Lodestone Lola

Jay Spenser

To Jim Farrell who flew *Flak-Bait,*
the real-life inspiration behind
Lodestone Lola; to all Martin B-26
Marauder flight and ground crew
members; and to their families, friends,
and fans. May the contributions of the
"Marauder Men" never be forgotten.

THE CREW OF *LODESTONE*LOLA*

Pilot:	2nd Lieutenant Jack Braden
Copilot:	2nd Lieutenant Frank Callard
Bombardier/ navigator:	2nd Lieutenant Rusty Savitt/ Flt. Officer Chilali "Chick" Spottedbird
Flight engineer/ top turret gunner:	Tech. Sergent Milton "Milt" Bidwell
Radio operator/ waist gunner:	Tech. Sergent Francisco "Paco" Gonzalez
Armorer/ tail gunner:	Staff Sergent Lewis "Jake" Jacobs

* **Lodestone**—*noun* ('lōd-stōn): A naturally magnetized piece of the mineral magnetite, possessing the ability to attract iron.

TABLE OF CONTENTS

Chapter 1:   Ardennes Forest, Belgium, July 2012 1

Chapter 2:   Kendrick, Vermont, September 2012...............4

Chapter 3:   Kingsholme, April 1944.....................................10

Chapter 4:   517th Squadron Interrogation Hut.................19

Chapter 5:   Operations, 328th Bomb Group.....................22

Chapter 6:   517th Squadron Barracks Site..........................26

Chapter 7:   Base Hospital, Kingsholme Field.....................32

Chapter 8:   T2 Hangar, Kingsholme Field 36

Chapter 9:   517th Squadron Mess Hall 38

Chapter 10:   Link Trainer Building, Technical Site..............40

Chapter 11:   Base Hospital...42

Chapter 12:   T2 Hangar...44

Chapter 13:   Aloft Over East Anglia 48

Chapter 14:   Kingsholme and Surroundings 51

Chapter 15:   The New Crew 56

Chapter 16:   Joyride...66

Chapter 17:   Escalation..70

Chapter 18:   Waddleston Hall 74

Chapter 19:   Colonel Canfield 82

Chapter 20:   False Start..86

Chapter 21:   Maximum Effort...91

Chapter 22:   First Blood 95

Chapter 23:   Road to Recovery 104

Chapter 24:   The Build-Up 110

Chapter 25:   Rising Stakes...117

Chapter 26:   Giving and Receiving...123

Chapter 27:   Preparations...129

Chapter 28:   No Escape 136

Chapter 29:   Operation Overlord 140

Chapter 30:   Aerial Armada 149

Chapter 31:   Over the Beaches..154

Chapter 32:   Fortunes of War..167

Chapter 33:   London...180

Chapter 34:   Remembrance 190

Chapter 35:   The Night Mission 194

Chapter 36:   Duel in the Dark..206

Chapter 37:   Cat and Mouse 217

Chapter 38:   The Choice 229

Chapter 39:   Happy Landings..235

Chapter 40:   Lest We Forget 238

Flak-Bait's Preservation

For More Information…

Author's Bio

Acknowledgements

Chapter 1: Ardennes Forest, Belgium, July 2012

Ahalf-dozen workers, men and women both, stood on a flat-topped salvage barge and peered down into the water. Also on this platform was an industrial compressor and the generator that powered it. Together they noisily pumped air down through thick hoses to inflate submerged flotation bags.

Framing the pristine mountain lake was an unbroken forest of great natural beauty. The hills and ridges of this wilderness betrayed no evidence of human presence aside from the shattered silhouette of a medieval fortress atop a distant peak.

Three small boats ringed the salvage barge in the middle of the lake. Barely big enough for their enclosed pilot houses, these vessels had a single occupant each. They stood on their afterdecks and, like their colleagues on the barge, stared down into the lake.

The maritime salvage team's collective reverie ended when a half-dozen scuba divers in wetsuits broke the surface. Tossing their flippers into the boats, they clambered aboard with help.

Yellow flotation bags appeared in the depths. Looming into view next was a ghostly green form with wings and a tail. Spontaneous cheers and shouts rang out across the lake.

Alerted by this, the American half of the salvage recovery effort gathered at the lakeshore. Dr. Quinn Wolcott, its leader, stood at center. Blonde, determined, and barely thirty years old, she shaded her eyes and bounced excitedly on tiptoes straining for a better view. A subordinate in jeans and a T-shirt handed her a pair of gyrostabilized binoculars.

"Thanks," Dr. Wolcott said, lifting them to her eyes.

She focused in time to see a World War II–era bomber break the surface. Her breath caught as a cascading wash of lake water ran off the artifact amid the bobbing flotation bags. Just the top of the plane showed above water so the inflated bags obstructed her view of it. However, she could clearly make out that it was a Martin B-26 Marauder bomber, and that its side-hinged plexiglass escape panels stood open atop the cockpit.

This meant the pilot and copilot had survived the ditching and escaped before their bomber sank. It all matched what Dr. Wolcott hoped to see. Grinning delightedly, she handed back the binocs.

* * *

The vessels had slowly towed the barge with its prize as close to shore as they could. Slings positioned by divers beneath the plane's wings and fuselage were attached to a large crane standing on the narrow shore, and the cable had been tensioned. This brace kept the airplane from slipping away as its flotation bags were deflated and removed.

Shouts in French by the Belgian salvage crew had the distinctive Walloon accent of the Ardenne region. It utterly defeated Dr. Wolcott's limited command of the language from many years of studying French in school.

She and her team of seven young Americans were a scruffy lot. Most of them wore T-shirts adorned with a colorful logo and the words *Historic Aircraft Recovery Trust*. Their ball caps and the cases of equipment piled on the beach likewise bore the HART emblem.

Despite her youth, Dr. Wolcott was the clear leader of this international collaboration. At her signal, the hired crane roared to life. Its operator slowly and carefully lifted the twin-engine bomber into the sunshine.

Silt-laden water gushed endlessly from the artifact. When the flow finally abated, lightening the load, the crane pivoted to rotate the plane over the narrow beach. People scuttled clear as it was gently lowered onto its belly.

Dr. Wolcott stared in wonder at the recovered artifact. Her assistant with the binoculars gaped in astonishment.

"Holy shit, Quinn, check out that battle damage!" he exclaimed.

"Shot to hell," Wolcott agreed, "but we can fix her."

The foreman of the Belgian recovery team approached. "Is this the airplane that you seek, *Mademoiselle?*"

Wolcott turned and gestured for a towel, which another team member tossed her way. Approaching the battle-scarred plane, she wiped dirt and algae off its nose on the left side to expose hand-painted nose art. They saw a scantily clad pin-up girl adorning the dramatically rendered name *Lodestone Lola.*

"Yes," Dr. Wolcott replied. "Yes, this is the airplane."

Chapter 2: Kendrick, Vermont, September 2012

Dr. Wolcott pulled into the barnyard and climbed out of her rental car, briefcase in hand. Dressed in casual business attire, she savored the country air redolent with the scents of pine, ferns, and moss. The only sounds were the soft sighing of the breeze and a few desultory late-summer bird chirps.

The rural farmhouse had deep woods all around and a mowed field between it and the barn, whose red paint had weathered to a faded purple. Both structures were so comfortably settled that they appeared part of the land itself.

Probably two hundred years old, Wolcott thought, admiring the impeccably maintained home. A Norman Rockwell painting come to life, it had three stories, a slate roof with red-brick chimneys, two wings, and a veranda with a screened-in porch at one side. The farmhouse's clapboard flanks were painted white and its window shutters were a glossy black.

A flagstoned path through the grass led her to the front steps. From inside, there came a pleasant multigenerational hubbub. The visitor knocked and the door opened.

Yes?" inquired an attractive but harried young woman with light brown hair.

"Is Jack Braden available? I mean Judge Braden?"

"Is he expecting you?"

"I believe so. I'm Dr. Quinn Wolcott."

"Lisa Graham, I'm his granddaughter," said the woman, opening the screen door wide.

She led Dr. Wolcott down the front hall and into the dining room. A tall ninety-year-old man stood behind its polished table. Before him were scissors, markers, wrapping paper, and cardboard boxes. More boxes were piled on the floor nearby.

Dr. Wolcott saw that he was sorting personal effects and placing them into the boxes, which he labeled and taped shut. At each of his elbows was a child providing dubious help. The boy looked to be seven years old and the girl about four. On tiptoes, she pulled a rolodex file from the table and began playing with its rotating cards.

"What's this, Great Grampy?" she asked.

"It's for addresses," he replied dryly, "but most of the people in it are dead."

"Oh," she said, losing interest.

Her older brother looked around. "Where's your wooden hammer?"

Braden found a judge's gavel and gave it to his great-grandson. Lisa took it from the boy, handed it back, and pulled her protesting children away.

"Hurry up now, daddy's waiting to take you swimming in the village," she said, and nodded over her shoulder at their visitor. "This is Dr. Wolcott, Granddad."

The young mother ushered the children through a door, closed it, and turned back to find her grandfather and his visitor looking uncomfortable in each other's presence.

"Did you get my letter, Judge Braden?" Quinn Wolcott inquired.

Braden scowled as he continued sorting and packing.

"I'm a fan of yours, Sir," Dr. Wolcott went on. "You've devoted your life to advocating for society's disadvantaged and spent years as a Vermont Supreme Court justice, all capped by a Presidential Freedom Medal. That's a lot to look back on."

Lisa smiled, pleased by the words. Her grandfather stoically continued sorting.

"Going somewhere?" Wolcott asked, looking at the packing in progress.

"An independent living facility," he replied, not welcoming the interruption. "What can I do for you, Dr. Wolcott?"

"Call me Quinn, Sir. I'm here about your World War Two service."

He frowned. "That's not something I care to discuss."

Dr. Wolcott set her briefcase on the table, popped the latches, and withdrew a stack of color photographs. She tossed them down and they spilled across the table.

Braden stared at the large-format photos, thunderstruck. Some documented the salvage operation in Belgium, while others showed the retrieved aircraft now disassembled and being worked on in a brightly lit hangar or workshop. His mouth worked.

"It's ... my ship," he exclaimed, finding his voice.

*   *   *

They sat on patio furniture in the screened porch, Braden in a love seat and Wolcott across from him in a chair. Between them was a low tile-topped table. She laid her briefcase on it.

Lisa entered with glasses of lemonade that she distributed before settling by her grandfather. They watched Dr. Wolcott reach into her case and set aside more photographs plus a little box with the handwritten word *Ask!* on it. Beneath these items were the photocopied documents she was after.

Although intrigued by the box, Lisa refrained from interrupting as their visitor got down to business. "I tracked down your military records at the National Personnel Records Center in St. Louis, Sir," she said, showing them a thick bunch of photocopied pages held together by a large binder clip.

She held up other documents in turn as she mentioned them. "I also have here the wartime history of your bombardment group, your airplane's maintenance logs, and your escape-and-evasion debrief following your return to Allied lines in July 1944."

"How wonderful!" said Lisa.

"Where'd you turn those up?" Braden asked, surprised.

"Most of them I found on microfilm in the Air Force Historical Research Agency at Maxwell Air Force Base in Alabama. Together with *Luftwaffe* after-action reports obtained from the Deutsches Museum in Munich, my team and I were able to locate and recover your bomber from a lake in southern Belgium."

"What will you do with it?" asked Lisa, picking up the photos.

"Restore her to flyable condition although she'll never fly again," Wolcott replied calmly. "Aside from battle damage, she's in surprisingly good shape with almost no corrosion thanks to the cold fresh water, silt, and lack of oxygen at depth."

"May I ask what your doctorate is in, Dr. Wolcott?" Braden asked.

"History primarily. I'm an aviation archaeologist by profession."

Lisa interrupted with a delighted laugh. She showed them a black-and-white 8"x10" photo of the bomber's crew. Dressed in flight gear with Mae Wests beneath their parachute harnesses, they posed with *Lodestone Lola*'s nose art, three kneeling sergeant gunners at front and three officers standing behind.

"Look, Granddad, it's you!" she exclaimed.

Her finger touched the middle standing figure, who wore a fifty-mission crush cap and cradled a scraggly looking dog in his arms. She looked to her grandfather. "Did you stay in touch with your crew after the war?"

"Initially, Sweetie. But life's busy and we lost track of each other long ago. No, the only member of the 328th I maintained contact with was Tom Prestridge."

"I liked him," Lisa said fondly. She turned to Wolcott. "He was a distinguished author and Harvard professor. He and his wife used to come up every summer and vacation with us at a lake resort we all like."

Judge Braden nodded. "Tom and I were in the same squadron. He was my best friend. My first friend, actually."

"So he isn't around anymore?" their visitor asked delicately.

"No," said Lisa.

"I'll ask you again," Braden demanded, "what do you want from me?"

Dr. Wolcott spoke frankly. "I need you to tell me about *Lodestone Lola*. Not the stuff I can look up. I know she's a Martin B-26B Marauder built in Baltimore in 1943. I know her wingspan, range, when she deployed overseas, what missions she flew, and how many flight-hours she logged. I even know how many flak patches she has."

She leaned forward intently. "What I *don't* know is the human side of the story. What was the war like for you? How did *Lola* handle? What combat experiences did you and your crew share?"

Pulling a digital tape recorder out of her case, she switched it on, set it on the table between them, and looked expectantly at him.

"After so many years, does it really matter?" Braden asked.

Their visitor sipped lemonade. "I also run a small air museum," she replied. "A key tenet of my profession is that the value of any historical artifact is directly proportional to the amount that's known about it. So yes Sir, it matters."

"Ask my crew. Ask Frank Callard. He made a fortune after the war—"

"You're the only one still living."

Her words took Braden aback. "My entire crew? Frank too? Are you certain?"

"Yes, Sir."

Braden scowled. "I don't have time for this," he stated, starting to rise.

"Stay, Grandpa, please." Lisa pulled him back down beside her. "Do this for the family—it's our history too."

The old man relented with a sigh. Taking his granddaughter's hands in both his, he looked at her with concern.

"It was a lifetime ago, Sweetheart, and I didn't like myself very much back then."

"It's okay, Gramps. We'll always be proud of you."

Braden nodded and composed his thoughts with dignity.

"Do you know what it means to 'engender opprobrium,' Quinn?" he asked.

"No, Sir, not a clue."

"It's when you do something that makes a whole lot of people mad at you all at once. That's what happened to me shortly after I arrived in England at the start of April 1944...."

Chapter 3: Kingsholme, England, April 1944

Open farmland dotted with ancient trees spread as far as the eye could see. The East of England lacked mountains and rivers but it abounded in fertile pastures, gently rolling hills, and scenic waterways. And because of its proximity to the European continent, the area hosted more U.S. bomber and fighter airfields than any other part of the British Isles.

By 1944, in fact, well over a hundred British and U.S. airfields dotted Norfolk, Cambridgeshire, Suffolk, and Essex. Fully a quarter of these were in Essex alone. With a rich history dating back beyond invading Romans to iron-age Celts, this bucolic county rose to prominence at the start of the Middle Ages as the Kingdom of the East Saxons, giving rise to its modern name.

Essex was home to Kingsholme Field. Officially designated U.S. Army Air Forces Station 485, the military installation covered 1,700 rural acres clustered around three runways laid out in a triangular pattern. Aligned with the prevailing winds, Kingsholme's main airstrip was 6,000 feet long. It crossed the arms of a vee created by two 4,200-foot-long airstrips sharing a common threshold.

Looping around these black-topped runways was an encircling taxiway of concrete twice the width of a Marauder's wingspan. This meandering perimeter track enfolded the field's control tower and signals square. The latter, a rectangular patch of concrete in front of the tower, displayed the airfield's identifying code, which for Kingsholme was the letters KH.

The signals square included a wind tee large enough to see from the air. Tower personnel positioned this wind-direction indicator manually to show airplanes flying above the field which runway to use and what direction to approach it from.

Outside the perimeter track behind the tower lay the jumble of wartime structures that together comprised the 328th Bomb Group's Technical Site. Next to it was the Headquarters or Admin Site. And fronting the taxiway on the other side was a large T2 maintenance hangar.

This complex at one corner of Kingsholme Army Airfield was its beating heart. Few other structures and installations were visible around the flying field, the only one of any prominence being a second T2 hangar identical to the first. Less obvious were a bomb dump, ammunition dump, two bowser fueling sites, and mounded earthwork firing butts for the testing and calibration of Browning .50-caliber machine guns.

And everywhere there were hardstands. Dispersed around the field to minimize the toll enemy bombers or strafing fighters might take, these paved aircraft parking spots offered angled access to the perimeter track so that bombers going either direction could enter or exit them with ease.

Located on both sides of the perimeter taxiway, these dispersals came in different sizes and configurations. Small ones comprised a paved right-angle vee that departed the loop at 45 degrees for three airplane lengths before turning back to rejoin the taxiway. These could comfortably accommodate two bombers, one to a side.

Most were longer concrete crisscrosses that could accommodate four to five ships. Kingsholme also had two that were bigger still. Angling into the grass from opposite sides of the field, they ran perpendicular to the taxiway to each provide eight or more B-26 parking spots. These very long crisscrosses left wide swaths of grass open by the main runway for wheels-up crash landings.

The reason for so many dispersals was the U.S. Army's decision the previous summer that every American bombardment squadron should have 18 airplanes, not 12 as initially specified. With four squadrons per group, this meant 72 airplanes per base.

When all of them were on the ground, they dotted the landscape near and far like a herd of somnolent beasts. Depending on where your airplane dispersal was, the silver or camouflaged bombers across the runway might appear relatively near or far distant.

*   *   *

The base lay in a timeless thrall because ships from three of the group's four squadrons were away. The world was silent, the cool breeze redolent with an earthy promise of spring. Cumulus clouds drifted by overhead, dragging their shadows like blankets across the countryside.

Staff Sergeant Myron "Rotten" Wrotnowski closed his eyes and listened to the birds sing while savoring the warmth of occasional sunbreaks. A burly noncom in his thirties, Wrotnowski sat atop a parked U.S. Army Air Forces Cletrac M2 aircraft tug.

Or, more properly, Sergeant Wrotnowski lounged on it, his arms comfortably folded over his belly and feet propped up, ankles crossed. An unlit cigar dangled from his teeth. He'd light it when the bombers returned.

The veteran mechanic wore rumpled grease-stained coveralls and a battered ball cap with its bill bent up. Both were olive green like the vehicle beneath him. Jeeps, trucks, fuel bowsers, staff cars, bicycles, and just about everything else that moved on Kingsholme Field were also Army olive drab.

The Cletrac itself resembled nothing so much as a bilious loaf of bread mounted on tank treads. A steel towbar clamped to one of its full-length fenders, likewise painted OD, confirmed this tracked vehicle's primary use.

Fast and nimble with a seven-thousand-pound drawbar pull, Cletracs were the USAAF's indispensable jack-of-all-trades. The tractors did more than just tow airplanes; they pulled them out of the mud when they got stuck. And when bombers crash landed, the tugs helped haul them off to the T2 hangars to be repaired or cannibalized for parts and stricken from the inventory.

Cletracs also supplied compressed air for aircraft tires and electrical power for starting aero engines. But what Wrotnowski liked most about them was their padded bench seat. It was a good spot to comfortably sweat out a mission on the ground.

This habit of the maintenance chief's was best savored in the serenity at an empty dispersal. Today, however, he shared it with a 2nd Lieutenant who looked too young to drive, let alone fly. The youngster stood a dozen yards away in full flight gear staring fixedly at the far horizon.

"They won't be back for a couple of hours yet, Loo-tenant Braden," Wrotnowski called in his brash Brooklyn accent.

"He shouldn't have taken my plane."

"He's the CO. He can do whatever he wants."

"It's our first combat mission," the young flier said, sounding aggrieved. "This is what we lived and trained for at MacDill. He had no right to bump me."

"Colonel Fowler likes to see how they're comin' off the assembly line these days," Wrotnowski replied reasonably. "Your ship bein' the newest on the field, it's only natural he'd take her up. So the CO bumps the copilot—which is you—and takes his seat. Happens all the time!"

Braden glared angrily at him.

"Look at the bright side," the sergeant added. "Your crewmates have the distinct honor of leadin' this entire bomb group their very first time in combat."

Braden's truculent silence caused Wrotnowski to lose patience.

"Look, the damn airplane belongs to Uncle Sam, okay?" the maintenance chief said, exasperated. "Youz guys may have ferried her across the Atlantic, but there's no way you'd have been allowed to keep a factory-fresh B-26B. New ships go to the senior airplane commanders—that's just the way it is. Replacement crews fresh from the ZI fly whatever's available."

The ZI, or Zone of the Interior, was Army speak for the continental United States. Having been overseas for a year, Wrotnowski had seen dozens of replacement crews like Braden's rotate in, fresh from stateside training. Not being part of the 328th's original complement of personnel, they didn't have a clue how things worked and were so green the cows were chewin' on 'em.

Braden continued his stiff vigil of the distant horizon.

*　　*　　*

In vivid sunshine, eighteen Martin B-26 Marauders cruised in tight formation at 11,000 feet. The lead ship—the tip of the spear—shone resplendently and was devoid of any artwork. Like all U.S. airplanes currently arriving in the European Theater of Operations, this silver B-26 lacked the green-with-gray-undersides camouflage paint applied to older aircraft.

Two camouflaged Marauders flew on the lead ship's flanks, one on each side to form a vee. Close behind them and slightly below were three more Marauders identically arranged, creating the six-ship double vee known as a squadron element.

Spaced out to the sides some five hundred feet farther back were two more of these six-ship elements. The low squadron flew at left and the high squadron at right. This staggered arrangement—known as the combat box—maximized overlapping fields of fire for mutual defense against *Luftwaffe* fighter attacks.

Approaching the initial point of the bomb run, or IP, the planes abandoned this wide defensive stance. Each squadron element turned onto the bomb run at a different time, rolling out to align one behind the other. The six-ship bomber formations from the high and low squadrons now flew in trail behind the lead element.

This realignment created a ground-track footprint just three airplanes wide for enhanced bombing accuracy. Bomb bay doors came open. Bombs fell away as the 328th successfully devastated a forward *Luftwaffe* airfield with no losses.

The wide combat box reassembled itself at the rally point when the bombers turned for home. Lighter now with empty bellies and some fuel burned off, they raced for the safety of the English Channel led by the group commanding officer in Braden's brand-new ship.

Anti-aircraft fire began blossoming. Red bursts of 88-mm flak left dirty black puffs that drifted past as the twin-engine bombers sped on. To throw off the aim of the flak batteries two miles below, the lead airplane executed slight but frequent heading and altitude changes that the formation followed with practiced ease.

Just behind the CO's ship flew a veteran B-26 with the name *Baltimore Blitzkrieg* rendered colorfully on her nose. Leading the second vee of the lead element, this green-and-gray ship displayed artwork of a two-fisted cartoon pugilist delivering a knockout blow to a hapless Nazi. Below it were two tightly packed rows of nose-down bombs, each one representing a combat mission completed.

Captain Buddy Hasbrook, *Baltimore Blitzkrieg's* assigned pilot, concentrated on maintaining position in the formation relative to the CO, whose silver airplane loomed high dead ahead through his front cockpit windows. The formation was tight and they were very close to the lead ship.

A jolt shook *Baltimore Blitzkrieg*. Over the engine noise came the clatter of flak peppering the plane. Hasbrook, a bear of a man in his early twenties, gestured for his copilot to leave his seat.

"Check for damage, Tommy."

Lt. Tom Prestridge, at age 28 the "old man" of the crew, started to unstrap, then pointed ahead in alarm. "The CO's been hit!"

Flames blossoming, the silver Marauder pulled up into a graceful loop high above the squadron before falling back through the formation, narrowly missing a bomber at its rear. It entered a spin and plunged out of control.

Hasbrook's last glimpse of the stricken plane had been through the plexiglass escape panel over his head. He thumbed the push-to-talk button on his control wheel.

"Pilot to tail gunner, the CO's been hit," he transmitted. "Let me know what happens."

"Tail gunner to pilot, Roger," came the interphone reply.

The rear-facing gunner in *Baltimore Blitzkrieg's* tail turret craned his neck to look down. His frown deepened.

In the cockpit, Hasbrook remained stunned. Prestridge shook his shoulder. "Hey, Buddy, we're deputy lead, remember? We have to take over!"

Snapping out of it, Hasbrook angrily shook the copilot's hand off. Advancing the throttles, he pulled up into the formation's vacant lead slot.

A reply came in their leather helmets. "Skipper? She hit and blew. No chutes."

Hasbrook's balled fist struck a violent cobra-fast blow against the padded brow of the instrument panel.

*   *   *

Bicycles plied their silent way around Kingsholme Field. The estimated return time was approaching and senior staff officers began gathering at the control tower railing. On the apron of the tech site just below, servicemen silently tossed a football around, pausing between listless passes to search the horizon.

The same agonizing wait occurred at the dispersals where ground crew members gathered to welcome their charges home. At his hardstand, Wrotnowski fidgeted impatiently on the Cletrac as Braden continued standing, shoulders slumped.

The pilot straightened suddenly. Dots marked the horizon low to the southeast as the distant drone of engines became audible. Wrotnowski hopped off the tug and joined the young aviator. Together they stood watching.

The returning bombers loomed ever larger and were soon so close that officers at the control tower railing lowered their binoculars. Heads craned as the twin-engine warplanes thundered overhead in wide sweeping turns. Their deep crescendo held the exciting throb of out-of-synch propellers as engines throttled back. In a wide swirl, the B-26s in the landing pattern began peeling off one after another onto final approach, one bomber touching down every twenty seconds or so.

Among the officers crowding the rail was the group's air exec, Lieutenant Colonel Mike Swan. He looked grim. "One missing," he said.

Most of the Marauders had now landed, fast-taxied to the end of the runway, and turned onto the perimeter track. Taxiing nose to tail, they turned off at their hardstands and shut down.

Amid all this, Braden and Wrotnowski studied the planes still aloft. The sergeant called out their names from long familiarity with the 328th's fleet.

"Gumball..., Outhouse Louse..., Spirit of '76..., War Weary..., Jersey Ginger..., Skid-Row Moe..., Tennessee Henhouse—" Wrotnowski broke off in alarm. *"Sweet Willie's* in trouble!"

Two red flares arced up from this B-26, which had a feathered propeller and hung-up landing gear. Another bomber then on final pulled up out of the way, yielding landing priority to *Sweet Willie.*

Braden and Wrotnowski watched the battle-damaged bomber belly in on the grass, keeping the main runway clear for landings to resume. Base ambulances raced out to meet the plane as it slid to a stop on its belly and one wing.

By now, most of the Marauders had turned off the track into their dispersals. Flight crews were exiting and conferring with their ground team as other bombers rolled by. On the hardstand Braden shared with the crew chief, Wrotnowski scowled as one of the planes taxied past.

"Christ, *Lodestone Lola's* got herself shot up again. That jinx ship can't poke her nose in the blue without coming back full of holes! She's a goddam pin cushion—"

The sergeant broke off, a stricken expression on his face as he looked up. Braden instantly understood the reason for his dismay: the last of the B-26s had landed and theirs wasn't among them.

Fear gripped Braden's heart. Wrotnowski grabbed at his arm but the youngster tore free and took off running across the airfield in his cumbersome flight gear.

Chapter 4: 517th Squadron Interrogation Hut

Braden burst into the large Nissen hut. The atmosphere inside was subdued and rife with the smells of coffee, cigarette smoke, and tension. Combat crews still in flying gear stood awaiting their turns to undergo post-mission interrogation while every part of the mission was still fresh in their minds.

Some flight crews were already answering questions around the tables in the room, each of which had an intelligence officer at its head. *Baltimore Blitzkrieg's* six-man crew sat around the nearest of these, which was the only one to feature a nameplate. It said *Maj. Linden Vander, S-2.*

Major Vander was the 328th Bomb Group's chief intelligence officer. Stern, prematurely gray, and entirely focused on the task at hand, he filled out forms with information gleaned from the fliers clustered around him, asking follow-up questions as needed.

At Braden's unexpected approach, the major looked up. His pencil hovered as he frowned impatiently at this tall young man, whose chest heaved with exertion and emotion.

"Yes, what is it?" Vander demanded.

"Pardon me, Sir, but where is my crew?"

"Identify yourself, Lieutenant."

A member of *Baltimore Blitzkrieg's* crew leaned forward and spoke quietly to the intelligence officer. Braden didn't know his name but recognized him from the communal quarters he shared with other junior officers.

"You're the copilot of the ship Colonel Fowler took up today?" Vander demanded.

"Yes, Sir."

"I regret to inform you, Lieutenant Braden, that after attacking the target and turning for home, the colonel received a direct flak hit and went down. There were no parachutes."

The news hit hard. Braden struggled for self-control.

"Losing Colonel Fowler is a huge blow to the war effort in this theater," Vander said, "and a tragic personal loss to every man in this group."

"He was the best!" someone called out.

Other airmen chimed in, expressing their feelings over the loss of a universally admired combat leader. Braden listened with growing disbelief as this spontaneous acclaim echoed through the Nissen hut.

Braden addressed the room at large. "What about *my* crew?" he demanded hotly. "Do any of you know their names? My pilot? My bombardier/navigator? My gunners who died with your CO?"

Major Vander stood up. "That's enough, Lieutenant."

Braden pressed heedlessly on. "Your precious colonel murdered my crew and nobody here gives a damn!"

Captain Hasbrook leapt up, upsetting his chair. Lunging at Braden, he grabbed him by his Mae West life preserver and drew him close. Braden stood six feet tall but the veteran pilot had three inches and a good thirty pounds on him.

"You rotten ingrate!" shouted Hasbrook. "Colonel Fowler died in your place. It's because of him you're still alive."

Braden shook his head, unafraid. "Fowler was leading the formation. If he hadn't bumped me and taken my ship, we'd have been at its rear."

Hasbrook pulled his arm back to deliver a blow that would have sent Braden sprawling. Tom Prestridge stepped hurriedly forward and restrained the pilot's wrist.

"Cut it out, Buddy," he said flatly.

"Striking a fellow officer is a court martial offense," Major Vander said. "I suggest you listen to your copilot, Captain."

Hasbrook glared at his copilot but dropped his arm.

The group's S-2 turned to the new replacement. "And you, Lieutenant Braden," he ordered, "report to the base surgeon. Have him give you something to knock you out for twelve hours, then see the air exec for reassignment. Dismissed."

Chapter 5: Operations, 328th Bomb Group

Lt. Colonel Michael Swan raced up in his jeep, hopped out, and strode into a large windowless building labeled *Headquarters Site—Operations Block*.

A dozen clerical noncoms jumped to attention as he entered. "As you were," Swan said, releasing them with a quick salute.

They returned to typing, filing, and writing information into the labeled fields of huge wall-mounted chalkboards. Striding rapidly down a hallway, Swan bumped into Major Curt Keller as he exited a door labeled Decryption holding a flimsy.

"Curt, what's this scuttlebutt about a maximum effort?" Swan demanded without preamble.

"It's true, Mike," the group adjutant replied, showing him the decoded flimsy. "Confirmation from Ninth Bomber Command."

Swan sighed. "I was hoping for a stand-down," he said, rubbing his face. "We just lost our CO, for Christ's sake!"

"Yeah, well, there's a war on."

"So I hear." He handed back the flimsy. "Are we alerted for tomorrow?"

"Nothing slated yet but the day is young," Keller replied.

They walked down the hall together to an office door labeled Air Executive. Sitting on a bench just outside was a handsome young man in spotlessly shined brown shoes and crisply pressed service trousers. The khaki-colored shirt and tie beneath his A 2 jacket were regulation precise with polished collar insignia. The brown-leather aviator jacket was zipped halfway up, and he held his officer's service cap casually in one hand.

Swan shot the youngster a passing glance as he escorted Keller into his office. He slid behind his desk while the group adjutant remained standing.

"That the kid?" Swan asked.

Keller nodded.

"He looks like a damned recruiting poster," Swan said, then frowned at his overflowing inbox. "What time are the intelligence and met briefings?"

"That's now up to you as acting CO. Before then, though, I'd like to move you into the Old Man's office. It's been cleared out."

A combat pilot and former squadron commander, Swan winced visibly at the suggestion. "Send in the kid on your way out."

*   *   *

Jack stood at attention holding a stiff salute while Swan silently reviewed two open file folders on his desk. He finally looked up and returned the salute. Braden relaxed.

"Stand at attention!"

The young 2nd lieutenant snapped to.

"There's not a man on this base who doesn't know your name, Braden," Swan said, his voice steely. "Pretty unusual for a shavetail replacement fresh from stateside, wouldn't you say?"

"Yes, Sir."

"From what I hear, you're damned lucky Major Vander didn't write you up for insubordination."

The junior officer didn't reply. Swan shook his head.

"You won't win any popularity contests but that's not my concern. My job's keeping the 328th in the air."

The senior officer indicated the folders before him. "Your Sixty-Six-Dash-One and Form Five show top marks in fitness and flight training. You'd be an airplane commander but for a..."

He consulted one of the folders.

"...'chronic unwillingness to assume responsibility.' What am I to make of that?"

"You'd have to ask the person who wrote it, Sir."

"It also says you filed more than a dozen requests for transfer to single-seat fighters, all of which were denied." Swan shot Braden a piercing look. "Do you have a problem being part of a bomber crew, son?"

The use of the word *son* was deliberate. Swan was just twenty-nine, but he'd enlisted before Pearl Harbor abruptly plunged the United States into a two-front global war. Advancement was rapid of necessity for prewar officers, and Swan's lofty rank of lieutenant colonel—soon to be full colonel if he became group CO—placed him squarely in loco parentis territory.

The word had its desired effect on Braden, who softened. "Colonel, I just prefer going it alone," he confessed, "in the air and on the ground."

"Let me explain something to you, Lieutenant," Swan replied. "The Army Air Corps decides what you are, which is whatever it needs you to be to win this war. Understood?"

"Yes, Sir."

In an outpouring of frustration, the air exec grabbed a fistful of paperwork from his inbox, waved it, and threw it back down. "Right now, I have enough airplanes, spare parts, bombs, and fifty-caliber ammo," he said angrily. "What I don't have is enough first pilots. Copilots yes; I got 'em coming out of my ears. But not qualified airplane commanders."

He leaned back in his swivel chair and assessed the young man. "The Marauder's the hottest ship in the inventory—an unforgiving beast that'll kill you dead if you're not on your toes. This means I can't just take any copilot, promote him to the left seat, and expect rainbows and buttercups. I need top-notch fliers!"

They locked eyes while the senior officer made up his mind. "Effective immediately," he announced, "you're a first pilot with your own ship and crew. Dismissed."

Braden didn't move.

"Well?" demanded Swan impatiently.

"Sir, I request a transfer."

The air exec's expression turned to disgust. "Cut and run, eh, Braden? Well, that's your prerogative. See Major Keller; he'll get your paperwork in the mill. Until the transfer comes through, you'll fly as ordered. That's all."

Jack saluted. Swan pulled a document from his inbox and focused on it, pointedly ignoring the junior officer until the young man took the hint and left.

Chapter 6: 517th Squadron Barracks Site

After settling into their billets and touring the base, one of the first things Jack Braden's crew did was sign to be issued rugged Army bicycles. Members of the air echelon were entitled to the drab green bikes, each of which had a basket on the handlebars and a battery-powered headlamp on its front bumper.

More rugged than civilian bikes, these Army ones were essential gear for flight-echelon personnel on military bases more than a mile long and wide. Pilots needed them to get to their airplanes. Ground crews found them invaluable for picking up spare parts during all-night maintenance sessions at far-flung dispersals.

Westfield Columbia of Massachusetts was the manufacturer of Braden's Army bike. Loving the freedom and solitude it gave him, the young pilot put it to good use learning the layout and extent of his new home.

Almost all 328th BG buildings clustered around one small part of the perimeter track on the west side of Kingsholme just north of the main runway. The HQ site with its massive operations block was here. It included the quartermaster building where Jack had picked up his bike.

Beside it was the Technical Site, whose control tower lay inside the perimeter track's loop to better oversee runway operations. The tech site also hosted one of the airfield's two T2 maintenance hangars. The other T2 stood in isolation half a mile away on the southern portion of the perimeter loop.

Each of these hangars had their own flight ramps for parking or staging bombers requiring maintenance or repair. The open land behind them served as graveyards for shot-up bomber hulks being picked clean of parts while awaiting the scrapper.

Braden left all that behind as he nosed his bike onto a concrete path leading into the base's pastoral surroundings. He pedaled leisurely, savoring the picture-postcard scenery as he passed by waving meadowgrass and through copses of tall trees.

The path led to his designated Living Site, the cluster of a dozen or so temporary buildings he called home. It resembled an orderly shantytown thrown up by squatters, which wasn't too far from the truth. *We're invaders here,* Braden thought, *friendly forces but invaders nonetheless.*

Concrete paths interconnected these Nissen huts to prevent Army boots from turning grass into mud during the rainy season. More dwelling sites like this one filled other verdant pockets around the field, just how many Braden couldn't guess.

It struck him as odd that U.S. airfields in England pushed into their English surroundings with nothing to mark the transition from U.S. military installation to rural Great Britain.

He'd been told that the living sites were all within easy walking distance of one or the other of the group's two Communal Sites, each of which had three mess halls capable of feeding two hundred Army personnel at a time during mealtimes. His group numbered some 300 officers and 1,300 enlisted men like all medium bombardment groups in England.

The communal sites offered basically the same services that town centers do back home. The busiest place at each was its Post Exchange, which was a general store. Braden could stroll or bike to either PX to buy clothes, shoes, toiletries, tools, bedding, stationery, candy bars, and almost anything else that fit within his $175-per-month combat pay.

You could buy a camera and have its film developed there, but the Army restricted what you could photograph. It was forbidden, for example, to take pictures of base facilities and aircraft. The intelligence boys had to clear your prints and negatives before the PX released them to you.

None of this mattered to Jack, who had no use for a camera because there was nobody back home awaiting snapshots. He spent most of his time in the PX's comfortable snack bar, which offered food and coffee. The only thing there that bothered him was the authentic U.S.-style soda fountain across the room. Malted milks and ice cream sundaes didn't tempt him.

Men physically his age but far younger by temperament gathered there. They played big band hits on the juke box, sucked down ice cream sodas through straws, and noisily reminisced about their bobbysoxer girlfriends back home. When this happened, Jack got up and left.

The communal sites had enlisted and officers' clubs for those wishing to unwind over drinks. One of the latter clubs bordered the HQ and tech sites to accommodate the higher ranks working there. All clubs offered snacks but only the ones for officers had restaurants. For full meals other than the usual GI fare, the base's enlisted personnel had to go eat at a local pub.

Jack made good use of his communal site's gym, showers, barber shop, library, and rations distribution center. The movie theater, amateur theatrics, live music performances by squadron bands, and pickup sports games didn't interest him.

Near his PX was an Army Post Office. He rarely checked the APO because nobody wrote him personal letters. If he did receive something, it tended to be official or commercial.

Overall, life at Kingsholme Field astonished him. While fellow GIs were roughing it in mud, jungle, tundra, and sand around the globe, life here in England was easy if you could just avoid getting shot up by *Luftwaffe* fighters or blown to bits by flak. One minute you're in combat and the next you're relaxing with comforts those infantry and artillery boys can't imagine. And compared to most bivouacs, Kingsholme's communal huts—however much aviators liked to grouse about their cots or squawk about overcrowding—were a suite at the Savoy by comparison.

Reaching his assigned Nissen hut, which the Army insisted on calling a hutment, Braden dismounted, locked his bike in the rack, and went inside.

*   *   *

Jack Braden shared his twelve-bed hut with the officers of three other flight crews. They sat on their cots or in chairs reading, conversing, writing letters, or playing cards at a single rickety table next to the freestanding coal stove. One man was strumming a guitar.

The relaxed hubbub ended the moment he entered. He crossed in silence to his own billet, which comprised a cot, footlocker, and shallow closet built into the hut's curving wall.

Braden frowned at the two neighboring cots. Their mattresses had been rolled up to expose the metal bedframes. On each of these was a B-4 bag and a parachute duffel. Handwritten labels bore the names of his fallen commissioned crewmates.

"Who packed up my pilot's and bombardier's things?" Braden demanded.

Silence greeted these words as the entire 328th Bombardment Group continued to shun him. Finally a first lieutenant stepped forward. He was well groomed, mannered, and mature in bearing.

"I did," the man said. "The CQ's coming by to pick 'em up."

CQ stood for Charge of Quarters, the ground-echelon noncom assigned to their 517th Squadron living site. Braden nodded, sat down on his cot, and rubbed his face. The lieutenant surprised him by clapping him on the shoulder.

"Come on," he said, "you need a drink."

*   *   *

"You're in Hasbrook's crew," Braden said as they carried their glasses over to their table from the officers' club bar.

The lieutenant nodded. "Tom Prestridge, copilot."

"Jack Braden," he replied, shaking hands.

"We're billeted in the same hut, Jack. We'd know each other already if you weren't such a loner."

Braden hesitated before asking the question most on his mind. "Did you see what happened to my crew?"

Prestridge sipped, avoiding his squadron mate's eyes. "Front-row seat," he finally admitted.

Braden knocked back his whiskey. "Did they suffer?"

"Everyone suffers. *Man never is, but always to be, blessed,*" Prestridge quoted, then relented. "Sorry, occupational hazard. I was a newly minted English lit professor when the war intervened."

"How'd you end up here?"

The other man shrugged. "I joined the Harvard Flying Club and one thing just led to another. You?"

"Worked my way through a backwater college till the Aviation Cadets finally accepted me."

Prestridge signaled for another round. "Were you and your crew close?"

"No," Braden said. "But we were a team."

The copilot nodded. "That's the important thing."

The second round came. Braden sipped and focused on the glass in his hand.

"They told us in training that each man doing his part would keep us safe," he said. "That was bullshit. They're all dead now, the poor saps."

"Yeah," Prestridge agreed. "I never thought the Colonel would buy it. It'll be tough finishing up knowing he's gone."

"Who's finishing up?" Braden asked, not understanding.

"We are. The crew of *Baltimore Blitzkrieg*. Forty-nine missions under our belt and one to go. Just four of us actually, as our radio operator and tail gunner missed missions recovering from injuries."

"Here's to you, you lucky bastards," Braden said as he started to raise his glass.

Prestridge restrained his wrist. "Don't!"

"Superstitious?"

The college professor looked down at the table. "Maybe…. The toughest mission is when fate gets one last crack at you."

Braden didn't speak but this smacked of weakness.

"When you first get here," the copilot explained, "you think crashing's for the next guy; that it can't happen to you. Then you see ships go down, empty seats at the mess, guys you knew who aren't around anymore, and you realize you're all too human—if the fighters don't get you, the flak will."

Braden stood up. "Thanks for the drink, Prof."

Prestridge clutched his arm. "You and Buddy Hasbrook got off to a rocky start, Jack," he warned. "Be careful—he's dangerous!"

Braden shook him off and left with a bemused smirk.

Chapter 7: Base Hospital, Kingsholme Field

Dr. Clifford Polling, an Army Medical Corps major and the 328th Bombardment Group's base surgeon, hastened through pouring rain. Something caught his eye. A scruffy dog, soaked and miserable, was trying without success to defecate on the sodden grass near the Sick Site, as the Army called his base hospital.

"Max!" the doctor exclaimed, scooping the forlorn animal up in his arms.

Polling carried Max up the wooden steps into his hospital. Bypassing the medical orderly at the front desk, he took the shivering creature directly to an examination room and plunked him down on the metal table. As he doffed and hung his sodden rain gear, a young Army Medical Corps orderly entered.

"No offense, Doc, but you shouldn't oughta bring that mutt in here," he said, frowning at the table. "It's against regulations."

"Dudley, I'm a major and you're a corporal so you can't stop me," Polling said. "This patient requires our help and I will not violate my Hippocratic oath due to a slight technicality."

Dudley looked at the animal. "What's wrong with him?"

"I found him just outside trying without success to evacuate his bowels. Hand me that towel."

The orderly did so and the doctor briskly toweled his patient dry. Max licked his hand gratefully.

"Max is always constipated," Dudley said.

"It's not his fault—this Army diet is poisoning him." He bent and spoke gently to his patient. "How many times must I tell you not to accept GI chow from the men?" Straightening, he extended an imperious hand. "Laxative!"

Dudley was ready with the pill and handed it over. Polling pushed it down the dog's throat and stroked its chin.

Over the background drumming of rain on the roof came the noise of a Jeep pulling up. Hearing this, Polling washed his hands.

"Find some real meat for him, Dudley—and be sure to let him out before the pill takes effect."

A scowling Mike Swan entered the lobby, looked around, and saw the doctor. "Got a minute, Doc?" he said without preamble.

"Sure, Mike."

*   *   *

The acting CO poured himself a mug of coffee from the freestanding coal stove in Doc Polling's office. He sat down facing the group's chief flight surgeon, who was behind his desk. The nameplate before him read *Maj. Clifford J. Polling, U.S. Army Medical Corps* followed by medicine's caduceus symbol of two serpents entwined around a winged staff.

Swan knew Polling to be a superb doctor and gifted leader. As base surgeon, he managed four flight surgeons—one per squadron—and 17 enlisted medical support personnel. When the air exec was wrestling with something, it was often this level-headed healer he turned to for advice.

Swan sipped his coffee and reacted melodramatically as if poisoned. "What happened to 'First, do no harm'?" he demanded.

The doctor chuckled. "You're not here to gripe about my coffee," he replied. "Care to get it off your chest?"

Swan nodded. "Just between us, Doc, something's in the wind and I need an expert opinion."

The doctor leaned forward. "Is this about the maximum efforts Wing has us flying?"

"No, we can mount two missions per day for as long as needed."

"Then what's griping you?"

"A buddy at Wing shared a rumor going around there. Ninth Bomber Command plans to abolish the fixed tour of duty."

"What?" Polling said, shocked. "What about 'fifty missions and you go home'?"

"That becomes 'combat crew members will fly until further notice'." He frowned apprehensively. "What effect will this have on group morale?"

"You're kidding, right?"

"I wish I were, Cliff."

Polling looked troubled. "Honest opinion?"

"Call it like you see it."

The doctor stood, poured himself a coffee, and sat down again, his lips pursed as he phrased an answer.

"Human beings need a goal, Mike," he began. "Something to shoot for—a light at the end of the tunnel, so to speak. Without it, morale plummets."

"Spell it out for me."

Polling shrugged. "Some men will accept this philosophically," he said. "Others will become bitter and perform poorly in combat."

"That's what I'm afraid of."

"There's more. The number of men reporting to Sick Call will spike. They'll complain of colds, aches, shortness of breath, blurred vision, and a host of other neurotic symptoms that to them are very real. Some will say they can give no more and ask to be processed out through the Central Medical Board. Others will simply refuse to fly, triggering a wave of court-martials nobody wants."

"That's all I need!" Swan scowled and thought for a moment. "You know how to win this war, Doc?"

"No. Do you?"

Swan nodded. "From where I sit, it's having flight personnel as interchangeable as the spare parts we install in our ships. If a radio operator buys it, pull him out and stick another one in. Same goes for the pilots, the bombardiers, the gunners…."

Swan set his coffee mug down and stood. "Keep my boys fit for duty," he said in an order that was half plea. "Whatever it takes, Doc, keep 'em flying. That goes for your whole team!"

The acting CO strode out leaving the chief medical officer, a caring family doctor in peacetime, visibly discomfited.

Chapter 8: T2 Hangar, Kingsholme Field

The huge hangar 170 feet wide and 290 feet deep rang to the echoing clamor of rivet guns, sheet metal work, power tools, and heavy rain on the corrugated metal roof. Three Marauders were being worked on simultaneously, as were subassemblies from other bombers.

At front was *Lodestone Lola*. A four-man repair team labored over her. Standing on scaffolds erected around the plane, these airmen were repairing her fresh flak holes.

Using tinsnips, they cut patches from 2024 Alclad aluminum sheet metal and riveted them in place. Once affixed to the airframe, the silver patches received a slap of chromate primer for added corrosion resistance.

Zinc chromate is a more yellowish green than the bomber's olive drab camouflage. This left *Lola* looking fine from a distance but suffering from a bilious case of the measles when viewed close up.

Myron Wrotnowski stepped in out of the rain. Dripping wet in his ball cap and shearling jacket, he saw and approached the corporal with a clipboard who stood supervising the work.

"Hi ya, Zeke."

"Hello, Rotten," the corporal said happily, "how goes it?"

"The stinkin' weather's getting my goat. What a country—it's so cold, I gotta sleep wearing two pairs of wool socks!"

"Yeah, it gets to me too. But when the group's grounded 'cause even the birds are walking, we get a chance to catch up."

The sergeant nodded at the bomber. "How's *Lola?*"

Zeke turned the clipboard to show Wrotnowski a Repair and Maintenance Form. "Internal systems damage has been fixed. We're nearly done with the skin work."

"Anyone ever count how many patches she's collected?"

"No, but it's more than any B-26 on this airfield and maybe the most of any Marauder in the ETO. Whoever named her *Lodestone* sure got that right—she's a flak magnet!"

Something occurred to the corporal. "Say," he continued, "did you hear they assigned *Lola* to that second louie who bad-mouthed Colonel Fowler? They tell me he's so young, he don't shave yet."

"Yeah," Wrotnowski replied noncommittally.

An airman on the scaffolding called down for guidance. Zeke hurried forward to confer with him.

Wrotnowski stood staring long and hard at *Lodestone Lola* as he wrestled with a decision. Making his mind up with a nod, he turned and strode back out into the rain.

Chapter 9: 517th Squadron Mess Hall

The day dawned fresh and clear. Waiting in line for his turn to enter the squadron mess, Braden became aware of a constant deep droning high above. The noise grew louder like thunder that never stopped rolling.

Everyone's attention turned skyward. Splashed in full morning sunshine, several hundred B-17s and B-24s flew high above as they formed up into ever bigger formations before heading out on strikes deep into Nazi territory.

In line with Braden were three airmen who, like him, were in their early twenties. These buddies talked nonstop as the breakfast line advanced to the mess entrance.

"The heavies are sure puttin' up a show this morning," the first proclaimed.

"Yeah, poor bastards," agreed the second flier.

"They may go deeper into Kraut territory than we do," opined the third, "but they fly twice as high. That puts 'em above a lot of the ack-ack we gotta slog through."

"Yeah, we're flak bait!" said the first.

The second continued to stare at the spectacle overhead. "I wonder what their chances are of surviving a tour of duty?"

"Ah, worry about your own!" replied the first.

He playfully snatched his friend's 50-mission crush cap off his head and slapped him with it as they entered the mess hall. Inside, they and Braden picked up trays, dishes, mugs, glasses, silverware, and napkins before advancing past orderlies behind a long counter standing by to fill their plates with whatever they wanted.

The friends were gabbing so much that Braden went around them to come away with eggs, sausages, baked beans, toast, fresh fruit, and coffee with milk. The eggs were real, not the reconstituted powder civilians got by on.

Braden sat down at an empty trestle table, glad to be free of the gabble. Then, having got their food, the trio of friends approached Jack's table, still talking too loudly.

"I got me a sure-fire survival plan," flier two said.

"Yeah? What is it?" demanded the third.

"The way I figure it, there's only so much time before your luck runs out. So I sign up for extra missions. That way, I'm done and gone before my number can come up."

"You're nuts!" exclaimed flier one. "The best way to survive a shootin' war is to keep your head down and don't volunteer for nuttin'!"

They sat down at Braden's table. "You're Braden, right?" one of them asked. "What about you?"

Jack blinked. "Excuse me?"

"What's your theory about how to survive?" he asked, being friendly.

Braden stood up with his tray. "Don't hang around with losers," he said and moved across the mess hall to a far table.

An indignant buzz arose in his wake but Braden didn't care. He didn't need anything or anybody.

Chapter 10: Link Trainers, Technical Site

What looked like a dozen oversized toys on fixed bases gyrated noisily and blindly in the brick-walled facility. Painted sky blue with mock yellow wings and tails like real Army training planes, they lacked propellers at front. Their wooden cockpit covers lacked windows. As they tilted and spun, they wheezed asthmatically.

These were the latest version of the famous Link trainer, the world's first practical flight simulator. Invented by American pilot and barnstormer Edwin Link in the 1920s, they were actuated by electric motors, bellows, organ stops, and compressed air just like the player pianos and automated theater organs for silent movies that his father's company once manufactured in New York State. It went out of business in the depths of the Great Depression.

Upwards of a half-million U.S. Army Air Forces fliers learned the crucial art of instrument flying in these single-seat Link trainers. Thanks to prewar commercial sales of the device, so too did the German and Japanese pilots that Americans now flew against.

One Link came to a stop. Its top opened and Braden climbed out, his fatigues drenched in sweat. He crossed the concrete floor to a retirement-age captain—an airline pilot before the war, Braden had heard—who sat at this simulator's control desk.

"Not bad, Braden," the instructor said, "but watch those steep banks. You won't live long in a Marauder if you do that in the soup at wartime gross weights."

"Yes, Sir."

"Next!"

Another pilot in line for instrument flight proficiency training stepped forward as Braden left. Cutting between buildings at the edge of the tech site, he encountered Max. The dog looked up and wagged hopefully.

"Go on, beat it, mutt," Braden said, his voice hard. "Get lost!"

He pressed on, only to find his way barred by a fellow flier who unexpectedly stepped out from behind a Nissen hut. Braden tried to go around the man but another flier appeared from the other side. They blocked his path.

Captain Buddy Hasbrook appeared next. Large and gloating, he leered at Braden with a malevolent smirk.

"Well well, if it isn't the asshole who called Colonel Fowler a murderer," he said. "Grab him, boys."

His minions restrained Braden, who struggled to free himself as Hasbrook moved in with sadistic glee.

*   *   *

Alone but for the dog, Jack Braden awoke, tried to raise himself, and lapsed back into unconsciousness. Max whined and licked his face.

Chapter 11: Base Hospital

It was evening and the overhead lights were on. Doc Polling and an Army nurse attended to Braden, who sat propped up in bed. Stripped to his waist, the young flier was bruised and battered from his head down his trunk. She finished taping his ribs and applied more plasters to his cuts and contusions as the doctor spoke.

"You say you didn't see who did this to you?"

"No, Sir."

"All right, if that's the way you want to play it." Polling pointed. "But these bruises tell me your arms were restrained while someone worked you over but good. Judging by the results, I'd say the guy was half gorilla."

"I'm okay, Major, really. How 'bout letting me out of here?"

The doctor shook his head. "Not with cracked ribs and possible internal injuries. You'll stay the night for observation."

"I'm all right, I tell you."

"Oh? And what makes you such an expert?"

Braden hesitated. "My old man used to whale me when he was drunk," he said. "Packed a mean wallop."

The doctor set aside his stethoscope and took Braden's pulse, timing the heartbeat with his watch. A phone rang elsewhere in the hospital. The nurse excused herself and hurried out to answer it.

"Why'd your father do that?" Polling asked.

"He said I didn't see things through. That I needed to learn responsibility."

"Does he still drink?"

"I don't know. He ran out on us when his business went belly up in the Depression."

The doctor released his wrist. "I'll pretend I don't see the irony in that."

The nurse returned. Braden winced with pain as she and the doctor helped him don a pajama top.

"That was Base Operations on the phone, Doctor," the nurse said. "Lieutenant Braden here is being transferred." She looked at their patient. "You're to await transport to the Combat Crew Replacement Center, Lieutenant."

Braden explored his battered face with a bandaged hand. His eyes narrowed. Rising anger and newfound determination played on his face.

"Call 'em back," he instructed her. "Tell them I've changed my mind—I'm sticking with the Three-Twenty-Eighth!"

Chapter 12 T2 Hangar

The cavernous maintenance and repair hangar had been dumped of all aircraft except for one B-26 cocked nose-out in a rear corner. This bomber dramatically framed a gayly festooned platform set up before it. It was dark outside but bright inside because the hangar's overhead lights were on.

A morale-building dance party was in full swing as the group's official band, the Skyliners, performed for hundreds of base personnel and young British ladies. Most of these visiting English girls were civilians in saucy tea dresses. Some wore the uniforms of the British Auxiliary Territorial Service, Women's Auxiliary Air Force, and the civilian Women's Land Army.

Young American women in Women's Army Corps or Army Nurse Corps uniforms also danced with members of the 328th. Some were based at Kingsholme itself in its single female living site. Most lived locally in nearby Essex, while others came from duty stations in the home counties or London itself.

The Big Band's current performance came to an end amid enthusiastic applause. An athletic young flier serving as bandleader jumped up onto the platform and strode to the microphone.

"Thank you to the Skyliners and thank you all!" he said over the PA system. "Before our final dance of the evening, I will ask that Captain Buddy Hasbrook and his crew please raise their hands, and that our lovely English guests join us in saying so long and happy landings to pals of ours who today completed their fiftieth and final combat mission!"

Deafening applause and enthusiastic cheers broke out as Buddy Hasbrook, Tom Prestridge, and two other fliers—not all the crew had flown the quota of missions—raised their hands to enthusiastic pats on the back and ebullient acclaim. The band launched into a nostalgic swing-era farewell to the evening.

*   *   *

Stars twinkled in the cloudless sky as Jack Braden watched from outside the hangar. Two weeks had passed since his beating, during which he'd healed and spent time exercising at the gym. Meantime, ongoing bad weather caused stand-downs and missions to be scrubbed, slowing Kingsholme's pace of operations to a crawl.

Braden wore his pinks and greens, the winter service uniform of the U.S. Army Air Forces. Specified for year-round wear in England, it combined a dark olive-drab gabardine wool coat with taupe khaki woolen pants that had a slightly pinkish hue. Braden considered it the handsomest military uniform ever created.

His in-theater training nearly over, he would soon be flying combat. With this in mind, he'd removed the stiffening grommet from his service cap earlier that day. That metal-band-and-rubber-ring grommet kept the military hat taut and perfectly flat on top. With it gone, the green fabric behind the cap's russet leather bill sagged like a failed soufflé.

Army fliers removed these grommets to be able to fly with headphones on over their service caps. The result was a glamorous Hollywood-ready look immortalized as the *fifty-mission crush cap*. It was a badge of honor that only Army Air Forces fliers could wear.

Braden had planned on celebrating by attending the dance, but the loner in him couldn't set foot inside the hangar once he got there. Instead of joining the festivities, he'd stood apart in the dark, watching, listening, ignoring his aching loneliness.

He now felt a bit of a fraud. Not having logged a single mission yet, did he have the right to wear a fifty-mission crush? Did he even belong here in the first place?

But what bothered him the most was what he'd learned over the dance's PA system: Tommy Prestridge, his one and only friend, was going home....

*   *   *

An attractive young British woman in uniform mouthed her farewells to her friends and new acquaintances before hurrying out. Her eyes not yet adapted to the dark, the twenty-year-old ATS girl bumped headlong into Braden.

"Oh! Pardon me, I didn't see you," she said, flustered.

She spoke with the proper, well educated, aristocratic tones of the British landed gentry. In the raking light from inside, she saw Braden's face.

"It's quite all right," he told her.

She looked a bit taken aback. "Do you often stand apart in darkness while others enjoy themselves, Lef-tenant?"

Braden smiled ruefully. "Well, I'm not exactly the most popular flier on this base, Miss...?"

"Is there a reason for that?" she asked, ignoring the question.

"I chew with my mouth open," he replied with a straight face.

"Yes, well..., I must catch my bus."

She hurried past. Braden's eyes lingered on her, his heart beating faster, until an abrupt cessation of music drew his attention back to the hangar.

*   *   *

Army personnel came to rigid attention on the dance floor as Mike Swan led an officer to the microphone. From a hundred yards away, Braden could already see that the newcomer was fortyish, overweight, and very displeased.

From the deference accorded him by the air exec, a light colonel, Braden guessed him to be a bird colonel or even flag rank.

"As you were," Swan said into the stand-up microphone. "I'm here to welcome Colonel Willis Canfield, our new commanding officer, to the 328th. Colonel?"

He turned the echoing PA system over to the colonel. Canfield stepped to the microphone and surveyed the gathering below with a dyspeptic frown.

"Good evening," he said curtly. "I have two announcements to make. First, I run a tight ship and expect the full cooperation of every man on this base. Is this understood? Second, your fixed tour of duty is hereby rescinded. As of now, all aircrew will fly until further notice. That is all."

The new CO strode off stage leaving shock and dismay in his wake. The effect on the former revelers was electric. Braden hurried into the bright hangar, sensing that this change of command boded ill for the 328th Bombardment Group. Angry male voices rose above the background hubbub.

"What a hard-ass!"

"He's no Colonel Fowler!"

"So it's fly till we die?"

A carefree evening away from the war had ended like an airplane crash. Even the female guests appeared shocked by what they'd heard. *This can't be good,* Braden thought, sensing trouble ahead for the bomb group.

Chapter 13 Aloft Over East Anglia

The Martin B-26 Marauder *Gremlin's Glee* hedge-hopped low over the English countryside at 260 miles per hour. The day was bright with spring colors and the world gleamed from recent rain.

Jack Braden was at the controls. Lt. Colonel Keith Nielsen, the CO of his squadron, observed him closely from the right seat.

Colonel Nielsen was compact, blunt, and sloppy in his dress and personal habits. His collar was mashed from donning his Mae West and parachute harness without care, and the goggles on his leather helmet were crooked on his forehead.

None of that mattered because in the air Nielsen was a superb flier and a courageous combat leader who commanded the utmost respect. "Don't be afraid to horse her around when she's light," he shouted over the noise and vibration of the engines.

His pupil nodded, seemingly relaxed.

Nielsen frowned at him. One never knew what to expect when putting a new replacement through a first-pilot checkout. This was particularly true when the aviator was also upgrading from the copilot's seat. These factors had Nielsen on guard every instant. His eyes missed nothing as he watched the young man's every move.

Standing behind them with his hands on their seatbacks was Technical Sergeant Milton Bidwell. A hardened veteran, Bidwell—an old man of thirty—was likewise appraising this pilot's actions.

A tall man, Bidwell stood in a crouch because the B-26's cockpit roof was low. It also had thick structural beam running fore-and-aft between its plexiglass top panels. On this beam were mounted switches and a massive concentric trim wheel whose handle he carefully avoided hitting.

"Take her up to seven thousand," ordered Nielsen.

Braden advanced the throttles and hauled smoothly back on the control wheel. Unencumbered by bombs, ammunition, a maximum fuel load, and three additional crewmembers, the plane surged upward, effortlessly propelled by two engines each rated at 2,000 horsepower. It leveled out minutes later against a backdrop of billowing cumulus clouds in sunshine over patchwork farms.

Braden reduced power and retrimmed. Swan reached forward just then and pulled the left throttle all the way back to idle. The B-26 slewed to the left.

"You've suffered an engine failure, Braden. What do you do?"

Jack reached up to rotate the overhead handle. "I use the rudder pedals to keep her lined up, crank in compensating trim, hit the fuel booster pump, and check my throttle and mixture settings," he replied. "If the engine's still dead, I feather the prop."

"Do it."

Braden pulled the left mixture lever back to idle cutoff, switched off that engine's ignition, and lifted a red protective cover on the control pedestal to press and hold the left feathering switch. A glance out his side window confirmed that the prop had stopped spinning, its blades now oriented edge-on to the slipstream to minimize aerodynamic drag.

Nielsen nodded approvingly. "You lowered the nose to maintain flying speed and kept the ball centered throughout. Well done."

"Thank you, Sir."

A knowing look passed between the squadron commander and the tech sergeant, who nodded in agreement. Focused on flying, Braden was unaware of this exchange.

"Crank the left engine up again and let's head back to the field," Nielsen said, the check ride over.

Under Braden's deft touch, *Gremlin's Glee* landed with a chirp of tires and taxied to the technical site's flightline. The engines came to a stop in sudden silence. Men threw chocks around its main wheels as the crew of three exited through the nosewheel hatch.

"You pass, Braden," Lt. Colonel Nielsen told the young flier on the concrete outside. "One last thing: in an emergency, come down as fast as you need to. Don't worry about ballooning—the drag of these huge props with throttles closed will keep you planted. Once you're on the ground, just lift the nose as high as it will go. You'll find the B-26 is all done flying."

The senior officer turned to the sergeant, who hadn't spoken a single word their entire time aloft. "How about it, Milt?"

"He'll do, Sir."

"You're fortunate, Braden," Nielsen said with a grin, "Sergeant Bidwell here has consented to be your flight engineer and top turret gunner. There isn't a more experienced man in the group. You'll meet the rest of your crew following combat familiarization."

"Thank you, Sir," Braden replied stiffly.

"You did well," Nielsen added kindly. "You should be pleased."

"Is that all, Sir?" Braden said, saluting crisply.

Nielsen saluted back, surprised. "Dismissed."

The young flier crossed to where he'd left his bike, mounted, and pedaled away.

"I don't get it, Milt," the 517th Squadron CO said. "What's with that guy?"

"From what I hear, Sir," Bidwell replied, "Lieutenant Braden hasn't cracked a smile since he arrived."

Chapter 14: Kingsholme and Surroundings

Buddy Hasbrook sat drinking at the bar of the Officers' Club. It was surprisingly full considering the time of the day.

A passing flier stopped beside Hasbrook. "Buddy!" he said. "I thought you and your crew would be halfway home by now."

The line of glasses arrayed before Hasbrook on the bar bore witness to a binge well underway. *Baltimore Blitzkrieg's* pilot looked dully up and recognized Captain Marvin Sterngold, a popular airplane commander from the 518th Squadron.

Hasbrook scowled as the flier sat down next to him at the bar.

"My bags were packed," he said, aggrieved. "They made us unpack 'em, Marv."

"Gee that's tough," Sterngold said. "But I can see why the brass did what it did, what with the invasion coming any day now. They'll need every one of us for that show, and I for one wouldn't miss it."

The captain signaled to the bartender, a corporal, who poured two more shots and placed them before the men.

"It can happen to us," Hasbrook said thickly.

"What do you mean?"

"Going down like the Skipper. It can happen to any of us."

Sterngold frowned. "Yeah, rotten luck. Great guy like that."

Polishing glasses nearby, the bartender saw their glum faces. "Feels like a funeral parlor around here, don't it?" he said.

"What?" asked the newcomer.

"Look around. What with this new CO and everybody having to fly U-F-N, every man here thinks he's gonna be next."

Fear flickered on Hasbrook's drunken features.

"Oh yeah?" Sterngold replied. "And just where did you get your degree, Dr. Freud? Come on, Buddy, let's toast to better—"

Hasbrook shoved to his feet and lurched unsteadily off. His surprised friend watched him depart.

*   *   *

Three-dozen Marauders flew in tight formation. Flak explosions began to blossom at their altitude a quarter mile away. From the cockpit of *Jenny Be Good*, Jack Braden watched it warily.

He was flying left seat again. Gabe Diaz, a veteran airplane commander, served as his copilot to take him though a first taste of combat. They shouted to one another to be heard over the engines, sparing the rest of the crew having to listen over the interphone to the combat familiarization training in progress.

"Kraut ack-ack is radar directed and accurate," Diaz stated. "It takes the flak batteries seventeen seconds to set the shells to explode at the right altitude, load them into their eighty-eights, and shoot them at us, plus another fifteen seconds for those shells to reach our height. That's why Marauder formations never fly more than thirty seconds at a constant heading and altitude when there's flak coming up."

"We zig when they expect us to zag?" Braden asked.

"Yeah, cat and mouse—we try to outfox them and they try to outguess us."

The formation shifted slightly. Braden followed it to keep *Jenny Be Good* tucked in close among the surrounding bombers.

"What about enemy fighters?" Braden asked.

"They're always lurking so keep your head on the swivel."

The Marauders filling the windows were startlingly close. Some were silver, others wore olive green camouflage with light gray undersides. Every detail of those nearby planes was visible right down to their flush riveting, access panels, and grease stains. It was like waltzing on a crowded dance floor.

A nearby burst of flak jolted Braden and his check pilot in their seats. Jack breathed, forced himself to relax, and continued flying with calm precision. Diaz observed this with a nod.

"Well done. I'll take it now."

Braden released the controls and allowed himself a smile.

*　　*　　*

A jouncing Army 4x4 truck, one of many, delivered Jack Braden and many other fliers to the Interrogation Hut. It was located between the technical and headquarters Sites. He jumped down from the tailgate in his flight gear.

This time he had a reason to be there, having just logged his first combat mission, but the cold shoulder he received inside shattered any illusion that he was no longer shunned. His turn came to sit around an interrogation table with the crew he'd just accompanied.

A junior intelligence officer posed questions about flak locations, intensity, observed damage, bombing results, fighter opposition, and anything else the crew remembered or had made notes of. These were discussed for concurrence and correction before the table leader jotted them down on his debriefing forms.

Outside, a crowd of released fliers laughed relaxing around two mobile canteens parked in the area designated for food vans. The first vehicle had American Red Cross markings and was by far the more popular choice. The second, a British NAAFI van manned by two uniformed women, had relatively few takers.

Braden, leather helmet in hand, his hair boyishly askew, approached the latter and was delighted to recognize the ATS woman who had bumped into him in the dark leaving the dance.

Braden grinned and fixed his eyes squarely on her at the counter of the open-sided van. She looked up, barely noticed him, and looked away to continue serving refreshments to other customers alongside her older colleague.

Braden greeted both women with a kind hello after the fliers ahead of him finished and walked off with their refreshments.

"Remember me?" he asked the younger woman.

"Of course," she said, "the Yank who isn't popular."

He glanced at the nearby ARC truck, which was doing land-office business. "By the look of it, neither are you."

"It's difficult to compete with coffee and donuts when all one has to offer is tea and crumpets," she admitted with half a smile. "Fancy a cup?"

"Please. No milk or sugar."

Wordlessly she filled and dispensed a porcelain mug. Braden blew on it and sipped, sizing her up and calculating his chances. "Live around here?"

Despite herself, she laughed. "Is that the best you can do, Leftenant?"

With a bemused smile, never breaking eye contact, he set his half-finished tea on the van's counter. "See you around."

The other server was attractive, well groomed, and nearing fifty. She studied her young companion as Braden strode away. "Likable sort, don't you think?"

"Is he?" the ATS girl replied. "I hadn't noticed."

The woman spoke with bittersweet fondness. "It's about time you did, Georgie," she said. "One cannot go on grieving forever, now can one?"

*   *   *

Occasional snatches of soft conversation and a wistful tune on a harmonica greeted Braden as he entered. The freestanding coal stove was running but it barely took the chill off the hut.

Most of the junior officers in his shared barracks were second lieutenants like himself with a single gold bar on their collars. Some were first lieutenants with a silver bar. A few others were captains wearing railroad tracks, as the two parallel silver bars were called.

Every one of these fellow officers ignored Braden except for Tom Prestridge, who nodded a greeting and smiled. Near him at the far end of the hut was Buddy Hasbrook, who glowered menacingly before turning back to a card game at the hut's table.

Braden crossed to his billet partway down on the right side. He grabbed his shaving kit from the shelf above his cot, took a change of clothes from his closet, and turned to go shave and shower.

A small wood-framed chalkboard on the wall by his cot stopped him. He'd wondered about it since arriving in England. Little more than a foot square, the slate had scrawled on it vertical chalk lines grouped into fours with a diagonal slash through them to total five of something at a time. Seventeen lines had been recorded before the tally ended.

Jack caught the eye of the harmonica player on the cot across the way. "The guy who had this billet before me," he asked, "he kept track of his missions?"

"Yeah," the man replied.

"What happened to him?"

"Plane exploded."

"What was his name?"

"I don't recall." The flier resumed playing.

Jack grabbed the eraser off the slate's shelf and energetically wiped out the last traces of an aviator who had made the ultimate sacrifice. Picking up a piece of chalk, he scored his own first combat mission. Satisfied, he grabbed his things and departed.

Chapter 15: The New Crew

Wearing flight gear, Jack Braden and Milt Bidwell jumped down from the back of a truck. As it drove off, they strode together to join the four mechanics readying Martin B-26B Marauder *Lodestone Lola* for flight.

"Sergeant Wrotnowski!" Braden said, surprised to recognize the sergeant he'd met previously. The man was directing the bomber's ground maintenance.

"Loo-tenant," Wrotnowski greeted, wiping his grimy hands on a rag pulled from the capacious pocket of his coveralls.

"What are you doing here?" Braden asked.

"The sergeant is your new crew chief," Bidwell explained.

Wrotnowski nodded. "Your previous ship went down. I needed a new one, so I requested and got *Lola* here."

A mechanic with corporal's stipes on his coveralls approached to hand Wrotnowski a clipboard. They briefly conferred. "Oh, and it's Rotten," Wrotnowski continued, turning back to the new pilot.

"What's rotten?" replied Braden, "this ancient flying machine they palmed off on me?"

Wrotnowski, his crew, and Bidwell all exploded in laughter, the crew chief loudest of all. "No," Wrotnowski managed to say. *"Lola's* great—the best!"

"Rotten is the sergeant's nickname," Bidwell explained tactfully. "It's casual out here on the flightline. Unless a senior officer is present, we dispense with formality between the ranks."

Braden nodded. He shook hands with his new crew chief. "Hi, Rotten, I'm Jack."

As they clasped hands, their eyes met in a wordless contract that told Braden all he needed to know about Technical Sergeant Myron Wrotnowski. No further assurances were required as to the man's competence or commitment to his airplane and its crew.

The crew chief indicated his team, the corporal and an airman, the Air Corps' term for an Army private. They too wore ill-fitting, grease-stained coveralls. "Meet Miguel and Butch."

Braden nodded to the two men, who grinned back eagerly.

Wrotnowski reached up to give the B-26's aluminum skin an affectionate pat. "*Lola* here is all ready for you to take her up."

Jack Braden scrutinized the bomber—*his* bomber, taking in the plane's colorful nose art and the many rows of bomb symbols. He studied the chipped paint and the countless battle scars.

"You think she's okay?" he asked dubiously.

"Yes, Sir," the crew chief replied heartily. "*Lola's* racked up more missions than any other ship in the group, and that's despite the Krauts personally having it in for her."

"Anyone killed aboard this crate?"

"Nope. But more than a few guys earned purple hearts in her."

"How is it she's available?"

Wrotnowski hesitated. "Her last assigned pilot kept gettin' shot up," he admitted. "Said he was spendin' too much time in the hospital and not enough fighting, so he requested and got another bird. Since then, *Lola's* only been flown on rotation. She'll be glad to have boys of her own again."

Braden shot the crew chief a puzzled look. *It's an airplane, not some living thing,* he thought, impatient with the maintenance chief for suggesting otherwise.

"Here's the Form 1-A, Loo-tenant," Rotten said, handing the clipboard to Braden. I'll go over it with you before you take off."

A jeep pulling up at the dispersal interrupted them. At the wheel was Lt. Colonel Nielsen, who shut down and jumped out. Four young men in flying gear clambered out after him.

"Lieutenant Braden, Sergeant Bidwell," their squadron CO said with a nod of greeting. "Meet your flight crew: Lieutenants Callard and Savitt, copilot and bombardier/navigator respectively, and Sergeants Gonzalez and Jacobs, your radio operator/waist gunner and armorer/tail gunner."

The newcomers acknowledged their names with nods.

"Ready to fly?" Nielsen asked his newest command pilot.

"Yes Sir," Braden said. "That is, if Lieutenant Savitt is prepared to navigate us."

Rusty Savitt, an amiable redhead with ruddy cheeks and merry eyes, grinned as he held up papers and a folded chart. A wedding ring glinted on his hand. "Headings, splasher beacons, and IFF code," he proclaimed. "I'm ready!"

"Stick to your assigned round-robin corridor," Nielsen ordered. "Stray from it and the British antiaircraft gunners are likely to send a few friendly reminders your way."

The colonel spun on his heel, jumped into the jeep, and drove off.

Braden and his crew chief performed a walkaround inspection of the hard-used bomber. They reviewed *Lodestone Lola's* Form 1-A, which showed no red ink. All systems were working. Braden signed off on it.

Bidwell at his side, the airplane commander contemplated his assigned crew members. They looked unsure of their new airplane and pilot both.

"I don't know you and you don't know me," Braden began diffidently, "but together we have a chance to help win this war. That's what I want and I'm guessing it's what you want too."

Grinning and chewing gum with his mouth open, Gonzalez nodded cheerfully.

"You probably know by now that nobody in the Three-Twenty-Eighth wants to fly with me," Braden continued. "You might be in the same boat or maybe you just drew the short straw. Whatever the case, it doesn't change what we have to do."

He paused before continuing.

"Colonel Nielsen's taking a chance on us, and he's given us Sergeant Bidwell here to make sure we don't screw up. This is Milt's second tour in 'twenty-sixes. His first was in the Pacific Theater flying Marauders from bases in Australia and New Guinea. Lean on him. I plan to." Braden turned to his flight engineer. "Milt?"

The senior sergeant had the relaxed confidence of a seasoned veteran. "I'm not much for words, men," he said, "but I can assure you that the B-26 is one of the most intricate jobs ever fashioned by human ingenuity. These are tough birds. Each one has its own personality. Some are jinx ships, some hangar queens, and some lead charmed lives."

He reached up and affectionately touched the Marauder. "Now *Lola* here is what we call a hard-luck ship," he explained. "She's a shopworn angel with a tarnished reputation. And guess what? Nobody wants to fly with her either. But don't sell the old gal short—she's a fierce scrapper who always brings her boys home."

The crewmembers contemplated the battle-scarred B-26 with expressions ranging from highly dubious to openly apprehensive. All except Gonzalez, who radiated enthusiasm.

"Gentlemen, let's fly," Braden said.

Together as a crew, they performed a preflight familiarization walkaround with the mechanics answering questions, after which they boarded the bomber and proceeded to their takeoff stations. Braden and Callard, his new copilot, buckled into the cockpit.

Milt Bidwell joined them, positioning himself behind their seats to oversee the startup procedure. Knowledgeable about the plane's highly complex systems, the flight engineer stood by to assist the pilots if and as needed.

In particular, it was the flight engineer's job to step down into the navigator's compartment and turn on the generator switches located on its aft bulkhead at the right time. For some inexplicable reason, the engineers at the Glenn L. Martin Company in Maryland had chosen not to locate them in the cockpit where they belonged.

Through his side window, Braden saw Wrotnowski make a hand signal indicating that the ground power cord had been plugged into Lola's left wheel well. This provided external electrical power for starting, sparing the plane's batteries. He nodded to the crew chief.

Callard, slightly built with worry-filled eyes, pulled out the startup checklist and nervously cleared his throat.

"Main inverter," he said, reading from it.

Braden flicked a switch. "On."

"Blowers," Callard continued.

"Low; cover in place," replied Braden.

"Oil radiator shutters."

"Open."

"Carb heat."

"Cold."

"Mixtures."

"Idle cutoff."

"Props."

"Automatic; full high RPM."

"Cowl flaps."

Braden glanced back at the cooling gills on the nacelle of the engine on his side. "Open."

"Master and battery switches."

"On."

"Throttles cracked."

Braden advanced the levers an inch. "Starting left," he said.

Sliding his side window open, he stuck his head out. Butch, Miguel, and Wrotnowski stood watching from the tarmac.

"Clear!" Braden called loudly.

They stepped back. Braden shut the window. "Fuel booster…; energize…; prime…; mesh," he said, working the switches as he spoke.

The starter turned the left propeller over until the big Pratt & Whitney radial engine spluttered to life with a throaty bellow. The prop became a blur. Within minutes, the other engine also idled.

Braden gave the signal to remove the chocks. Giving the props a wide berth, Wrotnowski's men darted in to pull the wooden blocks away from the main wheels. Thumbing the button on his control wheel, Braden set his interphone jackbox to select the command radio and touched the push-to-talk button.

"Station 485 Tower," he transmitted, "Cobblestone O-for-Oboe is ready to taxi."

For security reasons, AAF station numbers were used for tower communications rather than the airfield's common name, which identified nearby towns. Cobblestone was the codename for Braden's 517th Squadron (identified by the letters JP on the airplane's fuselage). Borrowing from RAF practice, O-for-Oboe referenced the individual aircraft code letter painted on the airplane's flanks along with the squadron code. Each bomber in a squadron had a different letter identifier.

Receiving his taxi clearance, Jack Braden taxied out onto the perimeter track and followed its meandering pavement around the field, stopping short of the active runway's threshold.

Setting the brakes, he ran up the left engine and the pilots checked the magnetos, cycled the props, and performed other tests before bringing the engine back to idle to repeat the process on the other side. Braden called for takeoff flaps.

"Station 485 Tower," he transmitted, "O-for-Oboe is ready for takeoff."

No other flight operations then in progress at Kingsholme, the reply was immediate. "O-for-Oboe, you're cleared for takeoff."

A new combat pilot in a veteran warplane taxied out to line up on the runway. Holding the brakes, he opened the throttles wide.

Lodestone Lola bellowed and shook with the restrained pull of 4,000 horsepower. Braden released the toe brakes. They raced down the runway, broke ground, and climbed away.

*   *   *

Jack Braden cruised seven thousand feet above the bucolic English countryside getting the feel of *Lola*. This Marauder wasn't as stiff on the controls of others he'd flown. She trimmed up perfectly and handled like a snazzy sports car. Even his seat felt designed with him in mind.

His apprehensions about the bomber melted away. *Lola* was a spirited creature who flew with mettle and joy. What was it Bidwell had called her? A shopworn angel? Yes, that fit.

Braden ordered his crew to their combat stations. Savitt came forward, nodded a wordless greeting, and turned to crawl feet first into the nose compartment, his office as bombardier/navigator.

Having proceeded through the bomb bays to the rear fuselage compartment, Bidwell was now manning his Martin 250CE top turret. With armament not installed for the practice flight, this was strictly a sightseeing excursion for him.

Francisco "Paco" Gonzalez was also in the rear compartment. He sat on a red cushion he'd scrounged from a worn-out armchair surplussed back at base. It spared the young Latin American radio operator from having to sit or crouch on bare deck plates while manning the machine guns at his waist windows.

This was where Gonzalez would be when over enemy territory. It wasn't as comfortable as his seat in the navigator's compartment, but he far preferred it because this was where he'd earn his keep as an aerial gunner.

Facing aft, he gazed down through the low plexiglass windows, watching woodlands, pastures, farms, villages, and occasional large towns slip by. Those windows were inset in large fuselage panels could be opened by pulling them inward and sliding them up until they latched. This locked them out of the way within the curvature of the fuselage.

Doing so created large rectangular openings on each side of the bomber just at floor level. They offered very wide fields of fire for Gonzalez's two hand-aimed .50-caliber machine guns, one to a side. With guns not installed today, he kept the windows closed for comfort and rotated the pivoting machine gun mounts out of the way against the fuselage sidewalls.

At *Lola's* back end of was the Bell Type M-6 tail turret. Master Sergeant Lewis Jacobs sat there behind thick armor plate and even thicker armored glass. His controls let him remotely aim and fire the power turret's twin machine guns. Lewis liked to be called Lew but he'd given up all hope of that. In the Army, it was either Jacobs or Jake.

This not being a real mission, Jacobs hoped to leave his duty station and explore *Lodestone Lola* in flight. It would be fun and give him a chance to get acquainted with his crewmates. There had been no time for that in the brief jeep ride with Colonel Nielsen.

Most of all, Jacobs wanted to see out the front cockpit windows. All through his Marauder transition training, he'd been frustrated by seeing where they had been but never where they were going. This practice flight was his chance to go up front and have that look around.

"Tail gunner to pilot," he transmitted via interphone, pressing the throat mike onto his Adam's apple for a clearer transmission.

"Pilot to tail gunner, go ahead," came Braden's reply.

"Permission to leave my station and tour the airplane in flight?"

"Denied."

"What a hard-ass," Jacobs muttered to himself.

In the cockpit, Braden wanted nothing more than to have his crew leave him alone. He didn't care what they thought of him. Even now, he could feel the copilot's eyes judging him.

Callard irritated him. The worried little man perched on his seat as if any moment he might jump up and run away. He hunched sitting on his hands, a look of perennial worry on his face.

But Callard was his copilot. The sophisticated, demanding B-26 required both pilots to coordinate and cooperate. Braden relented.

"What's your name?" he asked, shouting over the engines.

"Callard, Sir," came the reply.

"I know that. I mean what's your first name?"

"Frank."

"Okay, Frank. Want to take her for a while?"

"No."

Startled by the vehemence of this refusal, Braden looked more closely and realized that Callard was fearful if not openly terrified. This wasn't your average case of nerves, and even those weren't warranted on a training flight. It was a walk in the park compared to combat.

"What's the matter, Frank," he pressed, "are you sick?"

"I'm okay."

"You don't look okay."

"I can handle it."

"Take the controls."

"No!"

This second refusal left Braden nonplused. Bidwell's voice in their leather helmets interrupted him before he could react.

"Top turret to pilot," the top turret gunner transmitted, "we've got company."

Chapter 16: Joyride

"Pilot to top turret," Braden replied via interphone, "what's up?"

Sitting in the plexiglass dome overlooking *Lola* from the top of her fuselage, Bidwell watched as another Marauder overtook them in a dive. Using his handgrips, he rotated his turret to track this new arrival as it leveled off beside them, throttled back, and took up station off *Lola's* right wing.

"Another B-26," Bidwell replied. "It's got a yellow horizontal stripe on the tail."

"That's the 386th over at Great Dunmow," Callard added.

Leaning forward to peer past his copilot, Braden saw a young and eager face grinning back at him from the other ship's cockpit. He repeatedly pointed downward in an exaggerated motion while his copilot nodded encouragingly. Their plane sank from view.

"Looks like he wants to play," Braden said, then thumbed the push-to-talk button. "Pilot to crew, hang on!"

Callard braced himself hastily as Braden shoved his control wheel forward. Land rose up to replace the sky in the windshield. The horizon tilted as they surged into a banking dive following the newcomer. Flying with one hand and working the throttles with his other, Braden caught up to keep *Lola* tucked in behind the other pilot's left wing.

Rusty Savitt had been studying his navigation chart in the nose when the bottom fell out from under him. His body flew up, hands slapping the compartment roof, until gravity returned to plunk him firmly down into his seat. The chart landed draped over his head.

Savitt pulled it off. "Navigator to pilot," he demanded heatedly, "what in hell's name is going on?"

Braden was too busy to reply. Both bombers flattened out on the deck to skim at top speed over hills, fields, hedgerows, and the occasional English village.

"Hello, do you hear me?" demanded Savitt, still incensed. "I'm the navigator—I've got a right to know where we're going!"

Again no answer. He twisted around to look up the crawlway into the cockpit. Their new copilot was sitting there, braced for support, his feet flat on the floor. The pilot was doing the flying.

In the rear fuselage, Gonzalez lost his fight to remain upright on the deck plates. His cushion continued sliding every which way beneath him, sending him tumbling and rolling. He'd climb back onto it but it kept happening as the plane maneuvered. The roller coaster ride had him laughing uncontrollably.

In the top turret, Bidwell had braced himself well. He grinned broadly, enjoying the spectacular view from his catbird's seat.

In the nose compartment, it looked to Savitt as if they were scraping their bellies on the fields. Through *Lola's* nose, he saw an ancient Norman church loom up ahead. It rushed closer, the steeple advancing right at them. The rate of closure was so high that a collision appeared unavoidable.

"Holy shit!" screamed Savitt, who dove out of his seat.

The bombardier/navigator scuttled in terror to the bulkhead and turned to accept his fate. It seemed nothing could save them. Then the wingtip of the lead plane lifted and his ship ballooned up with it, leaving his stomach behind. The B-26s cleared the spire and dropped back down again to continue skimming low.

Savitt picked himself up and shakily reclaimed his seat, muttering nonstop obscenities.

Ahead was a farmer's wife feeding chickens while her husband bent to harness his draft horse. With a deafening crescendo, the two bombers shot by low overhead, briefly blotting out the sun.

Panicked chickens flapped and scattered in every direction and the normally stolid horse reared frantically. The woman screamed while her husband angrily shook his fist at the sky and swore.

The lead ship throttled back and pulled up into a steep climb over a patch of woods, trading speed for altitude. By the time both bombers leveled out at five thousand feet, they were cruising sedately. Braden slid abreast and again looked at the other fliers.

Seeing huge grins on the faces of both 386th BG fliers, Braden burst out laughing. His fellow pilot saluted, waggled his wings, and broke off.

"Top turret to pilot," Bidwell transmitted, "looks like they're heading back to the barn."

"We'd better do the same," Braden replied, then thumbed the transmit button again. "Pilot to navigator, I need a heading back to Kingsholme."

"Hang on, Skipper, I think I crapped my pants," came the reply.

Braden and Callard laughed out loud, the latter in an explosive release of tension. Frank looked amazed to find himself alive and unharmed.

In the rear compartment, Gonzalez saw Bidwell's body shake. He couldn't see his crewmate's face in the turret dome and it puzzled him until he suddenly realized that the Pacific veteran was laughing heartily—they'd both enjoyed the ride!

Turning back to his waist windows, the Latino caught the tail gunner's eyes on him through the cutaway rear bulkhead. Twisted around on the rear turret's padded stool, Jacobs gave Gonzalez a grinning thumbs-up before returning his attention rearward.

In the nose, Rusty Savitt's heart still pounded. Much as he hated to admit it, he admired his pilot's skill. The other Marauder's wing had scarcely wavered as Braden held close formation on it.

Savitt checked the heading indicator in his cluster of repeater instruments. Slaved to the plane's master gyrocompass, this instrument told him they were headed southwest. He scanned the horizon ahead and recognized Chelmsford, a town he'd visited. It lay five or six miles ahead, and twenty miles beyond that on the same course was the Thames Estuary at its widest. He could even make out the town of Southend-on-Sea.

Knowing where they were, Savitt quickly consulted his chart and eyeballed a course. "We're not far, Skipper," he transmitted. "Steer zero-zero-six degrees. You should see the field in three to four minutes."

The course Savitt had previously plotted on the chart caught his eye. Carefully drawn to keep them within the prescribed operating corridors, this unflown training round-robin made him shake his head. It was a wonder the Brits *hadn't* sent warning shots their way except that they would have had to fire their antiaircraft guns horizontally. Could they even do that?

"It's going to be a long war," Rusty Savitt muttered with a sigh.

Chapter 17: Escalation

Bidwell stooped between the pilots monitoring the instrument panel. AAF Kingsholme was now in sight.

"That other pilot was a damn fine aviator, Milt," Braden said, reducing power and cranking in compensating trim.

"You're no slouch yourself, Sir," the sergeant replied. "He was off your opposite wing yet you stuck to him like glue."

"I just hope nobody got our aircraft codes," Frank Callard said, very worried. "If they did, we'll be doing K-P for a month!"

They ignored him. Braden switched his jackbox from Inter for interphone to Command for external VHF radio communication. "Station 485 Tower," he transmitted, "Cobblestone O-for-Oboe is entering downwind for the main runway."

"O-for-Oboe, you're cleared to land," came the reply. "Traffic is a departing C-47."

"Roger, I have it in sight," Braden replied, watching the twin-engine transport—a military version of the DC-3—take off.

He scanned the sky entering the landing pattern and called for one-quarter flaps. Callard complied. Braden adjusted power and retrimmed for level flight at 160 mph on the downwind leg, flying parallel to the runway opposite to the direction of landing.

"I want you to make this landing, Frank," he told his copilot.

Instead of sliding his seat forward to take the controls, Callard just sat there. Bidwell frowned at this insubordination.

"You need to fly, Frank," Braden told him. "What happens if I get killed or injured?"

"I'd get us down," the young copilot said.

"Prove it," his pilot said sternly. "Now."

Callard didn't comply. Braden released the controls, leaned back, and folded his arms across his chest, all done flying. The young right-seater shot him a panicked look.

Braden transmitted via interphone. "Pilot to crew," he said, "Lieutenant Callard will be performing the landing."

He loomed threateningly across the control pedestal between them. "Take the controls, Lieutenant—that's an order!"

Trapped, Callard slid his seat forward, unfolded the rudder pedals that stowed away at the sides of the tunnel to the nose, and grasped the control wheel. There being no instrument panel for B-26 copilots, he glanced latcrally to read the instruments in front of Braden.

"Landing gear," Callard ordered, gripping the wheel tightly.

Braden worked the lever. "Gear down and locked."

Callard repeatedly looked past him, nervously judging his position relative to the main runway. When they had flown past it, he banked sloppily to the left.

Braden frowned. "You turned base too soon, Frank."

The copilot didn't reply. He pressed fixedly on with his jerky approach. "Half flaps."

Braden complied. "Half flaps."

"Full flaps!" Callard corrected, realizing during his turn from base to final that he was coming in too high.

"Full flaps," Braden confirmed, moving the flap lever to the bottom of its travel.

Marauders flew much faster than other bombers. The runway loomed quickly ahead and the airspeed needle oscillated as Callard ham-handed the controls.

"Watch your airspeed!" Braden advised. "Don't let it fall below one-fifty."

The copilot nodded nervously but continued flying erratically.

"Relax, Frank," Braden said calmly. "Make sure you've got at least one-forty over the threshold and we'll be fine. Easy now...."

Frank pushed the control wheel forward, fixating on his airspeed indicator. "You're diving at the runway!" Braden shouted. "Start your flare now!"

Callard hauled back just in time. *Lodestone Lola* flattened out, hit jarringly on her main wheels, and streaked down the long runway like a barreling freight train. The copilot chopped the throttles as the nosewheel lowered to the pavement.

They continued careening too fast. "We're not stopping!" the copilot shouted, panicking. "Emergency airbrakes!"

He made a desperate grab for the airbrake handle above and behind them on the roof's center post. A last-ditch measure, this system would ruin the tires and potentially damage the landing gear by discharging compressed air to lock the wheel brakes.

Braden knocked his hand away. "I have it," he said.

Callard gratefully relinquished the controls. Braden pulled the control column fully aft. *Lola*'s nose lifted high off the runway as if taking off again, but the plane stayed firmly planted on its main wheels. Together with the aerodynamic drag of the idling propellers, this nose-high attitude bled off the excess speed.

The nose wheel settled again to the runway. With judicious braking, Braden brought *Lola* to taxi speed and turned off onto the perimeter track. They had used the whole runway.

"Thank you, Colonel Nielsen," Jack Braden muttered.

Overhearing this, Bidwell recalled the squadron commander's post-checkout advice and grinned.

*   *   *

They cut the switches at the hardstand and *Lola's* propellers came to a stop. In the silence that ensued, Jack sat mesmerized. Feeling like the violinist who discovers a Stradivarius in a thrift shop, he knew he'd found the airplane of his dreams. *Lola* was everything he'd ever wanted in a flying machine and then some.

Callard unstrapped and climbed shakily out to exit through the nosewheel hatch. Watching this weak man of slight stature, Braden felt anger at his incompetence. Following him out, he dropped to the ground as Miguel and Butch inserted the wheel chocks around the tires.

Catching up to his crew, Braden pushed the copilot off balance with a hard shove. "How'd you ever make it through flight school, you yellow son-of-a-bitch?" he demanded hotly.

Hurt filled Callard's eyes, which made Braden even angrier. He leaned menacingly in.

"When things go wrong up there—and believe me, they will—it's every man for himself! You hear me, Callard? *Every man for himself!*"

Leaving his copilot crushed and humiliated, he flagged a passing jeep that was empty except for its driver. "Sergeant Bidwell with me," he ordered. "The rest of you can hike back."

Braden and Bidwell climbed into the back of the jeep. It jounced off across the grass, leaving Braden's abandoned crew perplexed.

"What a bunch of goldbricks!" Braden seethed, still fuming. "I can't trust them, Milt. I won't have it!"

"Colonel Swan says it's either them or we don't fly," the tech sergeant replied gently.

Braden shook his head ominously. "That Callard, he's going to get us all killed—mark my words!"

Chapter 18: Waddleston Hall

Dressed in pinks-and-greens and wearing his 50-mission crush, Jack Braden pedaled down a rural English lane on his Army bicycle. It was chilly but spring had asserted itself. Birds sang in profusion and the air was redolent with the bursting scents of new life and freshly plowed fields.

Still troubled and with no assigned duties that morning, Braden had climbed onto his bike. The need for exercise and a change of scenery made him put Kingsholme Army Airfield behind him and kept going with no particular destination in mind.

It still surprised him that there was no fence around his airfield or, for all that he knew, any U.S. Army Air Forces air base in the whole of the British Isles. The HQ and tech sites shared a fenced perimeter and an MP at the main entrance's guard shack at all times, but the rest of the airfield was wide open.

Braden had watched British farmers sow their crops right up to the perimeter taxiway and bomber dispersals. Friendships formed and greetings were routinely exchanged. British children visited the dispersals in awe and went away with Hershey Bars and whatever souvenirs the U.S. personnel could scrounge up for them.

It was good for relations with the British populace, Braden was informed. He suspected it was also that the crash U.S. program to construct airfields from which to assault occupied Europe included neither time nor budget for mass fencing. Sentries and security patrols provided a base's only protection against Nazi sabotage.

The lane Braden followed took him through a tiny hamlet. There were few cars parked along the road and only a dozen people on the pavements, as the British called sidewalks. Small as this village was, though, it felt more substantial than any town or city Braden had known growing up.

As he pedaled out its far side, the stone façade of an ancient apothecary shop informed him that he was in Kingsholme. He wondered about the grand name. Was there rich history behind it? Did it evoke veiled legends lost to the mists of time? Or was his airbase simply named after it because it was the nearest settlement?

Back in the rolling countryside, Jack stopped at an intersection. Signposts had been removed back in 1940 in anticipation of a Nazi invasion that the Battle of Britain preempted, so he had no idea where he was. There being no vehicles or people in sight, he turned randomly down a lane even prettier than the previous one.

His mind wandered to the joys of flying, which meant freedom to him. He'd thrived at primary, basic, and advanced flight training at different military installations across the United States, mastering increasingly complex military single-seaters. Multiengine transition training came next, followed by orders to Barksdale Field near Shreveport, Louisiana, to learn to fly Martin B-26 Marauders.

Upon graduation, he'd won his pilot's wings and received a commission as a second lieutenant. Assigned at the copilot of a six-man crew, they'd trained intensively together before picking up a factory-fresh Marauder at Hunter Field in Savannah, Georgia, and then flew it all the way to England via the Southern Ferry Route.

Jumping off from Florida, they'd flown to Puerto Rico, made three stops along the Brazilian coast, and navigated across open ocean to the tiny dot that was Ascension Island. From there they made two stops along Africa's northwestern coast before arriving in England. Barely 22 at the time, he'd felt like a modern-day Sinbad to have seen so many far-flung cultures and regions of the world.

It would have been perfect if only the Army had assigned him to fly Lockheed P-38 Lightnings, Republic P-47 Thunderbolts, or North American P-51 Mustangs instead of Marauders. Just one man in one airplane with no flight crew to be responsible for. *No useless copilot sitting beside you radiating fear,* he thought disgustedly.

But then *Lodestone Lola* came along. She was perfect. She'd won his heart. How lucky could a flier get?

High-pitched bleating, loud and distressed, intruded upon these thoughts. Coasting to a stop, he dropped his bike in bushes and followed the sound to a tall hedgerow. In it was a frightened young lamb trapped in dense brambles. The animal redoubled its frantic struggles as he approached.

"Whoa there, take it easy," he said, bending to investigate.

*   *   *

Braden pedaled up the long drive of an imposing country estate, his tires scrunching gravel. A flock of sheep grazed contentedly on the manor house's extensive grounds. Dismounting, he strode to the grand entryway and used a very heavy door knocker of polished brass cast to depict the face of a sheep.

A liveried butler opened the door. "May I help you, Sir?"

"I need to speak with the owner," Braden said.

"Might I inquire as to the reason?"

"It concerns a lamb."

"A lamb, Sir?" repeated the butler, puzzled.

"Yeah," Braden said brashly, "a lamb."

The servant opened the door wide to admit Jack, who doffed his fifty-mission crush. He was in the grand foyer of an ancient country home. At its center was a circular white table with a huge Chinese vase filled with hothouse flowers. Far above it hung a massive cut-glass chandelier.

The furnishings gleamed with frequent polishing as did the grand staircase that wound its way to a balconied second level. The profusion of antiques was tasteful and pleasing. It looked as though they had all been there forever. Oriental carpets with evident wear added to the country home's settled and comfortable charm amid the opulence.

The butler returned. "Sir Colin will see you in his study," the servant announced.

"Sir Colin?" repeated Braden.

"Sixth Baronet Brookleigh, Sir. This way if you please."

The lord of the manor was writing at a large wooden desk in a den crammed with books, souvenirs, and framed photos on the wall. Fiftyish, well groomed, and brusque in manner, he looked up as the butler escorted Jack into the room.

"I'm told you have something to tell me ... about a lamb?" he asked in a forthright tone.

"Yes, there's one trapped in the hedgerow by your main gate."

"Mowbray," Sir Colin called as the butler withdrew, "please ask the groundskeeper to meet us outside with hedge shears."

*　　*　　*

Sir Colin and the U.S. Army aviator worked together to free the lamb, which was now passive. With a last snip, the baronet freed the animal and his American visitor lifted it out. They removed the last snags of greenery from its fur.

Walking side by side, the two men strode toward the flock of grazing sheep, Jack acutely aware of the pounding heartbeat of the traumatized young animal in his arms.

"What kind of sheep are these?" he asked.

"Cotswolds," the baronet replied. "You may set it down now."

Jack did as instructed. The bleating baby ran to rejoin its flock, which with loud bleats opened to admit it.

"You have my gratitude, Lef-tenant," Sir Colin said, watching this reunion.

"No thanks necessary, Sir."

"I quite disagree," the baronet said. "In times like these, it's easy to forget that what one does to help a fellow living creature—be it man or beast—does matter. It's what makes us human."

Braden's expression and posture showed that this experience, coupled with the quiet words, hit home. The American swallowed, uncertain what to do or say next as the country squire turned to the house.

"Tea will be ready," Sir Colin said. "Come along."

* * *

Forty minutes later, Braden sat in relaxed conversation with Sir Colin over high tea. The two were comfortably ensconced in the mansion's drawing room. A fire crackled in the great hearth of a sculpted fireplace.

Through the door, now wearing elegant clothes and jewelry, entered the two ATS women from the NAAFI van back at Jack's base. He gaped in surprise at the younger woman, who seemed equally astonished to find him there.

"Ah good, you're home!" Sir Colin said, rising.

Jack stood too as the baronet warmly greeted his new arrivals, kissing each affectionately on the cheek.

"We have company as you see, my dears," he said, turning to Jack. "Lef-tenant Braden, allow me to present my wife Lorelei, Lady Brookleigh, and our daughter Georgiana."

The women barely had time to shake hands with their guest before the country squire ushered them to sit down.

"Come have tea and we'll tell you of a heroic hedgerow rescue."

* * *

A dipping sun glowed richly over the estate's formal gardens, which were fenced off for protection against the sheep. Jack and Georgiana enjoyed a leisurely stroll through the perfectly tended plantings. Spring birdsongs mingled with the distant snarl of playful Spitfires tracing curving and exuberant contrails high overhead.

"So this is Waddleston Hall," Braden said. "I've flown over the estate many times but had no idea you lived here. Or that the other woman in your mobile canteen was your mother, for that matter."

"No, of course you hadn't," Georgiana replied. "In England, one doesn't discuss such things before being properly introduced—which you cleverly seem to have wangled. In fact, father appears quite taken with you."

They mounted the terrace and walked along the mansion's rear façade. Georgiana stopped and leaned her elbows on the stone balcony rail, surveying her ancestral lands. Marauder engines bellowed hollowly in the distance as Jack stood with her, watching Sir Colin's sheep graze among ancient trees on Waddleston Hall's expansive grounds.

"Raising sheep must pay well," he joked with a straight face.

Georgiana laughed, then fell into a wistful silence.

Jack looked at her. "Your father's a bit of a philosopher, isn't he?"

"Yes, I suppose he is," she replied softly.

"What's the deal with him?"

"You Yanks ask very impertinent questions," she replied.

Jack maintained his inquiring expression and she relented.

"Father was wounded at the Somme in the Great War but won't speak of it," she said. "After that, he was a Cambridge don until the Nazis put paid to his lecturing. All that's left to him these days is raising his prize sheep." She bit her lip. "He hates this bloody war, Lef-tenant, but then so do we all."

"Hard to get away from it, what with Kingsholme Field less than a mile away. How'd that happen, anyway?"

"The Ministry of Defence requisitioned the land from my family," she answered. "Twelve thousand trees were felled to make your bloody airfield. I used to ride through those woods—they were our deer park."

The distant sound of Marauders being run up by mechanics was continuous. Jack looked at his watch.

"I should go."

They walked to open French doors and were nearly bowled over as a boy of sixteen or so raced out. The youngster pulled up short, abashed and out of breath.

"I say. I'm sorry, I didn't mean...," he began lamely. "I mean, I understand there's a Marauder pilot here. Are you he?"

Georgiana laughed. "My brother Rupert, Lef-tenant," she introduced. "As you can see, he's mad about aeroplanes."

Braden stuck out his hand. "Jack Braden, U.S. Army Air Corps."

"Rupert Brookleigh," the teenager replied with a firm grip. "I'm joining the RAF as soon as they'll have me. Just hope this war lasts long enough. Let me show you my room—I can see a Marauder out my window!"

Braden laughed. "I'll take a rain check."

They exited Waddleston Hall through the foyer, Rupert still talking.

"The Marauder's awfully pretty," he said. "Is she fast?"

"Very."

"Can she take punishment?"

"As much as a four-engine B-17 Flying Fortress. And she carries just as many bombs."

Extremely impressed, Rupert bubbled with questions until Georgiana sternly intervened. "Rupert, father wishes to see you."

"No he doesn't."

"Yes he does!" she said, exasperated. "Inside with you now."

Rupert left grudgingly.

Braden laughed. "Swell kid," he said as he mounted his bike. "May I ... see you again?"

She nodded. "I should like that."

She surprised him with a brief peck on his cheek as he set off, causing his bike to wobble. Jack got it under control and waved as he departed.

Georgiana watched him ride away, her troubled frown betraying concern for his safety. She turned and went in.

Chapter 19: Colonel Canfield

Sergeant Teddy Lansbury leaned against the 1942 Packard Clipper parked in the CO's spot at the main building of 328th Bomb Group HQ. The Army had provided the staff vehicle to Colonel Willis Canfield, and Kingsholme Motor Pool had assigned Lansbury to be its driver.

It astonished the ground-echelon sergeant, a car aficionado, that the new CO sent down from 99th Combat Wing had arrived in a Clipper. Colonel Fowler's vehicle, which Lansbury had previously driven, was a dowdy 1942 Ford Fordor.

Whatever the model, all Army staff cars wore exactly the same paint scheme. They were olive drab overall except for a large white star—the U.S. insignia—emblazoned on their back doors and the white serial numbers stenciled down the sides of their hoods.

Underneath this identical paint, the Packard was bigger, grander, and more powerful than the Ford, which was the universal staff car at U.S. bases across England. From magazines, Lansbury knew the Clipper to be the vehicle of choice of top generals like Dwight Eisenhower, Douglas MacArthur, and Hap Arnold.

This Canfield guy really rates, Lansbury thought. *Or maybe he's rich?*

An hour later, the young sergeant's enthusiasm had waned significantly. Ordered by the colonel to stay with the car, he was trapped there cooling his heels and fidgeting impatiently.

Lansbury wanted lunch. He needed to use the latrine. *That asshole could have released me if he didn't need me,* he thought, no longer in the least bit impressed with either the new CO or his big car.

*   *   *

Seven dumbfounded senior officers were arrayed around the CO's office. Colonel Willis Canfield regarded them from behind its desk, mouth pursed and lower lip thrust petulantly forward as if daring them to protest.

Across from him were Lt. Colonel Mike Swan, air exec; Major Curt Keller, group adjutant; Major Linden Vander, chief of intelligence; and all four squadron commanders. This last group of light colonels stood because the office lacked sufficient chairs.

Canfield was of average height with no distinguishing features aside from a perfectly trimmed pencil mustache. He tended toward obesity and had fat little hands with blunt fingers. His hair was a brassy blond shade that looked like it came out of a bottle. Cropped to regulation length, it was brushed upward at front and plastered into a wave just above his forehead.

This guy can't decide whether he wants to be Clark Gable or Van Johnson, Swan thought with disgust. He lacked the charm of either.

Vander broke the silence. "You can't be serious, Colonel!"

"Deadly serious, gentlemen. Effective immediately, our bomb runs will be sixty seconds longer than they currently are."

"What good will that do?" asked Swan. "Our best bombardiers need just fifteen to twenty seconds to line up on a target and plaster it but good. All you'll be doing is increasing the time we spend as sitting ducks."

"He's right, Colonel." Keith Nielsen agreed. "There's no evasive maneuvering on the bomb run. The ships have to fly straight and level for the bombsights to work. This makes us run a gauntlet through hell."

"Yeah, the Germans place flak batteries around potential targets," said another squadron CO. "If we extend the runs, those guns will murder us—losses will go through the roof!"

"Without any improvement in bombing results, I might add," Vander stated firmly.

Colonel Canfield's mustache twitched. His eyes narrowed and his face flushed. He looked about to explode.

"As you know, Colonel," Swan said, striving to be conciliatory, "initial points have to be recognizable landmarks on the land below. IPs show us where to turn onto our bomb-run heading. We can't just turn anywhere and know we're on the right track, and we certainly can't move geographical features around on the ground so they're one minute farther away from—"

"Silence!" shouted the colonel, exploding. He glared at them, radiating intense dislike and resentment. "You will identify and use *different* landmarks. Is that clear?"

Nobody spoke.

"Mark my words, gentlemen," their new commander went on, "a longer bomb run *will* improve accuracy. That's why I'm here—to show you pantywaists how to bring the Krauts to their knees!"

"Colonel Canfield," Vander said hotly, "as this outfit's chief intelligence officer, it is my duty to inform you that I consider this new policy to be ill-advised!"

The CO smirked, stood up, and crossed to the coat rack by the door. Retrieving his trench coat, he donned it and cinched the belt tight, adding Humphrey Bogart to the list of actors he wished to emulate. Carefully donning his fifty-mission crush at a practiced angle, the vain officer turned in the doorway.

"You have your orders, gentlemen. Dismissed."

*   *   *

Now in Mike Swan's office, these officers stood at the window watching the CO depart in his oversized staff car. They were still worked up.

"That moron will wreck this outfit!" Swan predicted.

"Not if I can help it," Vander said. "I'll have my boys gather up strike photos. We'll show him the 328th already has one of the lowest circular-error rates of any group in the ETO. He'll see that there's nothing to gain from what he's proposing, and that it will needlessly and senselessly squander American lives."

Keller shook his head firmly. "Won't work, Linden."

"Why not?" demanded the intelligence officer.

"I got a pal at Wing who knows him," replied the adjutant. "Says the guy's been pitching this crackpot scheme for months. Looks like the brass gave him a command of his own to see if it works."

"Or they just sent him down here to get him out of their hair," Nielsen quipped.

"Oh, brother, that I can believe!" Swan said with a chuckle. "But at least Ninth Bomber Command has reinstated the fixed tour of duty. That's one less headache for us."

"What is it now?" asked Keller.

"Sixty-five missions."

A clerical noncom poked his head into the office to hand the air exec a flimsy. Swan scanned it with a frown.

"We've just been alerted for a mission tomorrow," he said. "You're all dismissed except for you, Curt. I need your help to get the ball rolling."

Chapter 20: False Start

Twelve junior officers slumbered in their beds, their snores lost to the rain drumming on the Nissen hut's corrugated metal shell.

The door opened and a young corporal wearing a rain-drenched slicker entered. He held a list in one hand and a flashlight in the other. "Braden's crew," the charge-of-quarters read out in a deep southern drawl. "Briefin's at oh-five-hunnert!"

He shone his light across the cots occupied by *Lodestone Lola's* three officers. "Come on, y'awl, the war won't wait."

With more crews to rouse in other barracks, the CQ in his hurry hadn't bothered to close the door while he made sure the three men were awake and getting up.

"Shut that door!" shouted the flier whose cot was nearest the entrance. A shoe flung at the CQ arced through his flashlight beam, barely missing him.

"Jeez, ah'm just doin' muh jowb!" the Southerner muttered, hastily pulling the door closed with a slam.

Crews slated to fly were quietly informed of it the previous day so they could hit the sack early. But sleep was hard to come by, not knowing what lay ahead. It was a big sporting event coming up for the home team, except that this game could be lethal.

Braden dressed by the focused glow of his reading light. He sensed Callard's eyes on him but didn't acknowledge it.

"I wonder what the target is?" the copilot said.

Braden pointedly ignored the question as he buttoned his shirt. Rusty Savitt, always the peacemaker, spoke up. "That you'll learn at the briefing along with the rest of us," he said. "Don't worry, Frank, we'll do fine."

In the officers' lavatory, the three crewmates stood side-by-side at sinks as they and dozens of other fliers shaved and brushed their teeth. Their line of freestanding sink-and-mirror units ran down the center of the temporary building. Vertical metal support posts also mounting sinks and mirrors behind those Braden's crew used that also faced in toward the center.

Urinals and toilet stalls lined the side walls of this glaringly lit lavatory. Its tiled interior echoed with complaints, yawns, running water, and conversations that made it hard to hear.

Braden glanced at Callard in the mirror and saw his copilot looking particularly dejected. His attitude softened toward him.

"Look, Frank," Braden said, "an early takeoff doesn't necessarily mean a long mission."

"In this weather?" the copilot erupted. "We should all just go back to bed!"

The man at the next sink overheard this. "Bad weather here doesn't necessarily mean the target's obscured," he said, thinking he was being helpful. Callard kept on worrying.

In the officers' locker room, *Lodestone Lola's* officers dressed in silence, each man lost to his own thoughts as he donned his flight gear. They placed their personal effects in the lockers and picked up escape kits on the way out.

Next stop was the squadron equipment hut where the men stood in line to receive their parachutes across a counter from enlisted clerks. A corporal brought out Callard's parachute but didn't immediately hand it over.

"This here chute harness is out of date, Lieutenant," the clerk pointed out. "Hang on and I'll grab you a quick-release harness."

"No, I want this one!"

"Sir, the Army's phasing out clip harnesses," the noncom explained. "What if you end up in the drink with one of these jobs over your Mae West? You wanna drown trying to get out of it?"

"I'm keeping it!" Callard insisted. Fear tinged his voice.

Braden shot him a look as he accepted his own parachute on a quick-release harness from another attendant.

"Suit yourself, Sir," said the first clerk, shoving Callard's chute across the counter. "Next!"

Outside the rain fell unabated. Dripping wet, Braden, Callard, and Savitt met up with Bidwell, Gonzalez, and Jacobs in the squadron's combat mess. Full crews—officers and enlisted both—ate there together because the Army knew that camaraderie and teamwork are vital to unit morale and cohesion. Regardless of rank, combat crews needed to know and trust one another to perform well in battle.

Lola's crew settled around a trestle table. Gonzalez dug in lustily to a large breakfast. Callard picked halfheartedly at pancakes soaked in syrup before giving up and dropping his fork.

Braden ate eggs with toast and coffee. He chewed mechanically, not hearing the conversations going on around him. On his mind was a nightmare he'd had in the wee hours that woke him drenched in sweat.

In Braden's dream, flak and fighters brutally savaged *Lola*. She would hardly fly anymore and it took all his strength to keep her on an even keel. He alerted his crew via interphone to await the bailout bell.

To reduce stall speed and prevent his crew from landing too far apart after jumping, he ordered Frank to lower the landing gear. But when he tried, they found the wheels wouldn't extend because the hydraulic system had been shot out. The emergency gear extension system also failed.

This was bad for two reasons. First, the retracted nosewheel blocked the hatch located between the cockpit and the radio compartment. Sliding its plywood panels open would now provide a view of the retracted tire and strut but no avenue of escape.

Second, the B-26 lacked an autopilot. At every Marauder base, people knew crews who survived bailouts except for their captains, who died holding the stricken ship level long enough for the rest of them to jump.

It was an unspoken truth about the otherwise glamorous job of first pilot that plane captains should hold their ships level for their crews to hit the silk. Honeywell's Automatic Flight Control System performed this function for shot-up B-17s and B-24s, but the Army in its wisdom had decided that the B-26 didn't require an autopilot since it flew shorter missions that were less fatiguing for pilots.

In Braden's still-fresh dream, *Lola* communicated through the controls that she wanted to spin out. Knowing they were on borrowed time, he tried opening the bomb-bay doors from the cockpit, but the punctured hydraulics prevented it.

Bidwell came forward just then to say that, in the absence of hydraulic pressure to hold the doors closed, gravity and airflow had together pulled those doors sufficiently open for parachute jumps. Relieved, Braden had Callard ring the bail-out bell.

His heart pounded to find himself alone. He unbuckled with one hand and gauged his chances. It would have been one-in-three if that hatch hadn't been blocked. Making it all the way to the bomb bay and jumping from there? Zero.

His dream ended in a desperate but doomed dash for safety. *Lola* snapped inverted, thew him against the radio compartment wall, and pinned him there with fierce gyroscopic forces. Braden woke up in terror, feeling himself still spinning down.

It was just a dream, he told himself. He pushed his food away.

*　　*　　*

Lola's sergeants split off for their gunner's update. Her officers filed into their squadron briefing hut and found a place to sit on the benches separated by a central aisle. These faced a stage at the rear of the building. On it were chairs, a covered easel to show each plane's place in the planned formation, and the green curtain hiding a giant rear-wall map that, when opened, would reveal their target.

A nervous buzz died down as Major Vander jumped onto the stage and strode to its center. "Ten-hut!" he ordered.

Benches scraped on concrete as six-dozen fliers jumped to their feet and stood rigidly at attention.

"The mission is canceled due to weather. You are dismissed."

Braden's crew filed out. "We live another day," breathed Frank Callard, vastly relieved.

Chapter 21: Maximum Effort

It was still pouring when Jack ducked under *Lodestone Lola* and straightened in her nosewheel well to slide aside the hatch panels. Using steel flanges riveted at the rear of the well as steps, he climbed aboard facing aft, turned into the cockpit, and dropped down into his seat.

Shaking water off his fifty-mission crush, he put the wet cap back on. Loudly drumming rain coursed off the cockpit windows and clear overhead panels. It fit his mood as the nightmare still bothered him. He'd never worried before; why now?

Lola felt clammy to the touch. When the wind gusted, she shivered. Inside she smelled of metal, electrical insulation, cordite, dust, petroleum products, fear, and sweat. Braden reached out and patted her control wheel.

"False alarm, *Lola*. They'll be out soon to unload your belly."

Eighteen tons of heavily laden airplane creaked in the wind.

"I'll do my best for you, old girl," he continued. "In return, you bring us all home safe and sound if you can. Deal?"

An odd slapping sound made him glance down. A heavy flak vest now lay inexplicably on the cockpit floor. As he watched, another flew in through the open hatch to land by the first. Two more followed before a dripping figure clambered aboard.

It was Rusty Savitt, the redheaded bombardier. He and Braden met eyes, each startled to find the other there.

"Oh!" Savitt said. "Didn't know you were here, Skipper."

"What's with the flak vests, Rusty?"

The bombardier/navigator grinned. "Carpeting for my office. Gotta protect the family jewels—my wife and I are planning on lots of kids."

Crouching in the cockpit, he stepped across the vests, each of which weighed roughly 25 pounds thanks to steel plates sewn into the heavy green canvas. Squatting, he propelled them one after the other down the short tunnel into the nose compartment, then crawled down after them on his hands and knees.

"Don't let Rotten know," Braden called out. "Wartime gross weights mean we're heavy already. He won't appreciate you making it worse."

"Yeah?" came the shouted reply. "Well, it's my ass on the line and I'm taking measures."

Rising to leave, Braden glanced into the compartment where Gonzalez, his radio operator, sat when they were not over enemy territory. The AAF called it the navigator's compartment but Marauder crews generally didn't carry a dedicated navigator. The bombardier usually performed this function in addition to his own.

Perhaps for this reason, fliers at Kingsholme often called it the radio compartment. The flight engineer went in there to throw the generator switches at startup or shutdown. Other than that, it was strictly the radioman's domain unless they were over occupied Europe, when Gonzalez manned the waist guns.

The Latino's station was immediately to Braden's right. Facing the forward bulkhead of that compartment's port side, it comprised a small plywood-topped table with radio heads to control the bulky electronic communications gear mounted on racks elsewhere in the compartment. That desk also featured an old-fashioned telegraph key for constant-wave Morse code communications at long range.

Across from Paco's desk was a longer table on the starboard side. It was sized for navigational charts and would be used on those occasions when a dedicated navigator flew with them. Braden didn't ever expect to carry this seventh crewmember—only the lead and deputy-lead ships did that.

He descended through the hatch and dropped to the ground. Outside he went forward and watched through the clear nose as Savitt spread flak vests on the floor of his cramped aerial office.

The navigator glanced up, saw Braden, and smiled before seeing something else. He pointed and Braden turned to see the same sorry-looking dog he'd passed when Hasbrook and his goons had waylaid and beaten him.

Wet through and through, the homeless mutt looked pathetic and utterly bereft. Rusty Savitt appeared beside Braden.

"Max, come here, boy," the bombardier coaxed, crouching and gesturing.

The skinny animal approached and sniffed his outstretched hand hoping for a treat. Instead, he received an energetic petting as Savitt caressed him heartily with both hands.

"Hiya, Pal! How's life treating ya?" Rusty asked, glancing up to smile at his pilot. "Know why they call him Max?"

"No. Why?"

Savitt laughed as he straightened up. "It's short for 'Maximum Effort' because he has such a hard time dropping his bomb load."

Still chuckling over the joke, Rusty retrieved his bicycle from under the sheltering wing where he'd dropped it.

After he pedaled off, Braden picked Max up on an impulse. The shivering dog had short fur. He was mostly black with white socks and a white tip to his tail. His throat, cheeks, and the wide stripe up his nose were also white. His amber eyes were filled with woe.

Max arched upward in Jack's arms and licked his face.

*　　*　　*

The rain had stopped. Braden and Max stood at the rear of the squadron mess building. Both were dry and Braden had showered and changed. He held the dog in his arms as he spoke with Willy, an African-American airman patiently peeling potatoes beneath an improvised awning by the building's rear door.

"Max needs decent food, Willy," Braden said. "You sure the mess doesn't have an extra bit of meat for our group mascot here?"

"I can't, Sir. It's agin' regulations. Wish I could help as I purely do love dogs, but they'd drum me out of the Army."

Braded nodded, disappointed. "What do you hear from your cousin?" he asked, changing the subject.

Willy brightened, stopped peeling, and pulled an envelope from his pocket.

"He's flying Mustangs now," Willy said, proudly unfolding and scanning the letter. "They transitioned from P-40s, which are slow and don't fly high enough. Now he escorts Forts and Libs on long missions out of Italy. Says he hopes to become an ace."

He wiped his hands and extracted a photo from the envelope that he handed to Braden. The small black-and-white snapshot showed a smiling Tuskegee airman in khaki flight gear posing proudly with his brand-new Norh American P-51D Mustang. Braden savored the fighter's sleek lines, which explained the wide grin on his fellow aviator's face.

"That's grand, Willy," Braden said, handing back the photo. "Tell him I'm rooting for him in your next letter."

An hour later, Braden was pedaling down the same country lane where he'd encountered the lamb in the hedgerow. With him was Max, who was enjoying the unexpected sightseeing tour. Too big for the basket mounted on the bike's handlebars, Max sat so tall that Jack had to stabilize him with a free hand.

Chapter 22: First Blood

Linden Vander and other air-staff officers watched from chairs on the 517th briefing hut's elevated stage. At Mike Swan's signal, an aid pulled the cord that opened the curtain covering the giant map on the hut's rear wall. The room buzzed as more than seventy fliers got their first glimpse of the target.

Standing before this map, Swan lifted his pointer and tapped the far right end of the ribbons strung to show their intended course to the target and back.

"Today we hit the Hasselt marshalling yards in Belgium," he announced. "Ordnance is a mixed load of five-hundred-pound GPs and incendiaries. To avoid harming the Belgian civilian populace, bring your bombs home if you can't drop 'em where they'll give Herr Hitler heartburn."

He nodded to the aid, who removed cloths covering three easels on the stage. Two of them had very large aerial reconnaissance blowups of the railyard. As he spoke, the air exec tapped these to identify specific details.

"Hasselt is the key railyard between Antwerp and Germany. Knocking it out will disrupt *Wehrmacht* mobility in the region for weeks. Specific targets are this rolling stock here…, these repair shops…, and these engine sheds."

Lodestone Lola's three officers sat near the front. Braden observed dispassionately, Savitt took notes, and Callard fidgeted.

Swan crossed to a chalkboard at stage left that depicted the mission's 36-plane combat formation. Each T-shaped symbol on it represented a different bomber. A pilot's name and the last three digits of the plane's tail number appeared in chalk next to the symbol.

Representing the formation as seen from above with the planes' noses pointing toward the ceiling, this diagram showed the location of each B-26 in relation to the others in the two-box formation. *BRADEN* and *814*—the last three digits of *Lodestone Lola's* tail number—appeared at extreme lower left.

"Jesus," Callard whispered, "we're flying tail-end-Charlie in the low squadron of the first box!"

"Coffin corner," said Rusty Savitt, concerned.

"Quiet," Braden whispered.

"I'll lead the mission with Colonel Gallo flying deputy lead," the air exec continued. "Colonel Nielsen has the second box. That's it from me, boys, see you upstairs. Major?"

Linden Vander accepted the pointer from the departing air exec.

"Morning, gentlemen," said the S2. "Latest intelligence suggests the German High Command is recalling more *Luftwaffe* units from the Eastern Front to further beef up its homeland defenses. That means German aces with lots of Russian kills under their belts, so keep your eyes peeled."

Turning, he lifted his pointer to the large wall map. "You can expect heavy flak along the coast and at these usual hot spots. Avoid this area here... and this one where aerial reconnaissance suggests new ack-ack emplacements...."

*   *   *

The Marauders cruised in perfect formation and bright sunshine high above the English Channel. Braden thumbed his push-to-talk button.

"Pilot to crew, okay to test your guns."

Throat mics work by picking up vibrations, not from directly hearing external sounds like most microphones. In his helmet as he spoke, Braden heard his own words slightly garbled but they were clear enough to be understood. *Lola*'s nose gun, waist guns, and twin-gun top and tail turrets began independently firing brief bursts aimed away from other aircraft.

Each Marauder also had four fixed forward-firing machine guns mounted in low-profile blisters to the fuselage sides. These packet guns were rarely used and never tested because they fired straight ahead and couldn't be aimed away from the formation.

Lola shivered with the brief poundings and filled with the acrid smell of cordite. Around them, other B-26s likewise tested their .50 caliber Brownings.

"All right, you clowns," Braden transmitted, "knock off firing before you shoot down one of our own."

He turned and glared at his copilot. "And you, Callard," he said, not via interphone, "keep that stink of fear to yourself! Christ, why didn't they put me in single-seat fighters?"

Frank hunched miserably as the enthusiasm of his fellow crew members filled their leather helmets.

"Whoo hoo!" said Paco Gonzalez in high spirits. *"Por favor,* send me some pendejos that I can shoot down today!"

"If by pen-day-hoes you mean Kraut fighters," came Jacobs' earnest young voice, "I plan on bagging a few myself!"

Braden stabbed the button on his wheel. "Pilot to crew, cut the chatter, you bozos, and try not to screw up!"

His ill humor silenced any further expressions of camaraderie among new crew.

*　　*　　*

More than an hour later, the 328th Bomb Group was running the gauntlet of intense flak on its bomb run. Orange explosions blossomed around the B-26s, whose bomb-bay doors came open. These shell bursts instantly faded to dirty black puffs that slid by, each marking the location of a shrapnel blast that could effortlessly penetrate nearby aluminum hulls and human skin.

In the cockpit of *Baltimore Blitzkrieg,* Captain Hasbrook wiped his face with the back of a leather-gloved hand. He was sweating profusely. His copilot shot him a puzzled look because the big pilot was usually the picture of calm.

"Buddy, are you okay—" Lieutenant Prestridge began to say.

A clangorous concussion threw them hard in their seatbelts, followed by a cascading rattle that sounded like birdseed being poured over sheet metal. Hasbrook froze.

"I'll check for damage," Prestridge volunteered, unbuckling.

All was well in the empty navigator's compartment. The copilot ducked through the low bulkhead door into the bomb bay and stepped down onto its steel catwalk.

Open bomb doors beneath Prestridge admitted daylight. More still entered the windowless compartment through dozens of new holes punched through its walls.

His flight engineer was at the other end of the bomb bay. A seasoned veteran, the gunner had left his turret to come investigate. Prestridge saw him assessing the damage with a frown.

The copilot squeezed between heavily laden bomb racks that provided handholds for crossing the catwalk. "What was that hellish din, Sergeant?" he shouted, joining him.

The enlisted man pointed up. Prestridge looked and his mouth fell open. The compartment's metal ceiling had a large tear ripped through it. Torn aluminum flapped in the slipstream.

"Holy shit!" Prestridge exclaimed.

The flight engineer nodded and leaned close to be heard. "An eighty-eight came up through this open bomb bay and exploded out the top and sides of the ship, Sir," he said. "What we heard was hot shell fragments and debris raining down on these here bombs."

"How on earth did it miss them on the way up?"

"Search me," came the reply, "but if it hadn't, we'd never have known what hit us."

Prestridge nodded, sobered. "Damned lucky it didn't take out a wing spar or rupture the fuel cross-feed. Any injuries farther aft?"

"No, Sir, we're all fine."

They were startled by the 500-pounders around them releasing in mechanical sequence. Prestridge and the sergeant watched the heavy ordnance drop and fall away behind to mingle with bombs released by other Marauders.

Sliding by twelve thousand feet below was the large railroad marshaling yard. It erupted soundlessly with flashes, concussions, and rising smoke. Just before the bomb-bay doors closed, they witnessed a particularly violent explosion.

"Must have been a Nazi munitions train on the tracks," the sergeant said.

Prestridge returned to the cockpit, strapped back in, and plugged in his comm jacks. "Flak turned our bomb bay into a sieve," he told his pilot.

"Take over, Tommy," Hasbrook asked, sounding odd.

Prestridge slid his seat forward and took the controls as intense heavy flak played cat and mouse with the formation. It was closer than he liked, particularly after what he'd just seen.

Those gunners are too damn good, he thought grimly.

*   *   *

At the rear of the 328th's first box, the crew of *Lodestone Lola* was thinking the same thing when the flak ceased.

"Why'd the ack-ack stop?" Callard asked, puzzled.

Before Braden could answer, Bidwell's dispassionate voice came in their ears. "Pen-day-hoes, ten o'clock high."

"Focke-Wulfs, dozens of 'em!" Savitt added.

Looking out his side window, Braden saw distant dots flying beyond machine gun range parallel to their formation. With their greater speed, the single-seaters pulled inexorably ahead. The lead fighters began to break off in two-ship elements and wheel around to attack from dead ahead.

Leaders and wingmen broke apart as each picked its own target. Braden saw their wings sparkle with cannon fire as they swept through the formation at the very high combined rate of closure.

Turrets rotated and machine guns pounded as gunners of the 328th BG hammered away at the enemy fighters sweeping past. Breaking off at the last instant, the Focke-Wulfs rolled inverted and dove away, leaving in their wake a savaged formation in disarray.

The speed of frontal attacks was too great. In his top turret, Milt Bidwell swore as he missed a yellow-nosed bandit. "Top turret to waist and tail gunners, they're breaking and diving away beneath us," Bidwell transmitted. "I'll call them out for you."

Squatting tensely on the floor between his waist guns, Gonzalez got a quick burst off at a passing Focke-Wulf. In the tail turret, Lew Jacobs sighted on the same departing fighter plane. His twin-fifties pounded briefly before he quit, greatly frustrated.

"Tail to crew, call 'em out for me sooner, guys!" Jake said.

Up front, Savitt gripped the handles of his machine gun as he scanned the sky. The frontal attacks were utterly nerve-racking in their quickness. His heart leapt to see one Focke-Wulf maneuver hard and straighten out heading straight for them. Its pilot had singled *Lola* out as the most vulnerable target at the rear outer edge of the first box's low squadron.

"Pen-day-ho attacking from dead ahead!" Savitt transmitted.

The nimble FW 190 evaded withering fire from *Lola* and the surrounding Marauders. Its wing cannons flashed. With one hand, Savitt reflexively pulled his goggles down over his eyes and squeezed his Browning's triggers.

The pilots watched this attack from the cockpit. "Pilot to crew," Braden added after Savitt's transmission, "he'll break off low to the port side so here's your chance."

The Focke-Wulf's tracers converged on *Lola,* whose nose gun and top turret pounded. Braden fired the packet guns as well, hoping their flashes would dissuade the attacker.

Cannon fire brutally raked *Lola,* knocking her left engine out of action. The sledgehammer strikes threaded their way inward until the bomber's plexiglass nose violently imploded. In the blink of an eye, the nose compartment filled up with high-energy plexiglass fragments while the rear bulkhead disintegrated in a blast that blew Savitt forward from behind.

The impacting shell had exploded against the rear of Braden's instrument panel, filling the cockpit with smoke. Confirming a dead engine outside his window, Jack hit its fuel cutoff, feathered the prop, and rapidly cranked in compensating trim.

As he did this, the FW 190 flashed past and rolled inverted to dive away from *Lola,* leaving the formation behind. Paco Gonzalez, anticipating this, fired his portside machine gun. Jacobs also fired but had no time to aim.

Knowing he'd missed, the tail gunner was startled to see the Focke-Wulf falter and belch dirty black smoke from its engine. *Lola's* gunners saw the pilot jettison his canopy and bail out, tumbling head over heels until his parachute blossomed.

A cheer broke out on the interphone. In the cockpit where none of this was visible, Callard guessed what had happened and started to cheer too. Then his eyes fell on his pilot.

"You're hit!" he shouted. "The skipper's been hit!" he repeated via interphone for all the crew to hear.

In the rear fuselage, Gonzalez's grin vanished. Ripping his cords from the jackbox, he started to race forward only to bump into Bidwell, who dropped lithely out of his turret to also go help.

Gonzalez arrived first to find Callard doing the flying as Braden contended with a profusely bleeding thigh. Bidwell appeared a moment later holding a first-aid kit. The Latino stepped down into the radio compartment to make room for the senior noncom.

"He's losing blood!" Callard shouted.

"You just concentrate on getting us home, Sir," the top turret gunner replied calmly.

"I can't land this thing, Milt," the copilot wailed, "not with one engine shot out!"

Ignoring him, Bidwell knelt beside Braden and ripped his right pants leg away. Using his teeth to open a packet of sulfa drugs, he sprinkled the powder on multiple bleeding wounds. Quickly he applied gauze pads and a bandage winding that he tied off.

"Leave the kit," Braden ordered.

Bidwell nodded. Reaching into it, he pulled out a syrette and offered it to Braden. "Morphine if you need it."

The pilot shook his head. "What I need is a clear head. Get back to your station."

Braden took the controls again. "We'll take turns flying," he told Callard. "I'll make the landing."

*   *   *

Officers at the tower railing saw two red flares arc upward from a Marauder coming in on one engine. This damaged ship cut into the landing pattern as other planes broke off, yielding landing priority.

Grimacing with pain, Braden scowled at his useless instrument panel. What few gauges were still there no longer worked. Losing the airspeed indicator was the biggest blow. He now flew by feel, compensating for a dead engine whose mangled cowling negatively affected the plane's aerodynamics.

As they descended toward the runway, Callard saw a rescue crew jump into an ambulance parked by the control tower. He lost sight of the vehicle as Braden touched smoothly down. When they'd slowed sufficiently, the pilot angled off the main runway.

Lola rolled to a stop in the grass. The meat wagon arrived as Braden shut down and landings resumed around them. Callard exited and sagged to the grass, unable to do anything but sit there. The rest of *Lola's* crew stood wordlessly by as medical orderlies opened the plane's bomb bay and carefully lowered their barely conscious pilot down on a stretcher.

More people arrived. They helped carry the stretcher over to the ambulance and slid it in through the rear doors. Savitt, his face bleeding, was ushered aboard before it raced away.

Next came the 4x4 truck delivering Myron Wrotnowski and his maintenance team. With Butch and Miguel in tow, *Lola's* crew chief walked around his plane assessing the damage. When he finished, he pulled off his ball cap, scratched his scalp, and scowled up at the shot-up engine and missing nose.

"I gotta talk to that guy about takin' better care of government property!" Rotten said.

Chapter 23: Road to Recovery

Tom Prestridge crossed the admin site to visit the base chapel. Entering and finding it empty, he proceeded to the back office area, saw an open door, and knocked.

Sitting at the desk of a small office was a heavyset chaplain in his forties wearing captain's bars. He looked up from his paperwork, closed his fountain pen, and removed his reading glasses.

"Come in, Lieutenant," he said kindly.

Prestridge entered hesitantly. "Do you have a moment, father?"

"As much time as you need, son. As you can see, it's pretty quiet around here."

The lieutenant nodded. "Whoever said there are no atheists in a foxhole never flew combat. We're a pretty fatalistic bunch."

"When your number comes up, it comes up; is that it?"

"Maybe. Just seems to me like a rabbit's foot makes more sense these days than a confessional."

"Sit down, my boy."

Prestridge accepted the seat and sized up his elder as if debating whether to unburden himself. The chaplain smiled disarmingly.

"Let's start with your name," he prompted.

"Sure. Tom Prestridge, I'm a copilot with the five-seventeenth." He hesitated. "I need to talk with someone—with you, father—about my pilot."

The chaplain nodded. "Go on."

"It's difficult, you see, 'cause we've flown a lot of missions together and he's a popular guy."

"Good pilot is he?"

"The best!" The copilot's quick smile faded to uncertain worry. "At least, I used to think so…."

The chaplain opened a bottom desk drawer and pulled out a whiskey bottle with two shot glasses. He poured, pushed one glass to Prestridge, and settled back with the other.

"I'm all ears," he said.

"Buddy—Captain Hasbrook, our skipper—he and I are like Mutt and Jeff. In civilian life he plays pro football whereas I'm an academic. I do okay at the controls, but when Buddy flies it's amazing!"

"How so?"

The copilot struggled for words. "I fly the B-26 like I'm walking on eggshells. Not Buddy. He breaks it to his will…, makes it do things you wouldn't believe. It's almost like those big Pratt & Whitneys don't matter—he's hauling us off the runway by dint of the strength in his arms."

The chaplain's sympathetic reaction showed that he assumed Prestridge to be gay. "Are you two… close?" he asked delicately.

"Oh no. Buddy resents me because I'm smarter than he is. But he needs an audience and I'm sitting right there beside him, so he tolerates me."

"I don't understand then," the chaplain said. "What's the issue?"

Prestridge sighed. "Buddy and I were flying deputy lead behind Colonel Fowler the day he bought the farm. Buddy idolized him like all the rest of us. Ever since, he's been… different."

"Different how?"

Prestridge shrugged and shook his head. "I don't know, father. Little things. Like how he flies. And his temper."

"Oh? What's he angry at?"

"Maybe having to keep flying after we put in our fifty. All I know is he's changed, Sir, and the guys—his crew, I mean—well, frankly, we don't feel safe with him anymore."

A pregnant silence hung between them. "Would you like me to speak with Mike Swan or Doctor Polling?" the chaplain offered. "Some R-and-R at a flak house may help Captain Hasbrook to—"

"No," Prestridge said. "Don't get me wrong, father. Buddy's not flak happy. Look, maybe I shouldn't have come...."

The flier stood, opened the door, and turned to leave. He looked back, more troubled than when he had arrived. "You'll keep this under your hat?"

"Certainly."

Prestridge departed, leaving behind him an untouched drink and a bewildered chaplain.

*   *   *

Recovering fliers occupied the hospital ward's beds. An Army nurse rolled a cart down its middle clearing away dinner trays. Reaching Braden's bed, she frowned at his untouched plate.

"Not hungry, Lieutenant?" she asked.

"No, Ma'am."

The nurse removed the tray just as Doc Polling, who was making his evening rounds, approached the injured flier.

"Good to see you're awake, Braden," the doctor said cheerfully. "How are you feeling?"

"Where's my bombardier?" Jack asked without preamble.

"I picked all the plexiglass slivers out of Lieutenant Savitt's face and discharged him hours ago. Fortunately for him, his goggles were down over his eyes."

Braden nodded and grimaced with a spasm of pain. Polling observed it.

"I'll have the nurse give you something for that," he said kindly. "Oh, by the way, I have a gift for you."

106

The flight surgeon rummaged in the pocket of his white coat and pulled out a small item that he placed in the pilot's hand.

"Your X-ray showed a constellation of Kraut metal in your hide. While you were under, I dug out every chunk. This was the largest."

The jagged fragment of an exploded anti-aircraft shell was just over an inch long and half that in width. Braden studied it, turning it in his fingers. Something caught his eye as he was about to toss it onto his bedtable.

"I thought you might like it as a souvenir," continued the doctor, "so I had it cleaned and sterilized."

Braden still stared, thunderstruck. Stamped in the metal were the digits *1773*. They were all that remained of a longer string, presumably a serial number or manufacturer's mark.

"Thanks, Doc," Braden said before the doctor moved on to his next patient.

The ward's doors opened and the nurse reentered. She made a beeline for Braden with a wide smile. Behind her, he saw Sergeant Bidwell catch one of the swinging doors and hold it open. With him were the rest of *Lodestone Lola's* crew.

"Feel like company, Lieutenant?"

Braden put aside the souvenir. "I guess so."

She turned and nodded. The five men swarmed in and clustered around their pilot's bed. Savitt's face was bandaged but he couldn't stop grinning. Braden regarded them, unsure and uncomfortable.

"Five minutes, gentlemen," the nurse said sternly. "Our patient needs his rest."

"Right, Ma'am," Bidwell said, representing the crew. He turned to Braden. "How are you feeling, Sir?"

"Fine, Milt," Braden replied. He turned to his bombardier. "Not much room in the nose of a B-26, Rusty. How on earth did that twenty-millimeter shell miss you?"

"Damned if I know, Skipper," Savitt replied. "It ripped open the back of my shearling jacket but left me totally untouched."

Braden winced in pain. "The Krauts... owe you a jacket," he managed to say.

"I'll tape the bill to the next bomb we drop!"

Everyone laughed, thawing the ice between the crew and their commander.

"I don't know if I'll get a purple heart for this," Savitt said, touching his face. "But you sure as hell will for your thigh. And maybe a medal too."

When Braden didn't respond, Bidwell broke the silence. "Sir, did you hear that Paco got the pen-day-ho who shot us up? It's been officially confirmed."

"Really?" Braden said. He turned to the waist gunner. "Great work, Gonzalez."

"Piece of cake, Sir," the Latino replied confidently. "The way I figure it, we used up all our bad luck on this one mission. From here on, it'll be us dishin' it out and the Krauts takin' it."

This brought laughs from around the ward, which enjoyed the infectious high spirits of Braden's crew. Their enthusiasm buoyed Jack in particular. He turned to his copilot.

"Thank you for taking over, Frank," he said sincerely. "You really came through for us."

The copilot blushed, pleased by the words. "I told you I could handle her in an emergency," he said. "But I can't land a crippled ship—you did that."

"Yeah, with an instrument panel blown to hell and nothing but a compass working," Bidwell proclaimed. "Don't know how you managed it, Sir!"

Jacobs agreed with an eager nod. "I've been on lots of flights with lots of pilots and nobody ever made a better landing than that!" he proclaimed.

The rising volume of their boisterous good spirits prompted the nurse to intervene. "Time for lights out, boys."

Each member of Braden's crew touched him or clapped his shoulder as they filed out. He couldn't say anything. His throat constricted. He blinked at the ceiling and swallowed.

*   *   *

In the hours before dawn, Braden wept while trying not to make any noise. He grimaced angrily at his inability to stifle the torrent of emotion that left him sobbing uncontrollably, his tears soaking the pillowcase.

Several beds away across the aisle, another injured young flier was also awake. He lay there unmoving, listening silently with a veteran's profound empathy.

Chapter 24: The Build-Up

Lodestone Lola sat outside the T2 repair hangar still hooked up to the Cletrac that had towed her in. Wrotnowski and Zeke stood below her assessing the damage.

"Gonna call on the Air Repair Depot?" Wrotnowski asked.

"Nah, we can fix her here," Zeke said confidently. "I got some Category E birds out back I can cannibalize for a nose, instrument panel, and parts for the nacelle around a new engine."

"How long do you figure?"

"Hard to say," the maintenance chief said with a shrug. "We got an extra heavy workload these days, thanks to the new CO making the group fly these extra-long bomb runs. You should see all the holes we're patchin' up!"

"Canfield's all wet," Wrotnowski asserted angrily.

"So they say. Far be it from me to disagree."

Wrotnowski smiled as he contemplated *Lola*. "Take good care of her, Zeke."

"Don't you worry none, Rotten, your baby's in good hands!"

*   *   *

Standing before a brand-new silver B-26 named *Slugger,* Colonel Canfield struck another heroic pose as more flashbulbs went off. The day was bright but the flashes and strategically placed reflectors softened the shadows to accentuate the drama of the images.

Lieutenant Emory Pierce led the team of noncoms doing the photo shoot. Summoned without notice from the 328th Bomb Group's Public Relations Office, they'd hurried out to Canfield's hardstand at Kingsholme's northeast corner. It was the closest dispersal to the admin and tech sites. Canfield chose it to be able to see his personal B-26 Marauder out his office window.

Lieutenant Pierce's normal job was to feed articles and photos about the deeds of 328th personnel to hometown newspapers across America. More than just inform the public, this vital work by military combat outfits boosted home-front morale.

The new CO's unscheduled vanity project interfered with this activity. Pierce didn't like it one bit.

"Got 'em, Pierce?" Canfield asked, pulling off his helmet.

"Yes, Colonel, I'll have prints on your desk this afternoon."

"Including the cockpit shots of me at the controls? The ones that make it look like I'm actually flying?"

"Yes Sir."

Canfield nodded. Stripping off his Mae West and parachute, he bundled these props into the arms of Teddy Lansbury, his sergeant driver, who watched everything as he cooled his heels.

"Deliver the pics to me personally, Pierce," Canfield said over his shoulder, "and plan on staying. I'll need your help working up press releases for my home-state papers."

"Yes Sir," the public relations officer said, unable to conceal the disrespect in his tone.

It was lost on Canfield, who waited for his driver to dump the flight gear in the trunk, slam it, and hurry around to hold the rear door for him.

"Dismissed," the CO ordered, climbing in.

Sergeant Lansbury shot them a pained *"What an asshole!"* grimace before getting behind the Clipper's wheel and pulling away.

Canfield's narcissistic high-handedness hadn't played well with the PR team. Their head shakes and disgusted expressions as they stowed their gear in a jeep showed they shared this opinion.

* * *

Two weeks later, *Lodestone Lola* sat on her dispersal fully repaired. Her flight and ground crews stood admiring their bomber in high spirits. Zeke and his repair team were also there for the handover celebration.

Dressed in his service uniform and fifty-mission crush, Braden hobbled forward, a crutch under one arm. Using his free hand, he swiped a paint brush back and forth over a stencil that Wrotnowski held in place against the bomber's forward fuselage.

Rotten reclaimed the brush and peeled off the stencil to reveal yet another bright red bomb symbol at the far-right end of the bottom row of bombs. It brought the Marauder's mission tally to 163. Everyone cheered and applauded.

"This old girl's not done yet!" the crew chief declared proudly. He turned to Paco Gonzalez. "Your turn, kid."

With pats on his back, the young Latino gunner slathered the brush across a stencil held next to two swastikas denoting previous victories scored against Hitler's *Luftwaffe* by *Lola's* crews. Rotten removed it to reveal a bright new swastika denoting Gonzolez's confirmed victory. Whoops, praise, and good-natured ribbing ensued.

"Thanks, Sarge," Gonzalez said, grinning while chewing gum. "Thanks everybody." He turned to Braden. "I guess we showed the Krauts we're too tough for them. Right, Skipper?"

Braden laughed. "Right, Paco."

Jack Braden took a deep, contented breath, savoring the day. For once in his life—ironically amidst the chaos of all-out global warfare—he felt completely comfortable in his own skin and at peace with the world.

Pedaling across the grass after the celebration, he spotted the NAAFI van at the tech site and changed course. As he approached, he saw Georgiana and her mother in their uniforms closing up shop. They didn't notice him dismount and awkwardly walk his bike to the van, holding the crutch and doing his best not to limp.

Georgiana was the first to glance up. "Jack!"

The pent-up emotion behind this exclamation lifted Braden's spirits further. He grinned ingenuously.

"Hi, Georgiana. Hello, Lady Brookleigh."

"Good to see you out and about, Lef-tenant," the older woman said cheerily.

"I was so worried!" gushed Georgiana. "They told us you were in hospital."

"I'm fine. Another day or two and I'll be back on flying status."

"Are you permitted off base?" Georgiana asked.

"Yes, until tonight."

"Ride along with us," she urged. "Is that all right, Mother?"

"Of course. Climb aboard, Lef-tenant."

He rolled his bike to the van's rear and handed it up along with the crutch. With a radiant smile, Georgiana set these aside and took his hand in hers to help him up. Her electric touch and astonishing beauty at close range made his heart leap as he settled beside her.

Up front, Lady Brookleigh drove with the forthright privilege of British landed gentry. Through the large front windows, Braden saw other vehicles yielding way. Whether it was due to politeness, because they recognized her, or simply out of deference to NAAFI vans, he couldn't guess.

Turning into the lush grounds of Waddleston Hall, Georgiana's mother followed the long gravel drive around to the rear courtyard and parked by the stables. They entered through a rear door.

Jack found himself in a very large kitchen where Mowbray the butler sat at the head of a table enjoying tea with his household staff. Startled, they started to rise.

"Sit!" ordered Lady Brookleigh. "Where's Sir Colin, Mowbray?"

"In the sitting room, M'Lady, with some of his former students."

"We shall require tea," she said, not waiting for a reply.

*   *   *

Teacups in hand, Sir Colin and Jack—he with the crutch under one arm—stood by fire with three young fighter pilots wearing their smart RAF gray-blue uniforms. Rupert stood by, eagerly soaking up everything related to aviation.

Georgiana and Lady Brookleigh, having changed into civilian attire, sat with female visitors elsewhere in the parlor. As Georgiana chatted with them over tea and cakes, her eyes stole repeatedly to Jack. He glanced her way just as often.

"I must say, your Marauder is an impressive machine, Leftenant," one young RAF pilot was saying.

"So's your Spitfire," Braden replied. "We feel much safer with you escorting us."

"You make it easy," said a second British flier. "Every other bomber is so slow that we must S-turn to escort them. Yours is so fast that we all clip merrily along together."

The third, who sported a mustache, nodded. "I shepherded a battle-damaged Marauder home just the other day, matter of fact," he said. "One engine tits-up, airscrew feathered. Don't know many twin jobs that will do two hundred on both motors yet this cheeky Yank did it on one."

Braden guessed its pilot flogged his remaining Pratt & Whitney to get a wounded crewmember back to medical help, but he kept the thought to himself. It was Rupert who spoke next.

"Really?" exclaimed the sixteen-year-old, enthralled.

Sir Colin smiled indulgently. "Rupert's building a model of the Martin Marauder, aren't you, Son?"

"Yes, father, it's in my room. I say, would you gentlemen care to see it?"

To his delight, the men instantly set their teas aside in unanimous consent. As they exited the parlor, Jack caught Georgiana's eye as he hobbled and nodded toward the door. She extricated herself and joined them at the main staircase.

Ascending to the landing, which Jack accomplished with her help, the convivial party proceeded down a long hallway past antique furnishings, suits of armor, and *objets d'art*. Upon entering Rupert's room, Braden instantly recognized a friend on the bed.

"Max!" he exclaimed, crossing to greet the dog.

Max sat up and wagged happily as Jack and Georgiana perched around him on the bed, petting him. Max looked transformed—well fed and well loved with a pampered glow to his brushed fur.

"Thank you for bringing him, Jack," Georgiana said. "Honestly, he and Rupert are inseparable. They positively dote on each other."

Rupert had shown the balsawood model he was building to the RAF fliers, who—not being that much older than he—were keen to see it. Beaming with pride, the boy next brought it to Jack.

"What do you think, Lef-tenant?" he asked.

Being a Marauder pilot, Jack knew how much his reply would matter to the teenager. He took the model in his hands and made a big show of examining it carefully.

The model was large with a two-foot wingspan. Its fuselage stringers were perfectly seated and cleanly glued into the bulkheads that Rupert had cut out and notched. The wings and nacelles were equally well crafted although, typical of balsa models, the overall effect was a bit crude.

Jack nodded approvingly. "Excellent job," he said. "You've captured the Marauder perfectly."

Rupert glowed with pleasure. "I'm about ready to cover it with doped tissue," he added.

"How are you going to paint it?"

"Like the one I see out my window," Rupert replied, pointing.

A telescope stood on a tripod before the indicated window. Jack crossed to look out over the estate's gardens. He saw a vista of grass, grazing sheep, and ancient shade trees. Beyond a distant brook-fed pond with waterfowl and reeds were encompassing woods. And framed by a gap in it in the middle distance, Jack could make out a single green Martin B-26 Marauder.

It was all that was visible of Kingsholme Field. Jack bent to look through the telescope, which was locked on the airplane. Seen close up, he instantly recognized *Lodestone Lola*.

Braden straightened in astonishment. "That's my ship!"

The room reacted in surprise. Rupert proudly let Georgiana and the RAF fliers take turns looking through his telescope.

Chapter 25: Rising Stakes

Jack and Georgiana meandered together through the gardens of Waddleston Hall, she speaking softly and vulnerably. "We were childhood friends, our families close for generations. It was hoped we might fall in love... and we did."

They came to a stone bench and sat down. Her body posture conveyed deep grief. Jack waited for her to continue.

"Alistair was a bomb aimer," Georgiana said at last, avoiding his eyes. "He was kind-hearted and sensitive, although he hid it from the world. In so many ways, you remind me of him."

She took a breath and looked up. "The week before Christmas last, his Lancaster failed to return from a raid on Berlin."

"I'm so sorry, Georgiana," Braden said gently.

She turned to him. "It seems when I fall in love with a man, he dies. So when I heard you were injured, I thought..., I feared.... Oh Jack!"

She buried her face in his shoulder, weeping. He stroked her hair and didn't move, letting the tears run their course. She straightened, sniffled, and wiped her eyes.

"You don't have to worry about me," he assured her. "Here, I can prove it."

The American took something from his pocket and handed it to her. She wiped her face again and blinked at it. "What is it?"

"A chunk of German flak that hit my plane and struck me." He pointed. "There's a number on it, see?"

Georgiana looked closely at the jagged chunk of machined steel and saw the number *1773*. "So?" she asked, not understanding.

Without a word, Jack removed his dog tags from over his head and handed them to her dangling on their chain. She studied the stamped aluminum identity tag. It read *BRADEN, JOHN J.* Just beneath that was his U.S. Army serial number: *O-4131773*.

Georgiana looked up in surprise. "That shell had your number on it! Part of it, anyway."

Braden flashed a smile. "How many guys can say their number came up—literally—and they're still around?"

It was suddenly all too much for Georgiana, who stood abruptly. "I should get back," she said, flustered.

Jack rose too, took her hand, and pulled her in for a long and tender kiss. They parted, both changed.

"M'Lady," Jack said, making no move to detain her further.

"Yank flier," she replied crisply.

Her twisted smile poignantly reflected the fragility of love in an uncertain, strife-torn world. Without another word, she turned and entered the French doors of her ancestral country home.

*　　*　　*

One day a letter arrived for Jack. It was from Lilly Quill, his mother's niece. Lilly had heard he'd deployed overseas and tracked down his APO number.

He'd known her as Lilly Tyler. They were the same age and had been friends as children. Now a schoolteacher, Lilly was closing out her apartment in Ann Arbor, Michigan, and would soon travel by train with their possessions to Groton, Connecticut, to join her husband. A newly minted PhD in naval architecture, Elroy Quill had been hired by the Electric Boat Company to help design submarines for the U.S. Navy.

Braden wrote back, taking care not to run afoul of the intelligence boys who reviewed and censored all mail leaving

Kingsholme. Thus began a regular correspondence that brought him pleasure. He sat happily at the PX snack bar composing letters.

The other change in his life was the list of books that Tommy Prestridge recommended he read. Braden scoured the communal site libraries for knowledge, read voraciously, and discussed books with the college prof on walks or bike rides as they played with ideas. It filled the hole in Jack's education. He thirsted for more.

*   *   *

On the first of May 1944, Braden, Savitt, and Callard dragged into their barracks. Their exhaustion and sweat-stained clothes—rumpled from being worn beneath flight gear—showed them to be just back from a mission. Other returning fliers entered with them and proceeded wordlessly to their billets.

Frank Callard and Rusty Savitt flopped down on their cots and went to sleep. Braden picked up a piece of chalk and added another slash to his slate on the wall. The tally stood at eighteen combat missions. Sitting wearily on his cot, he rubbed his face.

Lodestone Lola had come home with more holes but nobody had been injured. As for enemy fighters, Braden's crew hadn't seen a single one since their encounter with the murderous Focke-Wulf.

In the briefing, Major Vander had stated that the German High Command was pulling its fighters away from coastal France and the low countries to bases farther inland. Recon flights and human intelligence by local resistance groups confirmed the news.

Did the Nazis know an invasion was imminent? Had they taken this action to keep their fighters from being caught in a preemptive invasion-day attack on forward airfields before they could become airborne?

The S-2 also reported that entire German fighter wings were being relocated from battlefronts to beef up Germany's homeland defense. This was bad news all around, but worse for the four-engine bombers that penetrated deep into Germany and beyond.

Spring had driven away the endless clouds and frequent fogs of North Atlantic winter weather. Forecasting conditions over targets on the Continent became more accurate. Having arrived in early April, Braden experienced this welcome transition, and with it the 328th Bomb Group's increased operational tempo. Two Marauder missions a day were not unusual as the Army Air Forces in England made up for lost time.

With a weary sigh, Braden stretched out on his cot and placed his fifty-mission crush over his face, the bill resting on the bridge of his nose. Despite it shutting out the light, sleep eluded him.

Three codenames filled his mind's eye as if chiseled in stone: *POINTBLANK, CROSSBOW,* and *OVERLORD.* Into these buckets fit every single mission that Jack had flown in his first full month of combat.

OPERATION POINTBLANK was the AAF campaign to destroy the *Luftwaffe's* fighter strength. Achieving air superiority would be essential before the Allies could mount an invasion of the European continent. Attacking *Luftwaffe* airfields was part of this operation. So was forcing Hitler to recall his fighters to protect the German homeland, abandoning offensive campaigns elsewhere.

Defense of the Reich, the Nazis called it. *Reichsverteidigung.* Jack spoke no German but the harsh word had stuck in his mind. These recalled fighters and their pilots had taken on vast fleets of U.S. daylight bombers. The horrific toll they exacted of young American lives could not offset the fact that war is ultimately a game of attrition, and here America had an insurmountable advantage.

Forcing the *Luftwaffe* to play defense threw its fighters directly into the path of Eighth Air Force Flying Fortresses and Liberators and their escort fighters. The Germans had the most devastating armament of the war, their fighters being equipped with 20-mm or 30 mm aircraft cannons. But the U.S. fifty-caliber machine gun was no slouch and it had the advantage of a far higher rate of fire.

Each Fort or Lib mounted a dozen machine guns. U.S. daylight attacks now sometimes exceeded one thousand bombers plus seven hundred escorting Mustang and other fighters. Every combat box in this bomber stream was arranged to afford each plane a maximum field of offensive fire while keeping them collectively close for mutual defense.

While the deadly threat of flak remained undiminished, America was inexorably whittling the *Luftwaffe* down even as it took a toll of the Mighty Eighth. The result was a grim battle of attrition and the winner would be the side that could build more planes, produce more munitions, refine more avgas, and train more pilots. On all these fronts, the rapidly industrializing United States had a marked advantage thanks to its larger population, abundant natural resources, and can-do attitude.

Braden's thoughts turned to the top German aces with their Iron and Knight's Crosses. Earlier in the war, those legendary fliers had been *Luftwaffe* chief Hermann Göring's greatest asset. Many had combat experience dating back to the Spanish Civil War.

Reichsverteidigung had taken a grim toll of this elite group and Hitler lacked sufficient young men, industrial capacity, and training resources to offset their loss. With fewer experienced fliers among the *Luftwaffe's* ranks, and America's fighter force ever more superbly trained and equipped, the tide had turned.

Braden would have given anything to be one of those Mustang jockeys. He also recognized that the heavies had a rougher go of it than did the medium-bomber crews. His gratitude to both groups knew no bounds.

His mind turned to OPERATION CROSSBOW, the Allied campaign targeting the German launch sites that kept springing up in the Pas-de-Calais area and north of it along the Dutch coast. The intelligence boys said that these were for an unpiloted "revenge weapon" that had yet to make its operational debut. Hitler planned to direct thousands of these winged bombs against London and other targets to break the will of the British civilian populace.

As soon as the Nazis built these launch facilities, the Marauders of the 9th Air Force showed up to plaster them but good. Officially designated *NOBALL targets* by Ninth Bomber Command, they were universally referred to as *ski sites* because their most distinctive feature in aerial reconnaissance photographs was an angled launch ramp that curved up at the end like the lip of a ski jump. The shadows of slanting sunshine highlighted this feature.

Striking NOBALL targets had kept the eight B-26 groups busy throughout April. These missions were short, which was good. The *Luftwaffe* surrounded them with lethal flak emplacements, which was very bad.

As for OPERATION OVERLORD, it was what everybody lived for: the invasion of Europe to liberate the continent from the grip of the Nazis. You could feel it as an air of anticipation at every military installation. It became more palpable with each passing day.

Like the opening buds of spring, May saw a blossoming certainty that invasion was imminent. Nobody knew for sure when it would be, but OVERLORD must be the reason so many of the 328th's recent missions targeted *Luftwaffe* airfields, bridges over rivers, railway lines and marshaling yards, communications centers, and gun emplacements. Disruption and interdiction to hamper the arrival of enemy supplies and reinforcements would be crucial to the success of the Allie landings.

Everything depended on OVERLORD, which General Dwight Eisenhower led with RAF Air Chief Marshal Sir Arthur Tedder as his second-in-command. Although every aspect of their planning was top secret, the sheer scale of the operation made it a difficult secret to keep. It would be like nothing ever imagined before.

When that happened, it would be no cakewalk. A mix of hope and dread filled Braden's thoughts as he fell asleep.

Chapter 26: Giving and Receiving

Returning Marauders wheeled overhead awaiting their turns to enter the landing pattern. In the middle of this coordinated ballet, Buddy Hasbrook looked out his side window and used his rudder pedals to slip his plane sideways to the left.

"Buddy, what are you doing?" Prestridge demanded, shocked.

"Flight leader signaled for echelon-left formation," his pilot replied.

Baltimore Blitzkrieg was positioned at the right side of the first vee of a six-ship element circling Kingsholme's runways. Hasbrook slid left out of his slot and cut in behind the lead airplane. This unexpected action threw the following vee into instant disarray. A collision loomed with *Titmouse,* its leader.

"Look out!" shouted *Titmouse's* copilot, bracing himself as the rogue Marauder barged in from his side.

"Holy *shit!*" screamed Hasbrook's tail gunner, who dove out of his turret and scuttled forward in terror.

Sitting in *Titmouse's* nose, the bombardier threw himself back just as *Baltimore Blitzkrieg's* black-steel tail gun barrels raked through where his head had just been, destroying its plexiglass nose and the metal structure supporting it.

Mike Swan and other officers witnessed all this from the rail of the control tower observation deck. His fellow senior officers stood frozen in disbelief. Swan spun on his heel and raced down the tower's external metal stairs.

When *Titmouse's* turn came to land, the bomber—its forward fuselage in tatters—touched down and rolled out normally. The group's remaining ships all landed without incident.

*   *   *

In the interrogation hut a half-hour later, pandemonium reigned as everyone spoke at once. At Mike Swan's nod, Linden Vander and his junior intelligence officers silenced the hut. Braden stood watching incredulously with his crew, some of whose members had observed it for themselves from the landing pattern.

"All right, what happened?" the S-2 demanded.

"Buddy Hasbrook nearly killed me and my entire crew, Major," came the hot reply, "that's what happened!"

Hasbrook stood glaring defiantly. Clustered by him, Prestridge and the rest of his crew looked distinctly uncomfortable.

Vander turned to Hasbrook. "Well, Captain? I witnessed it myself and can't say I disagree with the lieutenant here. What have you to say for yourself?"

"Flight lead's copilot signaled me for echelon-left formation," Hasbrook replied. "I was just following orders."

"Who led the element?" Swan demanded of the room at large.

"I did, Sir," replied Dusty Dietrich, a veteran flier. "We were just about to break and sequence into the pattern when it happened."

"Did you order echelon formation to be flown?"

"No, Sir!"

"What about you, Chuck," Swan asked Dietrich's copilot. "Did you signal for echelon left?"

"No, Sir! He was flying sloppily and crowding us. I just waved him off, that's all."

Hasbrook looked around the hut for support but found none. Even the goons who had helped him beat Braden up avoided his eyes.

Seething with anger and resentment that he couldn't hide, Hasbrook chafed under Mike Swan's scowl.

"You're lucky the consequences weren't worse, Captain, or I'd have you up on charges right now," Swan stated. "You're grounded pending review. Dismissed."

Captain Buddy Hasbrook saluted stiffly, livid with rage. Others stepped aside, giving the big man a wide berth as he left the hut.

*　　*　　*

"Thanks, Mac," Braden told the supply clerk two days later as the airman slid a parcel across the countertop.

"Sure thing, Sir," replied the enlisted man. "We got more of these than we can use, all framed and ready for hanging."

The size and shape of a painting, the parcel was neatly wrapped in brown butcher paper tied up with twine. Jack picked it up and exited the Quartermaster Supply Building to find Tom Prestridge leaning against their jeep, hands in his pockets.

Still Jack's only friend on the field, Tommy looked rakish in his teardrop-shaped AN6531 sunglasses and fifty-mission crush. His cap was pushed back to reveal locks of blond hair.

"You look like a damned recruiting poster," Braden said as he slipped the parcel into the vehicle's rear seat.

"It's these aviator sunglasses," Prestridge said, grinning. "Every time I put 'em on, I feel like Douglas MacArthur."

The day felt like a holiday. In a way it was, because the 517th Squadron had it off. Like all AAF bombardment groups in the ETO, one of the 328th's four squadrons stood down each mission, leaving the remaining three to perform it. This rotation allowed time for flight crews to recover and airplanes to be maintained, inspected, and refitted.

The two lieutenants climbed into the jeep. Prestridge started up and lurched into jouncing gear toward the main gate. The sun being bright, Braden fished in his coat pocket for his own matching pair of Army/Navy-issue sunglasses.

"How did you rate the jeep?" he asked, slipping them on.

"Called in a few favors," Prestridge replied. "To tell the truth, I'm glad to get away for a while. Buddy's being a real asshole."

"You mean his pattern screw-up?"

"Yeah, that was bad!" Prestridge frowned deeply. "But it's more than that—either I'm screwy or he's going off the deep end."

"For instance?"

"He's been telling everyone that Canfield is right and anyone who grouses about the extended bomb runs is yellow."

"Wow, that pretty much insults every man in the group."

"Yeah, it seems like he's going out of his way to pick a fight with the whole world."

Braden considered telling him how his pilot and two buddies of his had beaten him, but it would only further strain the relationship of two fliers who needed to work together aloft.

They mechanically returned the MP's salute at the guard shack. turned onto the country lane, and accelerated through the wooded countryside, leaving Kingsholme behind.

*   *   *

In Waddleston Hall's grand foyer, Sir Colin, Lady Brookleigh, Georgiana, Rupert, and the two Americans looked on as Mowbray nailed hooks into the wall. Having removed his gift from its wrapping, Jack handed it to the butler. Mowbray hung the artwork, adjusted it to be perfectly level, and stepped aside.

A heraldic crest now graced the foyer's wall. Above the framed and matted military emblem set against a white background were the words "328th Bombardment Group (M)." In a scroll below was the motto *Recto Faciendo Neminem Timeo*.

"Quite fitting, considering that your airfield occupies our ancestral lands," Sir Colin said dryly.

"What's the inscription mean?" asked the teenager.

"If you studied your Latin, Rupert," Georgiana told her brother, "you would know that it says, *Doing right, I fear no one.*"

With a last look at the artwork, the baronet gave an approving nod. "Fine words. Fine words indeed."

"They're what keep me going, Sir," Tom Prestridge said.

"Will you gentlemen take tea?" inquired their hostess.

"We'll take a rain check, Lady Brookleigh," Prestridge replied. "The motor pool needs its jeep back."

*   *   *

The Americans descended to the gravel, donned their caps, and strode to the vehicle. As Jack climbed in beside his friend, he heard hurried steps behind them.

"Jack, wait!"

Georgiana ran up to Braden's side of the jeep. "I have a gift for you," she said, out of breath. "Had to dash upstairs to get it."

She lifted her hand to show them a pendant dangling from a slender gold chain, then pressed it into his hand with both hers.

Her blue eyes locked on his. "You said so yourself," she said. "Your number came up yet you're still alive. This is good luck, Jack. Wear it always and you'll be safe."

Braden reached up and pulled Georgiana in for a kiss. She stepped back afterward, embarrassed but smiling, and waved farewell as Prestridge put the jeep into gear. Ignoring his friend's grin, Jack opened his hand to examine her gift as they drove off.

It was his chunk of flak, but a jeweler had polished it and turned into a pendant. Like the thin golden chain securing it, the previously dull souvenir gleamed brightly in the sunshine.

"You're one lucky guy, Jack," Prestridge said.

"You can say that again, Prof!"

His smile faded as something occurred to him. "What'd you mean back there when you said our group motto keeps you going?"

Tom Prestridge considered the question. "I'm not a brave man," he replied. "Flying missions was tearing me up. Then one day I'm tossing down drinks at the OC when I see our group crest on the wall of the bar—just like the one we gave to the baronet and his family just now."

"So?"

"So that Latin quote hit me right between the eyes. Very loosely translated, it means, *Do your best and don't sweat the stuff you can't control.*"

"And that helps?"

Prestridge nodded. "It's the whole secret. Alexander Pope knew it when he wrote, *Act well your part; there all the honor lies.*" He chuckled as another thought occurred to him. "It's probably also why he said, *The fool is happy that he knows no more.*"

Braden frowned and shook his head. "I don't buy it."

Prestridge looked puzzled. "Something sticking in your craw?"

"This selfless stuff," Braden said. "Look, when you come right down to it, all of us want the same thing, and that's to come through this war with our skins intact. Right?"

"Yeah. So?"

"So the way to do that is take care of *numero uno.* Don't stick your neck out for anybody 'cause watching out for the next guy gets you nothing but a kick in the teeth."

Tom Prestridge glanced at him, startled. *"Teach me to feel another's woe,"* he quoted, *"to hide the fault I see; that mercy I to others show, that mercy show to me."*

"Huh?"

The lit professor sighed. "Forget it," he said, disappointed.

Chapter 27: Preparations

Against ominous skies, AAF personnel hastily painted broad stripes over *Lodestone Lola's* olive-drab skin. This fifth of June 1944, all Marauders on Kingsholme Field were receiving these alternating white-and-black bands around their wings and aft fuselages.

Materials had been sent ahead to all bases without explanation. Instructions for their use followed shortly by a directive from Wing that electrified the base. Why decorate bombers with high visibility markings? It could only mean one thing and everybody was already calling them invasion stripes.

The 328th Bomb Group's S-1 (Personnel), S-3 (Operations), and S-4 (Logistics) staffs had gone into high gear with the arrival of this directive. Given an extremely short time frame for security reasons, they hastily organized and dispatched paint crews across the length and breadth of the field.

These ad-hoc paint crews drew people from security, clerical and supply, maintenance and repair, medical services, communications, and every other ground echelon function. Ordered to drop their normal duties, the startled enlisted men found themselves jouncing around the perimeter track in the base's fleet of Army 4x4s, which took them to every occupied hardstand.

Jumping down, they pulled ladders, masking materials, brushes, and heavy paint cans out of the truck before setting to work. Marauder ground maintenance crews, alerted to assist them, pitched in to further speed the process.

It being British Double Summer Time, the sun wouldn't set till ten-fifteen. This would ordinarily suffice, but gathering clouds and Base Meteorology's prediction of bad weather moving in made completing the task a race against time.

*   *   *

Base Ops hummed with excitement as officers and enlisted personnel, including Women's Army Corps, hurried about their duties. In the teletype room, Willis Canfield, Mike Swan, and Curt Keller stood watching the chattering machine.

The group adjutant ripped off each new page after it printed. When the transmission ended, he opened the door and flagged the first passing noncom. This time it was a young WAC corporal.

"Have these decoded right away," Keller ordered.

The young woman nodded and hurried off, papers in hand. The adjutant reentered the room and shut its door.

"So this is it?" the CO was saying, scarcely able to contain his excitement. "The big show?"

"Could be," Swan replied, knowing full well that it was. The air exec hid his own thrill because he didn't want to give Canfield the satisfaction of confirming what any idiot would already know.

Colonel Canfield frowned. "Wing pulled my personal driver and filing clerks away to slap paint on bombers. Why would they do that?"

The teletype began chattering again. Swan focused on it as he pointedly ignored the man he couldn't stand.

Curt Keller replied tactfully on Swan's behalf. "My guess, Sir?" the adjutant said. "It's to give Allied airplanes over the invasion beaches highly visible markings that let our ground forces know not to shoot at them. Those boys hitting the beaches are bound to be trigger-happy."

"So this is it? And it's happening at every military air base in the British Isles?" the CO asked eagerly.

"No, Sir," Swan replied. "There's no need for invasion stripes on B-17s and B-24s. Or British Lancasters for that matter."

"And why not?" Canfield demanded hotly.

Keller explained, again answering for his friend. "Because the *Luftwaffe* doesn't fly four-engine aircraft," he said. "Eisenhower will make certain that every dogface knows not to shoot at anything with that many propellers."

Canfield glowered at his air exec, belatedly discerning contempt in the underling's manner. But nothing could spoil his enjoyment for very long on this historic occasion. He became ebullient again knowing that he, as CO of an ETO bomb group, had a dramatic role to play that he'd brag about the rest of his life.

The chief intelligence officer hurried in holding papers.

"Major Vander," Canfield said, "I just sent your intelligence boys another flimsy."

Keller shot Swan a look. *I thought I did that,* it said.

"We're decrypting it right now, Colonel," Vander said, handing over what he'd brought. "Meantime, here's the previous batch. You may want to read that first one out loud."

Canfield nodded and cleared his throat. "Field Order Eighty-Eight-Dash-Three-Forty-Eight-S. Quote: 'Our ground and naval forces will cooperate to effect landings in force on the French coast. All air forces in the United Kingdom will exert maximum effort in support of these landings,' unquote."

He looked up, eyes shining. "This is it, Gentlemen, the Invasion of Europe is at hand!"

"D-Day," Keller said with awe.

The WAC orderly returned to deliver more decryptions. Being nearest the door, Swan accepted and glanced at them.

"Bomb loads and targeting info," he told the others. "Two missions; first takeoff at oh-four-twenty tomorrow."

"Christ, that doesn't give us much time!" Keller exclaimed.

"What's the weather outlook?" demanded Canfield.

Swan scanned the sheets. "The met boys say locally heavy rain starting tonight with low ceilings and marginal visibility through midday tomorrow."

"No matter," Canfield said, "nothing can stop the 328th."

Swan ignored this Hollywood bravado and continued scanning the flimsies. "If weather precludes our bombing from normal altitudes, we're directed to go as low as it takes."

"How many ships are we putting up, Mike?" Keller asked.

"Fifty-two plus reserves in case of aborts. Pathfinders too. They'll take off ahead of us and drop TIs for us to bomb on if it becomes necessary."

Keller and Vander both frowned. Bombing through clouds on pyrotechnic target indicators was no way to hit small targets, the specialty of the B-26.

This was lost on the CO, who was positively bouncing on his heels with glee. "Wow, what a show!"

Still scanning the decrypts, Swan looked startled. "This one's for you, Sir," he said, offering it.

Canfield grabbed and read it. The others saw his elation vanish before their eyes. "I…, um…," he said, shaken. "If you'll excuse me, Gentlemen, I'll be in my quarters."

After he departed, Vander and Keller both stared at the air exec. "What was that all about?" Keller demanded.

Mike Swan smiled. "Quote, the commanding officer of the Three-Twenty-Eighth Bee-Gee shall lead the first D-Day mission personally, unquote."

Vander grinned. "Looks like the brass finally got wise to him!"

*   *   *

Lodestone Lola's stripes had barely dried before the rain began. Intense gloom made the continuing preparations challenging at her hardstand.

Vehicle headlights, handheld flashlights, and *Lola's* own internal fuselage lighting—powered by the auxiliary generator in her aft fuselage—created a warm pool of light below her open bomb bay. Its glow splashed off the wet concrete on which Marauder 814 sat.

Within this illumination, figures in rain gear darted about their tasks in nocturnal activity repeated across the airfield. Nearby dispersals revealed teams working in the light of their bomb bays. Far-flung hardstands across the field glowed like late-summer fireflies, but preparations there were presumably just as intense.

The ground-echelon crews were keenly aware of the importance of their work. Preoccupied though they were with the coming day, they knew any guesses they might utter about the invasion would fall far short, so they said little and concentrated on their tasks.

Eleven specialists cleaned and lubricated the .50-caliber machine guns that went into *Lodestone Lola*. Weighing 62 pounds each, these Browning M2s were the lightweight version built especially for aviation use. Three of *Lola's* guns had handgrips. The remaining eight had solenoid backs allowing their remote use.

The armaments team installed two of the handheld guns on the waist mounts and the third up front in *Lola's* plexiglass nose. The solenoid-fired weapons went into the blisters low on the bomber's sides and in its top and tail turrets.

Sliding the slender barrels of these guns into perforated cooling sleeves attached to the power turrets themselves automatically aligned the weapons in their cradles, making quick work of installation that required just the tightening brackets and the bolts.

Next, the armaments team fed ammunition to these weapons. The packet guns drew from individual ammo boxes located inside the fuselage behind its streamline blisters. The top, waist, and tail guns all drew their ammo from the aft bomb bay through flexible feed chutes. Not used for bombs, this second bay ensured the plane's gunners of ample ammunition in combat.

While this crew worked, another arriving truck delivered *Lola's* Norden bombsight. In her lighted nose compartment, a technician installed and checked this device atop its gyrostabilized mount, all under the watchful eye of an armed and helmeted MP standing outside in the rain. One of America's most closely guarded secrets, the Norden never lacked special protection.

Also in the predawn hours, eight 250-lb GP bombs arrived from the bomb dump. These general-purpose munitions came on a low-slung bomb cart towed by a truck, from whose rear jumped the ordnance team. They positioned the cart beneath *Lola's* open bomb bay and began attaching solenoid-release shackles to the bombs.

Once the shackles were affixed, the crew used the bomb bay's winches to hoist the munitions into position. Armorers on the plane's narrow catwalk hooked them onto the racks before placing two M103 fuzes into each bomb for redundancy, one in the nose and the other in the tail between the stabilizing fins.

Having screwed a nose fuze into one of the hung bombs, a lieutenant on *Lola's* catwalk bent down and extended his hand for another. A yawning corporal reached sleepily into the wooden box on the ground. Having worked through the night, he could barely keep his eyes open.

The fuze slipped from his fingers as he held it up to the officer. Fumbling desperately, he managed with profound relief to trap it to his body, preventing it from falling to the concrete.

"Careful!" exclaimed the lieutenant. "These fuzes can explode if you drop 'em."

Wet and miserable in his soaked slicker, the corporal gulped and nodded, his chest heaving. He was now thoroughly awake and fully aware that, with all the bombs and fuel aboard *Lola,* the spot where they worked could have become a smoking hole in the ground.

*   *   *

At squadron living sites all over the base, CQs in rain gear threw doors open and called out the names of every slated crew's pilot. By the time the fliers dressed and shuffled out of their barracks, it looked as if all of Kingsholme had been roused.

In the communal-site lavatory, Braden threw up from a case of nerves. Miserable in his toilet stall, he heard retches echoing from other stalls where fellow fliers shared his pre-mission jitters.

Don't screw up! Braden willed himself.

He and his crew had breakfast in the 517th Squadron's battle mess. Frank was again too nervous to eat whereas Gonzalez went back for more. Conversation was sporadic and desultory amid the dreary drumming of rain on the temporary building's roof and the growl of aero engines being run up and tested by ground crews.

Braden finished his coffee and stood. His crew followed.

Chapter 28: No Escape

Colonel Willis Montgomery Canfield could not sleep. His past insisted on replaying itself relentlessly in his mind. It left him feeling his whole life to date had trapped him, and now it was leading him to his doom.

This kaleidoscopic jumble of memories whisked him back to the county fair where his uncle bought him a flight with a barnstormer. That was in 1927, shortly after Lindbergh had soloed the Atlantic. Overflying cornfields at age nine, and then the public's resounding adulation of Lucky Lindy, began a lifelong fascination with flight.

Or more accurately, with the fame and glamor associated with flight. Acceptance and adulation by the masses, he learned, was the province of aviators.

Canfield failed miserably at the University of Pennsylvania's Wharton School of Finance and Commerce. Only a quiet donation by his father won him his diploma, sparing his prominent family embarrassment. That document underlaid the protective façade he had built for himself. At the same time, it was a haunting reminder that he was the ne'er-do-well son of a prominent bank president.

Movies were Canfield's solace. As a youngster growing up in privilege during the Great Depression, he'd spent entire days at the pictures. You got a cartoon, newsreel, short subject, and feature film—sometimes even a double feature—for just two bits!

Movies were more than an escape for Willis Canfield. They taught him he could be whoever he wanted. Cinema's leading men showed him the way. From them, he learned how to speak, move, and present himself to the world.

In 1938, Clark Gable, Myrna Loy, and Spencer Tracy clinched his career choice with their smash hit *Test Pilot*. He saw the movie over and over again before sharing his decision with his family.

Then twenty-one years old, he angered his parents by passing up the stultifying job awaiting him in the family business. His father refused to pay for flight lessons, so Willie decided to let Uncle Sam teach him at the public's expense.

How had it gone so wrong? Canfield's breath came in gasps of overwhelming fear squeezing his chest. He dug his fingers into the pillow as a sob escaped his lips. *Why didn't I leave well enough alone?* he thought. *Why did I keep pushing that extended-bomb-run concept?*

Ironically, the idea that got him in trouble wasn't even his own. Somebody talking at the next lunch table at Wing had proposed it as idle speculation. Then casting about as a way to promote himself, Canfield immediately seized upon it.

Because Willis Canfield needed above all to be noticed, talked about, considered brilliant, and continue to rise. If others didn't snap to and hang on his words, he felt that he scarcely existed.

Who knew the top brass would give him a combat command to evaluate the theory he pushed so hard? That horrifying possibility never occurred to Canfield, who very much did not want to die.

His overwrought mind brought him to winning his wings and receiving a commission in the late 1930s. Newly minted Lieutenant Willis Canfield had piled up flight hours in single-seaters like the AT-6 advanced trainer and P-40 pursuit ship. Meanwhile, his father conveniently died and left him wealthy. This stroke of good fortune opened to him a lavish existence at country clubs, where he could posture to his heart's content as a dashing sportsman pilot.

That ended abruptly with Pearl Harbor. Confusion reigned as a woefully unprepared nation belatedly girded itself for war. The military services were challenged to build up exponentially even as they reinvented themselves. The rigors of military life increased for Canfield and his time off base was curtailed.

The increasing sophistication of Army aircraft, equipment, and procedures also strained his ability to keep up. Before long, there was no hiding the fact that he simply wasn't a very good pilot, but promotions came nonetheless along with greater responsibilities.

Worst of all, Canfield found himself assigned to fly medium bombers. He had barely passed multiengine training in the Beech AT-17 Bobcat before orders arrived detailing him to MacDill Field in Tampa, Florida, for checkout in the Martin B-26 Marauder.

MacDill had row upon row of these menacing green bombers, each with a large white two-digit identification number on its tail. They populated acres of concrete before the huge base's hangars.

Young Americans fresh from training in flying, navigation, gunnery, and bomb aiming flooded in. They were molded there into combat crews. But not Canfield, whose pronounced lack of flying ability spared him that fate.

Recently renamed the U.S. Army Air Forces, the Air Corps as it was still informally called nearly washed Canfield out. He scraped by through convincing his instructors that he was destined for staff assignments. Only after being assured he'd be a desk pilot did they give him a pass.

The Marauder terrified Canfield. At MacDill, they called it the Widowmaker, the Flying Prostitute (the joke was its wings were so short that it had no visible means of support), and One-a-Day-in-Tampa-Bay. This last moniker came from training accidents at his base, which was on a peninsula projecting into Tampa Bay.

During Canfield's time at MacDill, that fleet of training bombers suffered one fatal crash after another. One new bomb group then being formed suffered 15 Marauder crashes in 30 days! It unnerved Canfield, who never came close to mastering the plane.

Martin's bomber was too much airplane for him and everyone knew it, but a crippling lack of officers in the higher ranks made the AAF keep promoting him. Within a year of making light colonel, eagles replaced the silver oak leaves on his collar.

As a full colonel, he sweated bullets that the Army might post him to a combat outfit overseas as its commanding officer. To his enormous relief, Willis Canfield instead found himself assigned to the administrative staff of the Ninety-Ninth Bombardment Wing, Essex, England. When he arrived, they made him a back-office paper pusher and gave him a staff big enough to do all the work.

Life was good again. During this deployment, Canfield logged the requisite four hours per month at the controls of an airplane to qualify for flight pay. He did this in the Wing's small fleet of Piper L-4 Grasshopper liaison planes. A military version of the Piper Cub, the L-4 was a fabric-covered light plane with two seats, one behind the other, and just six instruments. He could handle that.

Canfield didn't do it for the money. Staying on active flight status let him once again posture as a hotshot flier. He played this role to the hilt with anyone who'd listen, invoking his Marauder transition training at MacDill for credibility. When drunk, he'd describe one exploit after another that he concocted out of whole cloth. He sounded like another Jimmy Doolittle.

Only he wasn't Doolittle. He was Willis Canfield, a fraud and a failure. He knew it deep inside and it ate him up.

Chapter 29: Operation Overlord

Hundreds of solemn figures in flying gear made their spectral way to the operations block for briefing. The only light came from passing vehicles whose dim headlights, masked for the blackout, scythed through the rain.

Lola's officers filed into the 517th Squadron briefing hut and sat down. On stage were Colonel Canfield, Lt. Colonels Swan and Nielsen, and one of Vander's intelligence boys, a captain.

"Attention!" ordered Nielsen.

Benches scuffed as several dozen officers jumped to their feet. The squadron commander nodded approvingly. "As you were."

They resumed their seats and the briefing began.

"Colonel Canfield and Lieutenant Colonel Swan are here this morning to wish us luck," Nielsen said. "They're also speaking at the other briefings so I'll turn the stage over to the CO without further ado. Colonel?"

Willis Canfield nodded stiffly. His mouth worked but nothing came out. He looked unwell. A confused buzz began in the room that lasted until Mike Swan stepped forward.

"Gentlemen," the air exec asserted, "the largest naval assault in history is now underway in Normandy!"

Loud cheers and a feeling of electric excitement swept the room. Swan waited for it to die down.

"Your hard work has won this group the honor of being among the first combat aircraft to hammer the invasion coast on D-Day. Ninth Bomber Command has authorized me to tell you that seven

B-26 groups are being dispatched to execute precision dawn attacks at or near one of the assault beaches—"

Another huge cheer interrupted him.

"We in the 328th will be putting up three formation boxes—"

Yet more cheering. Again Swan waited.

"A-20 Havocs will attack targets farther inland," he went on. "As for Ninth Troop Carrier Command, all fourteen C-47 groups have been dropping paratroopers and supplies all night. They're still at it now, as a matter of fact. Some of these Gooneybirds tow gliders filled with yet more troops, light vehicles, artillery, and supplies. The British are doing the same thing with their own soldiers and equipment."

Swan paused for dramatic effect as another cheer died down.

"The upshot is this," he continued. "By the time our troops hit the sand, thousands of allied soldiers will already be behind enemy lines helping to secure the invasion beaches and cut them off from enemy reinforcement."

Thunderous applause and youthful whoops topped the previous cheering. Swan allowed himself a smile of pride.

"The massive scale of OPERATION OVERLORD—and this morning's phase of it, OPERATION NEPTUNE—is unparalleled in human history. While the outcome is as yet uncertain, we can all be proud of the U.S. Army. But let's not forget for an instant that we're just one part of this show."

A roomful of earnest young Americans in flying gear hung on his every word. Their eager faces buoyed the air exec. *Was I ever that young?* he wondered at the grand old age twenty-nine.

"Over the English Channel," he said, "you'll see U.S. Navy, British Royal Navy, and British Commonwealth ships. Belgian, Free French, Czechoslovakian, Norwegian, and Polish volunteers are among their crews. And those landing craft delivering our boys to the beaches? That's the U.S. Coast Guard in action!"

He paused to let the full weight of history sink in. The briefing hut fell silent.

"I want us to reflect on what the free world is doing today," he continued somberly. "Regardless of nationality, we are all brothers in arms in our love for and defense of democracy."

A thunderous final cheer broke out. It snapped Willis Canfield out of his funk. He stepped forward. "Good luck, men!" he said.

The room fell silent. The CO scowled.

Swan spared Canfield further embarrassment. "The Colonel and I have a tight schedule," he concluded. "We leave you in the capable hands of your squadron commander. See you upstairs, boys!"

They departed. Lt. Colonel Keith Nielsen, brusque as usual, picked up a pointer and nodded to an intelligence clerk. The rear wall covering slid aside to reveal the huge map they knew so well. Every flier in the room studied it intently.

A pinned red ribbon traced a southerly flight path to Normandy, where five invasion beaches were outlined and labeled with code names. From left to right beginning at the base of the Cotentin Peninsula, these were UTAH, OMAHA, GOLD, JUNO, and SWORD.

"U.S. forces will establish a foothold on the European Continent at these beachheads designated Utah and Omaha," Nielsen said, touching them with his pointer. "The U.S. First Army's Seventh Corps will assault Utah Beach as the Fifth Corps takes Omaha. At the same time, British and Commonwealth forces will secure their beachheads farther to the east. The British Army has Gold and Sword while the Canadians have Juno."

Nielsen lowered the pointer. "Our boys hit Utah and Omaha at H-Hour, which is precisely zero-six-thirty this morning. British and Commonwealth forces land at the same instant. Immediately prior to this, Ninth Bomber Command is tasked with knocking out the coastal cannons overlooking Utah Beach. Eighth Air Force units will do the same for Omaha. They will also assist at the British and Canadians at their beaches."

The briefing hall erupted in consternation.

"Why are the heavies horning in?" demanded one flier.

"Yeah," called a second, "this should be strictly a Ninth Air Force affair!"

"It's what we specialize in," added a third. "Leave it to the B-26s, A-20s, and P-47s—we can do what they can't."

One respected flight leader stood up. "The Eighth has zero training or experience in low-altitude tactical support," he said. "You have to be nimble to take out pinpoint targets—those guys fly furniture vans."

The room fell silent. "I agree with you," Colonel Nielsen said. "We should at least be covering both U.S. beaches. But this is the biggest show of the war, and the Mighty Eighth is politically too powerful for Eisenhower to make them sit on the sidelines."

Frank Callard shook his head in disbelief. "Let's hope things go well at Omaha," he commented, "because they'll be flat out of luck if they require precision air support."

"You got that right," Braden replied fervently.

"For this first mission of the day, the 328th will put up forty-eight ships in three boxes," the colonel continued. Reclaiming the pointer and lifting it high to the wall map. "The first and second boxes will separate at landfall to attack these two coastal gun emplacements near Ouistreham."

The pointer shifted. "The third box, which I'm leading, targets this gun emplacement at Montfarville. In case we find these targets socked in, each box has its own pathfinder for blind bombing."

At Nielsen's signal, the intelligence clerk removed a sheet draped over three easels. The first two supported large recon photo blowups while the third showed a three-box formation diagram.

The 517th Squadron CO put down his pointer. "This is important so listen well. We finish laying our eggs just before the first landing craft hit the beach. If you can't drop your load on the first pass, bring 'em home again because there's only time for one crack at this. Takeoff is at zero-four-twenty hours."

He raised his wrist. "Time hack."

Every flier in the room looked at their own government-issue watch. When its second hand reached 12, they pulled up on its crown to stop its movement.

"On my mark, the time will be precisely zero-three-zero-eight minutes," Nielsen said. "Now!"

Having adjusted the minute hands, the fliers pushed the crowns back down. Every wristwatch in the room was now synchronized with that of the mission leader.

"Navigators and bombardiers shall remain for detailed briefings and packets. That is all, Gentlemen. Godspeed."

*   *   *

Lodestone Lola wasn't at her usual dispersal. Neither were the other B-26s slated for the mission. They sat on other hardstands, their positions dictated by the required order of takeoff. Only if these were performed in the proper sequence could they build up into the large formations that routinely assemble over East Anglia.

Through darkness and pouring rain, Kingsholme's 4x4 trucks delivered crews to their temporary hardstands. An airman sitting beside the driver checked his clipboard and called out the names of the airplane commanders for each dispersal they reached.

Braden heard his name. His crew and several others jumped off before the truck lurched away.

In front of them sat *Lodestone Lola*. All B-26s appear fast just standing still, but in Braden's proud eyes she was the most rakish. Even in darkness, *Lola* took his breath away.

She was first in line of the four bombers at their hardstand. Due to the foul weather, Braden ordered his men to board right away instead of waiting for stations time. They gratefully complied as *Lola's* ground crew emerged from a canvas shelter at the edge of the dispersal.

"Loo-tenant!" Sergeant Wrotnowski said.

"Hi, Rotten."

"Great day for flying," quipped the crew chief.

"Yup," Braden replied with a smile. "The only thing worse than taking off in this weather would be to miss the big show."

Pilot and crew chief walked side-by-side as they circled *Lola,* discussing her systems. Hard work and close collaboration over two months of frequent missions lent them the comfort of friendship and mutual respect.

Standing beneath *Lola's* sheltering wing, Miguel and Butch watched them take their time, oblivious to the rain. Satisfied, the pilot thanked his ground team for their labors throughout the night.

"She'll take good care of you, Jack," Wrotnowski assured him.

"Good luck, Sir!" Miguel and Butch both chimed in.

A lump tightened in the pilot's throat. He nodded.

The plane felt cold to the touch as Braden climbed aboard. Seeing Savitt and Gonzalez at their stations in the navigator's compartment, he ordered them to join Jacobs in the back. Bad weather and darkness added risk to this takeoff, he explained, so they were to sit with their backs to the aft compartment's forward bulkhead until *Lola* was safely aloft.

Frank and Milt were in the cockpit. The flight engineer stepped aside to let Jack slip into his seat. He ordered Milt to strap into one of the vacated seats in the navigator's compartment, then called Chick out of the bomber's nose to take the other seat.

Heavy rain assaulted the bomber's aluminum and plexiglass. *Lola* shivered with every gust of wind as they waited. Braden fidgeted in his wet flying gear, but he knew from experience that he'd be fine once *Lola* came to life. He'd be fully occupied with no time to worry.

In contrast, Frank felt sure he would die. The *Wehrmacht* would presumably do everything in Hitler's power to prevent the Allies from kicking open the gates to *Festung Europa*. The weather was also squarely on Adolf Hitler's side, and by now he and his generals presumably knew *exactly* which stretch of coastline to defend. Not the Pas-de-Calais or Antwerp, but Normandy with its strategic port of Cherbourg.

There was something else, something that Callard realized after the Focke-Wulf attack, which made him even more certain his number was up. His darting eyes compared his duty station with that of his pilot.

Behind a Marauder pilot's seat is an upright flat-black shell of thick steel to protect the airplane commander from machine gun bullets, cannon shells, and exploding flak. The left side of the bomber's forward fuselage has conformal steel plates to protect his body and legs. And directly in front of him is the instrument panel.

A B-26 copilot enjoys none of these protections. His exposed seat has neither rear nor side armor, and there is nothing before him but the open crawlway into the nose.

An instrument panel isn't armor, of course, but Jack Braden would have died a gruesome death had it not been there to prevent the Focke-Wulf's round from striking his body and exploding against the metal seat he occupied.

If that shell had entered the nose angled the other way, they'd have had to scrape what was left of Frank Callard up with a spatula. Every time this dreadful realization intruded upon his thoughts, another pang of stark terror of the *Oh shit!* variety jolted him.

A brilliant green flare arced into the darkness above the control tower. "Engine start," Braden ordered.

"Ready with the checklist," Callard heard himself reply.

*   *   *

Seeing the flare, Rotten and his men emerged from the tent to position themselves on the pilot's side of *Lola* forward of the propeller. Through the cockpit windows, the crew chief saw Milt Bidwell come forward and speak to the pilot, who nodded. Braden slid his side window open and stuck his head out.

"Putt-putt's running," Braden shouted, confirming what the crew chief already knew. "Stand by to crank up number one."

*   *   *

More than fifty Martin B-26 Marauders—including spares that would return and land if any of the slated bombers experienced mechanical problems—started their engines. The splutter of starting radials across AAF Kingsholme rose to a roar as over a hundred 2,000-hp aero engines came up to speed. The result was a wall of noise that emanated from everywhere at once, penetrating the body and vibrating in the bones.

Lola's Pratt & Whitneys idled as her flight crew completed the same checks that Rotten's crew had performed mere hours before. The startup checklist complete, Jack gave the thumbs-out signal for chocks to be pulled.

Staying well clear of the propellers, Miguel and Butch darted in from each side and returned to watch from the sidelines, the rope-connected wooden chocks slung over their shoulders. The bills of their ball caps tilted up as another brilliantly green flare lit the sky.

Releasing the brakes, Braden nudged his throttles and *Lodestone Lola* rolled off her parking spot toward the perimeter taxiway. He braked just short of it.

"Who do we follow again?" Frank asked nervously.

"*Outhouse Louse*, tail number seven-eight-three," Jack replied.

One after another, Marauders turned out of the prior hardstands to taxi past on their way to the runway, their running lights bright.

As one dispersal emptied out, more airplanes emerged from the next one down the line, and then subsequent ones, augmenting the growing conga line of Marauders wending its way to the runway.

The previous hardstand spilled its bombers onto the taxiway. *"Outhouse Louse,"* Callard confirmed as the last of these passed by.

Releasing his brakes, Braden followed that ship onto the rain-slicked perimeter track. Nose-to-tail, every B-26's steel brakes squealing plaintively as its pilot maintained separation, this ungainly parade wound its way around Kingsholme Field.

Chapter 30: Aerial Armada

Leading the 328th, *Slugger* was the first Marauder to reach the threshold after the pathfinder ships took off. Turning onto the runway, it held short. Gusts buffeted it as its landing lights shone down a tunnel revealing dark asphalt and grass. They highlighted the pouring rain and rendered the surrounding darkness intense.

"This isn't flyable!" Colonel Canfield exclaimed. "They've got to scrub this!"

"We'll know soon enough, Sir," replied copilot Hank Lamb, an amiable young first lieutenant with a deep New Hampshire accent. "A green flare means go; a white one means mission scrubbed."

"I'll radio the tower," the CO said, reaching for the radio.

"No Sir! We're to observe strict radio silence, Colonel, you know that. That's why the tower uses signal flares."

Canfield frowned, irritated at the lowly underling for correcting him. But Lamb was right; aside from emergencies, he could only use the radio to coordinate in flight with the 1st Pathfinder Squadron if necessary.

Feigning kindness, Canfield had let Lieutenant Lamb perform the startup and pre-taxi checks and lead the group in a snaking line to the runway. Hoping for a promotion to first pilot and a crew of his own, the gung-ho youngster had eagerly accepted. It never occurred to him that the CO of the 328th Bomb Group didn't trust himself to touch the controls of a B-26 even on the ground.

All the way around the track, Canfield wrestled with his fears. Now lined up on the runway, he resolved not to slip and let them show again. But as he sat in his personal bomber awaiting the order to take off, he rued his career choice.

Another green flare arced high over Kingsholme and descended slowly, illuminating waving curtains of rain. Canfield cringed, His heart pounded.

"I'll do the takeoff if you like," Lamb suggested helpfully.

Not trusting himself to speak, Colonel Canfield merely nodded.

Astonished to have this offer accepted, the copilot opened the throttles wide and released the brakes. Heavily laden with bombs and fuel, *Slugger* surged down the length of the runway with a roar and clawed its way into the enveloping darkness.

Hank Lamb's instrument training kept him alert to the dangers of pilot disorientation. He flew dividing his attention between the view ahead, or lack thereof, and the gyro instruments in front of Canfield. He was careful not to look anywhere else as that might topple his own internal gyros.

Without help, he brought up the Marauder's flaps, adjusted its trim, and switched off the landing lights, leaving the running and recognition lights on. The former splashed color into the clouds, green to starboard and red to port.

Seen from the next ship to take off, *Slugger's* lights seemed to wink out after it broke ground. Every twenty seconds, another silver or green B-26 in bright new invasion stripes raced down the main runway to also be swallowed up by darkness and cloud.

Baltimore Blitzkrieg's turn came. The venerable Marauder nosed onto the runway and held short until the plane before them broke ground far down the field.

"*Cry havoc and let slip the dogs of war,*" Prestridge quoted.

"Fuck you, Tommy," said Hasbrook.

The big bear of a pilot brought his engines to full bellow and they too hurled themselves into the dark.

Braden's turn came a dozen ships later. *Lodestone Lola* came up to full rated power straining against her brakes. Squeezing the charm dangling around his neck for luck, he released the toe brakes and raced to follow the flock.

Darkness and driving rain enveloped them as Braden flew calmly and steadily on instruments. Following the prescribed procedure, he climbed out straight ahead as Callard and Bidwell, the latter having come forward, strained to peer through the clouds.

At the predetermined height, Braden leveled off, trimmed, and began a timed turn to the left in hopes of linking up with other B-26s flying the rectangular pattern above Kingsholme's splasher beacon. The previous two ships—*Lola's* companions in one vee of the formation chart—had already leveled off and flown straight ahead on the extended runway heading for longer distances before they turned, the element lead farthest of all.

By turning sooner, the second ship intercepted the first on a perpendicular track at the same speed and altitude. With any luck, they had seen each other and linked up. If not, those ships would climb individually until they broke out above the clouds and could form up in the clear. The time lost might ultimately place them in the wrong spot in the formation, but that didn't matter.

The predawn weather conditions turned this interception into a nightmarish groping through darkness and murk. They might easily miss the other bombers and need to climb on their own. They might even collide with one of them.

Nerves stretched to the limit, the pilots and their flight engineer strained to make out the two planes as they crossed from right to left in front of them. Callard was the first to see hints of running lights and called them out with relief.

"Good job, Frank," Braden told him.

He banked into a 90-degree turn and tucked *Lola* behind the lead ship's left wing. Their vee leader led them into a steady climb, clearing the previous altitude for more bombers to form up. Due to the weather, there would be no further attempts at assembly until they broke out in the clear.

Callard realized to his surprise that he felt alert but not fearful. What's more, he'd performed his duties flawlessly. As for Milt Bidwell, he was his usual calm and unflappable self.

"Who knows how many bombers and fighters are doing this same thing we are right now," Braden said. "Go upstairs, Milt, and scan for potential collisions."

Bidwell nodded and went aft. Compelling as the view was from the cockpit, he knew he'd be of more use in the top turret with its sweeping 360-degree view.

"Thanks for your help, Frank," Braden said after Bidwell left.

"You too," the copilot replied. "You're doing all the hard work."

"You seem less apprehensive than usual."

Callard laughed. "Call me crazy, Jack, but I feel safe today. I guess I'm just too excited—thrilled actually—to be scared right now. It's this amazing day where we're all making history."

Braden checked his own feelings. *Yup,* he thought, *we'll all do everything we can to make this a historic success.*

Taking a deep breath, he flexed his fingers on the controls and relaxed. Callard's words pleased him. It was the first time a member of his crew had addressed him by his first name rather than just Skipper or Boss. For some reason, it gladdened his heart.

$*$ $*$ $*$

Clouds caused the running lights of their ghostly formation to flicker and occasionally wink out. These fearful instants quickly passed as their vee element progressed upward at climb power, still tracing a racecourse pattern over their base's splasher beacon.

Each pilot flew as steadily and predictably as he could. One slip, one moment's inattention, could spell disaster for all. It was brutally tiring and Braden wondered how long he could keep it up.

At thirteen thousand feet, the sky lightened as they rose through luminous peaks and broke out in full moonlight above a dazzling undercast. Looking like snow-covered mountains, this floor of billowing cloud whizzed by beneath *Lola's* keel.

They had entered an unearthly realm suffused with a golden glow of a setting full moon. It extended as far as the eye could see. Within it, Marauders darted like schools of minnows as ever more B-26s, singly or in vees, popped up into view.

Braden took all this in quickly. As he'd anticipated, their flight leader was throttling back. He did the same to maintain formation as the three bombers leveled out together. He saw *Outhouse Louse* flying on the far wing of *Jersey Ginger,* their lead ship.

"It's... *beautiful,"* Callard exclaimed in utter awe.

Braden nodded, allowing himself time to take it in. "Magical, actually. I never imagined I'd ever see anything like it."

Raking shafts of moonlight created an atmospheric and wildly romantic backdrop to the coming day's harsh realities. Hundreds of bombers, mostly B-26s, milled about like bees with a purpose as they continued forming into large swarms.

"Can you believe it!" Bidwell said, hurrying into the cockpit.

Braden grinned. He'd never seen his flight engineer display excitement or any other emotion before. None of them had.

"We're above our splasher," Braden said. "Where's the group?"

"Four o'clock, one quarter mile," Bidwell replied, conveying what he'd seen from his turret.

Callard peered out his side window and nodded. "We're close. I see tail markings from other groups mixed in with ours."

"Must have gotten lost," Braden guessed. "They're tacking on to make sure they don't miss the show."

"Nobody wants to miss this one," Bidwell agreed. "When I think how few B-26s we had to fight with at Midway and then in the Southwest Pacific, this is beyond mind-boggling!"

Chapter 31: Over the Beaches

In *Slugger's* cockpit, Colonel Canfield was increasingly worried. His young copilot focused on his watch and didn't notice.

The 328th bomb group had assembled and was ready to go, as were six other ETO Marauder groups. A-20 Havocs and fighters and heavy bombers were also visible. All flew holding patterns over their home bases awaiting the moment to launch.

"Hundreds of crates all overloaded with gas and bombs," the CO muttered, sounding aggrieved, "and we gotta let down through the soup. Christ!"

"The worst of this weather is supposed to pass before dawn, Colonel," the copilot said. "The clouds are going northeast and we're headed south."

"I was at the briefing too, Lieutenant!"

"Sorry, Sir."

Lamb saw the formation of a sister bomb group—the 344th by its white-triangle tail markings—turn and descend into the undercast. *Lucky devils,* the copilot thought, *Eisenhower chose them to lead the Marauder parade!*

Other groups followed suit at intervals minutes apart. One after the other, they vanished from sight as their launch times arrived. The copilot stopped frowning at his watch and dropped his wrist.

"Time to descend," he announced.

The CO didn't move or reply.

Lamb frowned, not understanding. "Want me to take it, Sir?"

"Yeah!"

Astonished by this additional honor, Lamb flew with the heady knowledge that all three boxes of the 328th Bombardment Group (Medium) were following his lead. He turned the formation onto its briefed heading and descended into the clouds.

Not a word passed in the cockpit as Lamb pondered what was happening. The CO's words, actions, and appearance suddenly added up to just one thing: the man was scared to death. Lamb was amazed that he hadn't seen it before.

Boy, will I have a story to tell, he thought. *Wait till the guys at the officers' club hear about Canfield!*

The guy was a fraud, but Lamb couldn't worry about that now. Concentrating on the gyro panel, he maintained a constant wings-level course descending on instruments. As the altimeter unwound, his navigator gave him periodic heading and position updates.

They passed through occasional squalls as the enveloping clouds lightened with the first hint of gray. A giant orange fireball suddenly blossomed on Canfield's side, filling the cockpit with a baleful glare.

"Jesus, what's *that!*" the terrified CO cried out.

"Two ships must have collided, Sir," Lamb replied.

*　　*　　*

In the cockpit of *Baltimore Blitzkrieg,* Buddy Hasbrook—his face illuminated by the orange explosion—shoved his leather helmet off his forehead and wiped his face using the back of the gloves he wore for luck. Sweating profusely he struggled for breath.

Distracted by the fireball, Tom Prestridge only belatedly realized that his pilot was distressed.

"Buddy, what's wrong?" he asked.

"Shut up and keep your eyes peeled for other ships!"

Suspecting his pilot might be suffering a medical emergency, the copilot looked more closely and arrived at a different conclusion: Buddy Hasbrook was scared.

*   *   *

Aboard *Lodestone Lola,* Frank Callard watched the last traces of orange fade away in the claustrophobic murk. His exhilaration fled and he felt grief. *Those poor guys!* he thought, wondering which bomb group they'd belonged to.

Braden's instinct was to distract his crew. "Pilot to navigator," he transmitted calmly, "position check."

Neither Savitt nor Gonzalez was aware of the collision. The compartment they shared had only a slit window high up on that side. At his navigator's station, Rusty finished a position plot.

"Navigator to pilot," he transmitted, "I make us off the Sussex Coast just east of Brighton. We're on course and should arrive at the IP at the designated time."

"Pilot to crew," said Braden. "We're over the Channel now so assume your combat stations. Don't test your guns unless and until you can clearly see a thousand yards."

The waist gunner and bombardier/navigator rose at the same moment, Gonzalez heading aft to his waist position and Savitt forward to the nose compartment. They bumped into each other.

"Perdón," said the Latino.

"I hope you rack up more pen-day-hoes, Paco," his crewmate said, kind as always.

"Thank you, Sir."

Entering the cockpit, Savitt paused to exchange good-natured banter with Braden and Callard. He apologized to the latter for making him slide his seat all the way back so that he could access the crawlway down into the nose compartment.

When Braden descended below 4,000 feet and they were still clouds, he frowned. Callard wasn't paying attention to the altimeter or he'd be more than just anxious.

In *Lola's* aft fuselage, Bidwell climbed into his catbird seat just as Gonzalez arrived. He saw the tail gunner grinning at him.

"Are you thrilled?" Jacobs immediately blurted.

"Yes, Jake, I am," Gonzalez replied with a grin, "this will always be the most exciting and important day of my life."

"Me too, Paco. But I'll take Kraut fighters any day over weather like this."

Jacobs climbed into his Bell tail turret. Gonzalez slid the floor-level waist windows open, positioned his red cushion just where he wanted it on the deck plates, and sat down.

After plugging his cords into the interphone jackbox, the Latino rotated his Brownings on their pivoting swivel mounts so that the barrels pointed out the windows. Satisfied, he unwrapped a stick of gum, popped it in his mouth, and chewed lustily.

Lodestone Lola's position in the 328th's formation was halfway back on the inboard side of the third box's low squadron. She and all the ships tucked in around her relied on their formation lights to maintain position. Orders were to switch them off the moment they emerged in the clear. Whenever that would be….

The mist brightened and instrument conditions gave way to tattered cloud above gray windswept water. Dawn's first light revealed vessels everywhere. Literally thousands of ships of all sizes and descriptions pulled wakes through rough seas as they steered for Normandy. A great many more were there already, stationed parallel to the coast as they shelled the German defenses.

Exhilaration and an overwhelming sense of history sent chills through the members of *Lola's* crew. There was no doubt they were witnessing one of the pivotal moments in human history.

*   *   *

"We're still descending!" cried Colonel Canfield.

The commanding officer had been shouting for a while that they were too low. Now that they could see, he didn't seem reassured.

"The clouds are forcing us lower as we approach the French coast," Lamb explained, no longer deferential to his CO.

Canfield had feared they'd descend continuously through fog right into the water. Having avoided this fate just presented new dangers. The colonel knew his orders: if visual bombing could not be effected from the optimal altitude of ten thousand feet, they were to go in as low as it took.

As low as it took!

"This will put us within range of every Kraut with a rifle!" Canfield exclaimed, seriously considering aborting the mission.

"Personally, Sir," the copilot replied, knowing the effect his words would have, "I'd be more worried about machine guns and twenty-millimeter ack-ack. They're everywhere down low."

Canfield gulped and made himself as small a target as he could. His knuckles were white as he gripped his seat. The copilot suppressed a smile and shook his head.

Normandy was fast approaching as they descended over ships lined up perpendicular to the coast, many vessels deep. Their turrets glinted and flashed as large-bore cannons pounded targets beyond Utah Beach, which was dead ahead. Geysers spouted in the water around them as Nazi shore batteries returned fire.

*   *   *

Smoke from shelling draped the land beyond Utah Beach. Aboard *Lola,* Callard saw a U.S Navy destroyer that had suffered direct hits and been cut in half by explosions, yet its guns continued firing as it sank. This naval bravery deeply affected the copilot.

Busy at the controls, Jack Braden had little time for sightseeing but he did snatch glances down through his side window. He saw a cruiser deliver a broadside barrage from both foredeck turrets. Flames leapt from its barrels and the ship rocked back, pushing a visible swell of water out beside it.

They raced across landing craft dragging their wakes to shore so slowly that they looked stopped. In a fleeting glance, Jake and Paco saw that every landing craft was packed with helmeted soldiers and equipment. Then land flashed beneath their keel.

At an altitude of 800 feet, the 328th formation's three boxes split up to attack their separate targets. Enemy fire rose from all points of the compass. Glowing tracers arced up to greet them.

*   *   *

Lt. Colonel Nielsen led his dozen B-26s to attack the Nazi shore battery near the French village of Montfarville. Among *Gremlin's Glee's* crew were a lead navigator and a lead bombardier, both hailed as among of the best in the entire 99th Combat Wing.

Pushed down to six hundred feet above ground level by the weather, the bombers skimmed Normandy toward their target. Nielsen banked hard over the IP and rolled out on the bomb run, his squadron following in trail. When the box saw *Gremlin's Glee* open its bomb-bay doors, they opened theirs.

Not a threat at usual B-26 bombing altitudes, twenty-millimeter flak was deadly at low level. Vicious and agile, those antiaircraft weapons sent shells exploding everywhere just when the bombers were to take evasive action. Small-arms fire hosed toward them way from every point of the compass.

Explosions jolted Nielsen's ship like a bad stretch of road as the bombardier bent to his sight. Their chances of making it to the target looked worse by the moment but they were as yet unhit.

The vees flying behind the squadron CO included *Lodestone Lola* and *Baltimore Blitzkrieg,* two of the highest-mission Marauders in the ETO. The formation pressed on with undaunted determination.

In *Lola,* Braden betrayed no more emotion than he did on training flights and milk runs. Aboard *Baltimore Blitzkrieg,* Buddy Hasbrook was hypervigilant and hyperventilating.

Just as Nielsen was silently thanking Martin Aircraft for building such a tough bird, a bright flash in the distance caught his eye. A B-26 from another group had received a direct hit and blown up.

The squadron CO forced the tragedy from his mind. Time for reflection would come later. *We've got one shot at this,* he thought. *All those boys hitting the beach down there are counting on us to get it right!*

Nielsen worried that they would overrun and miss their target because bombing from very low altitude provides far less time for a bombardier to identify and lock onto a target. He pushed this concern aside and concentrated on following the needle of the pilot's directional indicator prominently located on the instrument panel before him.

A simple instrument, the PDI had a vertical needle between reference markings that would deflect left or right. Driven by the bombsight itself, it guided the pilot into gentle course corrections with the slightest of banks and judicious use of the rudder. Keeping that needle centered was crucial to hitting a target.

*   *   *

Bent over his Norden bombsight in *Gremlin's Glee's* nose, Captain Bradford Banks ignored the jostling flak bursts. Using his gyrostabilized electro-mechanical computer's adjustment knobs, he sighted through the eyepiece. It provided a magnified view of a swath of French countryside ahead.

With the skill and concentration of a surgeon, Banks fine-tuned the rate at which the Norden's rearward-scrolling horizontal cursor tracked over the ground passing below. When done, the repeating cursor line moved at precisely the same rate as the terrain, neither leading it nor slipping behind.

Other adjustment knobs on the right side of the Norden let him negate lateral drift caused by a crosswind. These and other actions, sent as guidance to Nielsen's PDI, led their commander to put his squadron on a track parallel to and upwind of the target.

Banks had memorized landmarks from reconnaissance photos. These appeared in the bombsight's viewfinder. Knowing the target would come next, he watched it slide into view. There was no mistaking it because the fortified coastal battery's cannons were issuing smoke and flashing nonstop as they directed high-velocity shells against the Allied invasion fleet.

Banks marked the target. He had made himself a spectator because the Norden would now decide when the bombs fell. His job was simply to watch in case the crosshairs deviated from dead center over the target, but they never did. With astonishing precision, this top-secret engineering marvel stuck to targets like thumb tacks stuck into a map.

An angled mirror angle in the Norden's optical system adjusted to keep the flak battery in view as long as possible on the run. Having previously set the bombsight's trail arm to a numerical value representing the ballistic characteristics of 250-pound bombs, Banks straightened and watched the top of the Norden.

A metal index tab slowly rotated upward from the bottom on a curved display. When that moving tab came abreast of the fixed tab representing the bomb type's glide characteristics, a circuit was tripped and—Banks having set his intervalometer to Salvo—all *Gremlin's Glee's* bombs automatically fell away.

The tabs met and the Marauder surged up under the release of weight as its ordnance fell.

"Bombs away," Captain Banks announced.

This phrase was voiced to let the crew know they could close the bomb bay and maneuver freely to get out of Dodge. Hollywood showed bombardiers shouting it just before or during bomb drops, but in real life it was after.

"Tail gunner, how did we do?" Colonel Nielsen demanded as he banked toward the rally point.

"Tail gunner to bombardier," came the reply, "bull's-eye, Sir!"

*   *   *

Colonel Canfield's component of the 328th BG was on its bomb run attacking an Ouistreham battery. Flak was everywhere.

Still doing all the flying, Hank Lamb was exhausted and badly needed a rest. That wasn't in the cards, not with Colonel Canfield cringing and cowering in sheer terror.

Smoke obscured the target, complicating the lead bombardier's sighting. They dropped anyway as there was no time to go around for another pass. The bombs fell wide and failed to damage either the German cannons or the site's adjoining fortifications.

As they turned away, Willis Canfield lost his battle with fear and became hysterical. Lamb tried his best to calm the CO down but the man had cracked wide open. Incoherent and hysterical, he sobbed piteously, pleaded for help, and barked nonsensical orders.

"It's okay, Colonel, we're heading home!" Lamb insisted again and again, trying to get through to him.

In his compartment, the navigator glanced around to see whether this was a good time to interrupt the CO with a course for home. From his seat at the right side of the radio room, his view through the rectangular metal cockpit entrance framed Canfield's seat not too many feet away. What he saw baffled him. Frowning, he tried to make sense of it.

Greatly distressed, the CO was batting away his copilot's hand as the other flier tried to shake his shoulder. The navigator heard shouts but engine noise prevented him from making out what was being said. Nevertheless, the group leader's extreme agitation was unmistakable.

A violent flak burst pushed *Slugger* up. She reared like a horse before falling off in a bank to the left. The navigator, thrown against the cushioning fabric of his compartment wall, rubbed his head as the ship came level again.

Hank Lamb had dropped everything to regain straight-and-level flight. He didn't see Willis Canfield hastily unstrap or realize he was getting up until the man fled the cockpit in abject terror.

"Colonel, where are you going?" Lamb called after him.

The CO tripped and toppled down the steps to the navigator's compartment, landing against the radio operator's desk. Rising, he fell backward against the hapless navigator, who had stood up to help him.

"Colonel, Sir—" the navigator began, but the CO ripped free and was gone.

With the bomber righted, Hank Lamb did a quick survey of the instruments and added power to climb back into position as the formation leader. The navigator poked his head into the cockpit.

"What's up with the colonel?" he asked.

"Where is he?" demanded the perplexed copilot.

"Damned if I know, Hank. He scuttled into the bomb bay like the devil himself was after him."

*   *   *

Beefy wing spars made for a low entrance to the bomb bay of the Martin B-26 Marauder. Diving through it, Canfield straightened up on the catwalk and squeezed between the racks. His seatpack parachute kept snagging, making passage difficult.

He had no destination in mind, just a blind need to run away from danger and responsibilities. Crying as he entered the rear fuselage compartment, he sagged to the floor, his back against its forward bulkhead. Chest heaving, he groped beneath his flight gear for a pack of cigarettes and lit one with shaking hands.

This unwanted and unloved scion of a wealthy Philadelphia family had grown up under an emotionally absent mother and a physically abusive father who told him every day in countless ways that he was worthless. Those enduring hurts ate him up. Whatever his achievements, he knew he was always a fraud.

He'd never felt so alone as at this moment. Two very close bursts peppered the fuselage around him with shrapnel's deadly rattle. Cringing, he cried out and dropped his cigarette.

Canfield felt sick to his stomach. His head swam and he breathed in labored gasps as painful memories of a life-gone-wrong again flooded his brain. All the pain, all the rejection....

Certain that this mission was worse than anything the ground-pounders on the beaches below could possibly suffer, he put his face in his hands and wept at his own sorrowful plight.

*   *   *

Slugger's waist gunner glanced casually around and was stunned to see the 328th's commanding officer, a bird colonel, sitting there racked by terror and sobbing like a baby. Reaching wordlessly up, he tugged at the pants leg of his colleague in the top turret. That sergeant gunner slipped down out of his perch and together they gaped at the stricken CO.

"What should we do?" asked the waist gunner, shouting to be heard.

"Damned if I know!"

*   *   *

In the cockpit, Hank Lamb divided his attention between flying and wondering where the colonel went. He braced himself on the control pedestal to lean into the middle for a better view aft. As he did so, his hand accidentally brushed the bail-out bell switch. Its strident ringing resounded throughout the bomber.

*   *   *

Canfield knew what that bell meant: they'd been hit—he needed to abandon ship before it blew up or crashed!

Springing to his feet, the commanding officer of the 328th Bombardment Group dashed past the gunners and dove headlong out an open waist window. The sergeants gaped in astonishment, unable to believe what they witnessed.

In the cockpit, Hank Lamb hastily silenced the strident alarm and followed up with an interphone call.

"Copilot to crew," he said, "disregard the bail-out bell—I hit it by accident." He paused before continuing, sounding embarrassed. "Any of you guys know where the CO is?"

"Waist gunner to pilot," came the reply, "he just volunteered for the infantry!"

Dangling from his parachute as he descended over the most dangerous territory on earth, Colonel Willis Canfield watched his ship and formation fly safely home without him.

*   *   *

Aboard *Lodestone Lola,* Frank Callard couldn't believe their luck. "No fighters, no fighters…," he repeated with incredulous joy via interphone. "I was sure there'd be fighters."

"Yup, the *Luftwaffe* was a no-show," Bidwell confirmed heartily from his top turret.

"We really plastered that gun emplacement!" gloated Jacobs, who was still assessing the retreating target from his unique vantage point. "We saved those ground-pounders a lot of work."

"We saved Army and Navy lives," Rusty Savitt added.

Braden happily ignored this breach of interphone discipline. He and his crew had done well—they deserved to blow off steam with some light banter.

In the nose, Rusty Savitt laughed merrily, taking turns with the others to make comments. The weather had cleared and the day was bright. He relished the scene spread before him through the bomber's nose as they continued low over Normandy.

The bombers began climbing to the rally point where the squadron elements would reassemble into a tight three-box formation and fly home. Leaving his seat, Savitt stretched out, elbows on the floor, to peer down through *Lola's* plexiglass nose.

Just ahead was the English Channel, where he'd soon have a perfect view of the invasion fleet. He thumbed his push-to-talk.

"Man, what I wouldn't give for a camera!" he said ebulliently. "If Liz and I ever have kids, they'll never believe—"

With a soft ping, a bullet hole appeared in the plexiglass. Savitt slumped, eyes open but dead, a matching hole in his forehead.

Chapter 32: Fortunes of War

The sun was low. Georgiana pulled up before the Plough and Plover Pub in her father's 4¼-Litre Bentley, which she drove herself over the protests of the chauffeur she'd left behind. Hurrying inside, she approached the publican as he polished glasses behind the bar.

"Where is he?" she demanded without preamble.

"In the back, M'Lady."

The pub owner stepped out from behind the bar and led the way. "Been drinking much of the evening, poor devil," he said as they walked. "All I could get out of him was your name and that of someone named Lola. Do you know who she is?"

"Yes, I'm afraid I do. The other woman."

The pub was crowded and noisy. Jack Braden sat alone in a rear booth looking utterly bereft. The young American's uniform and hair were askew. His hand cupped a glass and a half-finished bottle of scotch sat before him on the table.

He looked dully up at their approach. "Oh, hi, Georgie ... Ana."

"Hello, Jack."

"Want a drink?" he offered, jostling the bottle as he tried to pick it up.

"You've had quite enough," she said firmly and turned to the publican. "Help me get him to my car."

They levered the Yank flier to his feet. Georgiana grabbed his 50-mission crush in passing and together they walked him out. Jack protested loudly all the way that he wanted more to drink.

Braden passed out before they reached the car. With effort, they placed him in the front seat. Georgiana tipped the publican, who thanked her with a nod of his head.

It was twilight when they reached Waddleston Hall. Georgiana parked in the rear courtyard among the outbuildings. A groom hastened forward and helped her maneuver Braden into the stables.

Twenty minutes later, Georgiana and Jack sat facing each other on bales of hay. The lights overhead made him wince and he held his head. In the background came the gentle sounds made by content horses in their stalls.

A servant arrived with a silver coffee service. She set it down on the bale next to her mistress. "Will there be anything else, Miss?"

"No, Sarah. Please don't mention this to anyone in the house."

"No, Miss," she said and withdrew.

Georgiana poured a cup of black coffee and handed it to Jack. "Drink up."

Accepting it, he sipped, winced, and tried to hand it back. "No thanks."

"You cannot return to base in your present condition, so drink!"

"Who says I'm going back?" Braden replied, avoiding her eyes.

Georgiana was shocked. "You can't be serious."

His defiance crumbled to abject misery. Lowering his head, he cried in strangled sobs. Georgiana watched him as she struggled to understand.

"What happened today, Jack? Did you fly in support of the Allied landings?"

Braden's hand trembled as he set down his cup. "My bombardier bought the farm over Normandy," he said flatly.

"Oh! I'm so sorry."

He glared at her, his anger flaring. "Sorry! Is that all you can say? You don't have a clue, Georgiana—people die up there!"

Her patient expression showed she knew this all too well. "What can I do for you, Jack?"

"Nothing. I'm leaving."

"Going where?"

"Anywhere but Kingsholme Field. I can't show my face there again."

"You're running away?" she asked, startled.

"I have no choice," he said, his voice rising. "Don't you see? I'm no good, not for you or my crew, not anybody!"

"You'll be a deserter in time of war," she said, aghast. "Do you realize the consequences?"

"Sure, a life sentence at Fort Leavenworth, Kansas. Maybe that's what I deserve. Rusty was my responsibility, my ... *friend*. What am I supposed to tell his wife Liz when I write to her, which I have to do?"

"Have you talked with anyone else about this?"

"No. I tried to tell Major Vander at interrogation I couldn't find the words."

He sagged forward, put his face in his hands again, and succumbed to alcohol-fueled misery. "I can never go back there," he wailed. "I failed. I don't belong. I get people killed!"

Georgiana let his strangled, tortured sobs run their course. She spoke when they subsided.

"People die in wars, Jack," she said softly. "That doesn't make it your fault."

"It is," he said angrily, "it always is!"

With a flash of insight, Georgiana stood and crossed to sit beside him. Putting her arms around him, she hugged him to her chest. "You've lost someone before, haven't you?" she asked tenderly. "Someone very dear to you?"

"I... had a kid brother who died because of me," he admitted with difficulty. "I screw up—I'm no good!"

"How did he die, your brother?"

Jack looked sharply up, haunted by memory. "When I was seven, we were in the car," he said. "I remember my dad shouting at me to shut up but I wouldn't. I wouldn't."

More tears welled and slid down his wet cheeks. "We crashed through a fence and flipped in a farmer's field. My kid brother—" Braden made himself finish the sentence. "He didn't make it."

Georgiana sat devastated by what she'd just heard. "But your father was driving," she replied. "It was his fault, surely."

An adamant shake of his head rejected her words. "No, it was mine. Dad said so…, told everyone. His drinking got worse after that and he left us. My mother never recovered and died a year later."

So you've been on your own and carrying this guilt since you were eight, she thought, her heart going out to him.

Aloud she said, "And you think that was your doing? Listen to me, Jack. Listen to me! Your father was a drunkard and that's what drunkards do—blame others for their mistakes!"

She knelt earnestly before him and took his hand in both hers. "Don't you see? *He* crashed that car, not you. *He* shattered your family, not you!"

Hunched in a posture of intense self-loathing, Jack avoided her eyes.

Georgiana frowned and tried a different tack. "Seven-year-olds fuss—that's perfectly normal," she said. "But fussing doesn't make cars crash—driving while inebriated does that."

Jack didn't move, but Georgiana now sensed he was listening to what she said. Her words were penetrating.

"You aren't him, Jack! Your father abandoned his family and fled his responsibilities. You're not like that." She squeezed his hands. "You're kind, caring, and responsible. My father thinks you're perfectly wonderful, and as you know he's never wrong."

A chuckle erupted through Braden's grief. They met eyes as he rode an emotional roller-coaster. He wiped his streaming cheeks.

Georgiana stood and again took his hands. "Repeat after me," she said sternly. "It is *not* my fault. It *never was* my fault. My father was a drunkard and *I am not he!*"

Braden frowned in confusion. There was a childlike vulnerability to him that she had never before seen in this self-assured Yank.

"You were his *victim*," Georgiana said calmly. "Just as much as your brother and your mother, you too were his victim. He and you didn't destroy your family; he alone did that. So repeat after me: *It is not my fault and I am not my father!*"

"It's ... not my fault," Jack said, haltingly and without conviction. "I'm not him."

"Again!"

"I am not my father," he said less tentatively.

"Believe it yourself and then convince me of it!"

Georgiana had him repeat the affirmation over and over again, which he did with growing confidence and conviction. He broke off, a startled look on his face.

In that instant, she saw him embrace the truth. A chuckle of disbelief broke from his lips as acceptance showed on his face. Tears flowed but he now seemed serene.

Jack visibly relaxed and cleared his throat, his emotions under control. Georgiana laughed happily to see this and handed him her handkerchief. "Better now?"

He sat up straight and nodded. His breathing was centered and regular. To his astonishment, a lifetime's crushing weight had gone. He felt so light, he feared he might float away.

Georgiana watched the handsome Yank rise to his feet, resolute now and sober. Her car keys jingled as she pulled them from her purse. "I'll run you back to base."

They walked side by side to the Bentley, everything different.

*   *   *

Braden skirted the Officers' Club on the way to his billet. Its door flew open as rowdy D-Day revelers spilled out into the night. Caught directly in the light from the doorway, Braden heard their shouts of recognition.

"Hey, Buddy, look! It's your jinx in the flesh no less!" one drunk flier shouted.

"Hell, nothing's been right since that guy rotated in," added another.

Hasbrook stepped forward and blocked Braden's way. "We have unfinished business," he said, his voice slurring.

"Not now, Buddy. You're drunk and I'm hung over."

Braden tried to pass by, but the large man gripped his upper arm painfully. "We'll settle this like men."

"Oh really? With your two goons restraining my arms again?"

Hasbrook's anger flared. "You calling me a coward?"

"Yes, I'm calling you a coward," Braden replied.

*   *   *

A crowd gathered as word spread like wildfire that a fight was brewing at the technical site. On the concrete pad by the control tower where ambulances and emergency vehicles were stationed, Hasbrook and Braden stood warily facing each other as more men arrived by the minute, Jack's crew among them.

"You're yellow, Braden," Hasbrook taunted loudly, playing to the crowd. "You and Callard the Coward both!"

Jeers and catcalls broke out all around them. It was clear that Hasbrook was their favorite and Braden's unpopularity had not diminished. It bothered him that it extended to his crew.

"You're right about my copilot, Buddy," Braden replied hotly. "He's terrified to climb into a B-26. But he does it anyway and he's racked up a lot of missions, some pretty tough. And for that, I give him more credit for guts than any man in this group!"

Startled disbelief showed on Frank Callard's face as these words hit home. Jake patted Frank's shoulder. Gonzalez grinned and passed him a stick of gum. Milt Bidwell caught his eye and nodded.

Frank broke out in a happy smile. His crew's support, and that of their pilot in particular, meant the world to him.

Tom Prestridge arrived, looked around, and hurried anxiously over to join them. He nodded quick greetings with a worried frown.

Hasbrook, meanwhile, turned to a noncom. "Marek, go into the control tower and switch on the floods."

"But Captain, the blackout—"

"Turn 'em on, I say! There ain't a Kraut within a hundred miles of here."

A minute later, the floodlights sprang on and the two pilots squared off, both wobbly. Outmatched and in no rush to engage, Braden circled his outsized foe, a calculating look on his face. His stance and body posture said he knew how to fight.

Hasbrook lunged forward. Whoops and yells egged him on as he launched a series of murderous punches at Braden, who ducked and sidestepped them all just in time. As the sparring continued, it became clear that both men were too impaired to really fight well.

Grumbles of disappointment arose among the onlookers. That changed when a lightning-fast punch from Hasbrook connected, sending Braden reeling back at least twenty feet.

"Buddy'll kill him!" Prestridge exclaimed, stepping forward to intervene.

A strong hand gripped his bicep. He turned to see Milt Bidwell. "No disrespect, Sir," the sergeant said calmly, "but don't write our Skipper off just yet."

Things worsened materially for Braden as Hasbrook caught him and delivered savage blows. Jack broke free and counterattacked with punches that landed had little effect.

With surprising agility and a long reach, Buddy snagged Jack by the shirt and drew him in. His fist back to deliver a haymaker, but before he could deliver it, he tripped over his own feet and stumbled backward, pulling Jack down on top of him. The crowd roared with laughter as this unexpected blunder increased the fight's entertainment value.

The adversaries rolled and struggled until Hasbrook successfully straddled Braden. Pinning him beneath him, he delivered with savage glee what he felt sure was a knockout punch, although Braden threw his arms up to take the blow. Staggering to his feet, Buddy turned to the onlookers and basked in their acclaim.

To everyone's surprise, Braden popped right up and jumped onto Hasbrook's back, attacking him furiously from behind. This struck the crowd as hilarious and they roared again with laughter.

Hasbrook threw Braden off, but his opponent landed on his feet and moved too warily to be caught again. To the crowd's surprise, Braden now took the offensive. Darting in, he landed one hard punch after another, his fists connecting a dozen times in a row.

The tide gradually turned against the bigger man, who began to sag. Chest heaving, Braden attempted to deliver a crowning blow of his own but missed as the larger man fell to his knees. Jack lost balance, spun around, and tripped backward over Buddy, who—on all fours starting to get up—was perfectly positioned to trip him. They both ended up in a tangled heap on the ground, utterly spent.

The crowd surged forward laughing uproariously. Led by Jack's crew, they elevated him onto their shoulders and proclaimed him the champ. Jack grinned and held his arms high in triumph.

Hasbrook's few loyalists helped him up. He shook them off and glowered angrily, nursing his injuries. The crowd ignored him.

A jeep raced up just then with Mike Swan was at the wheel and Curt Keller beside him. Now a full colonel and the 328th's new commanding officer, Swan jumped angrily out of the vehicle.

"What the blazes is going on here?" he shouted. "Somebody turn off those damn lights!"

As Swan spoke, a flaming torch loomed in the night sky behind him. Alerted by the crowd's reaction, he and his adjutant turned to gape at a ghostly form descending to the airfield. It resolved into a very large, darkly camouflaged airplane with one engine on fire.

The crippled RAF bomber made jarring contact with the grass. The near-side main landing gear immediately collapsed, dropping a wing tip that dug a furrow in the grass. The careening plane slewed in an uncontrolled arc toward the signal square and control tower.

The Avro Lancaster came to rest a mere forty yards away. After a shocked instant, sirens wailed at Kingsholme and Army personnel raced to man the crash vehicles by its tower.

Fire fully engulfed the inboard engine on the high or far side of the wrecked four-engine bomber. Flames broadened toward the fuselage as fuel gushed from broken wing tanks.

Two RAF crew members escaped through a rear fuselage door and raced to the safety of the crowd. The Army crash vehicles stopped short of the bomber. American voices could be heard.

"Watch out—she's gushing fuel!"

"Stand back, that ship's gonna blow sky high!"

Reacting, Jack looked around and dashed to a nearby Cletrac and pulled an emergency axe from its clips. Sprinting to the burning Lancaster, he leapt up onto its sloping wing, ran up it to the fuselage past the fire's searing heat, and raced atop the plane's canted roof to its glazed cockpit.

Crewmembers beneath the plexiglass roof pounded desperately at a jammed overhead escape hatch. Braden gestured quickly with his axe and they fell back. He swung repeatedly until the plexiglass panel broke away.

Throwing down his axe, Jack reached in and pulled out five RAF crew members, one after the other. They scrambled past him and raced down the wing, Jack following. Framed by rising flames, he jumped off and ran for all he was worth across the grass.

The bomber exploded violently, hurling him flat. Pushing up, he turned to watch it burn.

*   *   *

In the warmth of the well-lit base hospital, Doc Polling and a nurse attended to the seven Royal Air Force crew members. They sat in their flight kit, blankets draped over their shoulders as they sipped hot mugs of tea or coffee.

With them were Mike Swan, Linden Vander, Curt Keller, and Jack Braden. The latter wore adhesive bandages freshly applied to his bruises and scrapes. They were the result of his fight; he suffered no injury during the daring rescue.

"The blighters stay out of sight, you see," an RAF sergeant was explaining in a Cockney accent. "You 'ave no idea they're there until suddenly the sky lights up. By then, it's too bloody late."

The Lancaster's pilot, an officer with a patrician accent, nodded. "Some of their night fighters have upward-angled 30-mm cannons that rip open a bomber's belly like a gutting knife."

The pilot sipped tea and stared at the wall. "But that's not what this devil did."

"What did he do?" asked Mike Swan, fascinated.

"*Luftwaffe* night fighters frequently stalk our territory. We took off heavily laden from the East Midlands for a strike deep into Southern Germany. Over the Channel, a red light on my dashboard warned me we were being scanned by enemy AI."

"AI?" repeated the doctor, not understanding.

"Airborne Intercept, our invention you chaps call radar. I alerted my crew, but this cunning Jerry stayed below the visible horizon. We never saw him until he suddenly popped up and riddled us, exploding our left inboard Merlin. Then he disappeared without finishing us off."

"He either ran out of shells or more likely was low on petrol," guessed another member of the RAF crew. "Or he thought he'd bagged us and returned to base to pop champagne corks."

"We jettisoned our bombs over the water and turned back," the RAF pilot continued, "but the engine fire grew out of control. We had no alternative but to crash land quickly."

The pilot met Swan's gaze. "Thank you, Colonel," he continued with gratitude. "I shouldn't have known where to set down had your airfield lights not been on."

"That was strictly an accident," Swan said gruffly and scowled at Jack. "You can thank Lieutenant Braden here for getting into the goofiest prizefight this unit has ever witnessed!"

"We owe you our lives, Lef-tenant," the British pilot said.

His crew chimed in with heartfelt thanks of their own.

*   *   *

On the steps outside, the Americans paused to button their coats against the night's chill.

"Per ardua ad astra," Swan said, quoting the RAF motto. "That must mean *Into the air the hard way."*

"Dueling in the dark—what a lousy rotten way to fight a war," Vander stated disgustedly.

"You've got to hand it to the Brits," agreed Keller.

"How long will engineering need to clear my field?" Swan asked.

"Just one day," Keller replied. "The RAF's coming by to help disassemble and cart away what's left of their Lanc."

Swan turned to the junior officer among them, who according to protocol had remained silent. "And you, Braden," the group CO said. "You're more trouble than you're worth. I should have sent you packing that day we first met. Hell, maybe I still will."

He relented suddenly and grinned. "Except that I wouldn't know where to send the Silver Star I'm putting you in for."

"I imagine the Brits will also give you a medal," Vander added with a warm smile.

"By the way, the colonel and I watched the end of that fight of yours," Keller said. "If the Keystone Cops make movies again after the war, you and Captain Hasbrook have a bright future."

The senior officers laughed. Mike Swan clapped Jack Braden heartily on the shoulder. "Swell job, kid!"

*   *   *

Still sporting bandages on his face two days later, Jack set out for a donut and coffee at the PX before a scheduled meeting with his crew chief at the hardstand.

It was a perfect day, warm and fragrant with spring in full bloom. Everywhere he walked, fliers greeted him, even those from other squadrons whom he knew only by sight. They all treated him kindly.

Jack's smile said he could get used to it.

*   *   *

He and Myron Wrotnowski were alone at the airplane dispersal. Their meeting was bittersweet. It began with Rotten wordlessly shaking Jack's hand, surprising him. The crew chief squeezed and held it with inarticulate silence that spoke volumes. Braden clapped his arm and nodded gratefully. Rotten grinned.

They walked around inspecting *Lodestone Lola*. "We put a new nose on her," the crew chief said. "The hole was small and we could have patched it, but who needs to live with the reminder?"

"We all miss Rusty," Braden said sadly. "He was the best of us."

"You're all the best," Rotten replied feelingly. "Don't let it go to your head, but I couldn't name a finer bunch of red-blooded Americans. Me and the boys, we're proud to be your ground crew."

Braden's smile was melancholy as he contemplated *Lola's* shiny new nose glass. "Who cleaned away the blood?"

"There wasn't any. But we gave that compartment a good scrub anyway—right after I tossed out all those damn flak vests. Fat lot of good they did." He hesitated. "Any idea how it happened?"

Braden nodded. "They said the bullet was an eight-millimeter Mauser round. Probably fired from a Karabiner 98k, the standard Nazi infantry rifle. It was a freak shot and the bullet was partly spent before it hit Lieutenant Savitt, but it had enough momentum left to penetrate his skull and kill him instantly."

"Some goddam Kraut soldier made the shot of the century and doesn't even know it," Rotten said disgustedly. "If I could get my hands on that Nazi bastard!"

Jack swallowed. "It won't be the same, Rotten," he admitted. "It's taken the heart out of all of us."

Wrotnowski thought for a moment. "That's war, Lieutenant," he said philosophically and not unkindly. "Youz guys need to put it behind you and get back in the saddle." He reached up and gave his B-26 a loving pat. *"Lola's* sad too, aren't you, baby?"

Chapter 33: London

Flight Officer Spottedbird had piercing black eyes that placidly observed the world. Boyish with straight black hair, *Lodestone Lola's* new bombardier/navigator was tall, thick without an ounce of fat on his muscular frame, and had skin the color of a glowing tan. His grin was infectious.

The paperwork gave his first name as Chilali, which he told his new crewmates meant "Bird" in Kiowa. He took pleasure reading his mother's letters from the reservation aloud to them. They began "Dear Lallo" but the nickname he ended up with was Chick, which *Lola's* crew chose for him.

Chick Spottedbird was a flight officer, that odd warrant-officer rank above the enlisted grades but below the commissioned ranks. He'd been with them just a week, but being so different from Rusty Savitt made his arrival a smooth transition. Not tempted to draw comparisons, his crewmates took to this fun-loving Indian warrior from Oklahoma, who they quickly realized was fearless and funny.

Chick diffused the uncomfortable double-standard among *Lola's* officer ranks—his pilots were lieutenants and he wasn't—by joking that the Army didn't want Indians drinking up all the firewater at the officers' club. He further joked that he'd have those lieutenant's bars already if Eleanor Roosevelt had more clout with her husband.

The flight officer rank was an expedient measure that allowed the Army Air Forces, which had to expand tremendously, to relax its requirement that all officers have at least two years of college under their belts. Most F/Os were later commissioned in the field.

The training that flight officers underwent and the standards they had to meet were identical to those of everyone granted a commission. From his first mission onward, Chick proved this by performing his duties every bit as capably in *Lola's* nose as his badly missed predecessor. And since the Army had no formal policy as to where flight officers could drink, he also found himself warmly welcomed at Kingsholme's two officers' clubs.

In the immediate aftermath of the invasion, the 328th's mission shifted to include providing ground support to U.S. forces through tactical bombing to help them break out and continue advancing beyond the beaches. This period, time had a new calendar: D-Day-Plus-One, D-Plus-Two, and so on.

Chick Spottedbird didn't worry that his predecessor's fate might befall him. He wasn't cocky like so many new replacements arriving from stateside. Instead he was serene and focused, which made him good at plastering targets. These were now sometimes indicated by nothing more than fabric panels placed by ground troops as reference markers to indicate battlefield targets.

Back from one such mission, Braden, Callard, and Spottedbird entered their Nissen hut. Chick tossed his things on the cot that had been Rusty's and reached for his guitar.

"No time for that, Chick," Braden reminded him. "Pack fast, boys, we have a train to catch."

He added a quick chalk stroke to his missions tally—the slate now recorded thirty-nine—before hastily tossing clothes and shaving gear into his B-4 bag and zipping it up.

*   *   *

Dressed in pinks-and-greens and carrying their B-4s, *Lodestone Lola's* crew—except for Milt Bidwell, who decided to visit a buddy in the 387th at Chipping Ongar—exited Liverpool Street Railway Station. The echoing cacophony of steam engines under its long roof gave way to the bustle of a proud but assailed city as they exited the main entrance.

They had tickets and suggestions for the 48-hour leave from the Special Services Office at Kingsholme Field, which booked them at the Great Eastern Hotel in Bishopsgate. Braden asked a Britisher for directions right outside the station. Wearing a homburg, the Londoner gave an answer that sounded like a foreign language, but his folded umbrella pointed unerringly at the stone-facade ground floor of a red brick building across Liverpool Street.

"Wow, that's convenient!" Gonzalez said with a grin.

The hotel was solid and quiet inside with a ponderous elegance harkening back to the heyday of the British Empire under Queen Victoria. Braden and his crew felt out of place, but the kind and deferential staff there welcomed them as honored guests.

Braden knew why. The Special Services clerk at Kingsholme had explained that American servicemen were paid roughly twice as much per month as their British and Commonwealth counterparts. Yanks were known to spend generously and lavishly, a trait that earned them warm welcomes throughout England.

Throwing their bags into their rooms, they hurried back down and split up outside the hotel. Gonzalez, Jacobs, and Spottedbird wanted drinks, dining, and dancing whereas their pilots looked forward to taking in the historic city's sights.

Callard asked the hotel doorman for advice after the others had left. Instead of answering, the liveried staff member hailed them a London taxi. "Trafalgar Square," he instructed the cabbie, holding the door for the Americans.

A ten-minute ride took them to Trafalgar, where they paid off the cabbie. This congested square teamed with pedestrians and vehicles although bomb damage and rubble were evident up the side streets. A huge statue of Admiral Lord Nelson presided over all from atop a high column. He stood serenely untouched.

Braden imagined what a psychological blow it would be to the British Empire if Hitler's forces were to topple Nelson from this lofty perch. *May that never happen,* he thought.

Along with train tickets, Braden had received a map of London back at base. Unfolding it, he navigated them to the River Thames. Frank Callard turned out to be as big a fan of walking as he was, and their woolen pinks-and-greens were the perfect weight for the cool, breezy weather.

Big Ben and the Houses of Parliament loomed before them as they followed the curve of the river's embankment. As they drew closer, they saw that the famous clock tower's façade was scorched and some of its windows were broken. The face of the clock on their side was shattered although it displayed the correct time.

"I haven't heard Big Ben ring once," Braden realized. "Do you think the mechanism is damaged?"

Callard shook his head. "The Nazis attacked it along with the Houses of Parliament before we entered the war," he said. "They roughed the tower up as you can see, but it still stands and its bells work. The British just decided they won't peal until the war is over."

They wandered through St. James Park, talking and enjoying the greenery and bursting blooms. Broken clouds sailed a sky with the sun breaking through every so often.

"How did you know all that about Big Ben, Frank?"

The copilot shrugged. "It's just something I remember, Jack."

Ever since Braden's epic fight with Buddy Hasbrook, he and his copilot addressed each other by their first names. Jack liked having this unexpected and supportive friend in the air and on the ground.

He found Frank Callard to be intelligent, kind-hearted, and quick to laugh. What's more, he knew vastly more about the world than Jack himself did, modestly attributing it to his love of reading. Their talks roamed freely. They took joy playing with ideas and insights.

When their bombardier had died in midsentence, it was Frank who crawled down into *Lola's* nose to check on him. He'd sobbed helplessly over the interphone at finding Rusty Savitt dead, crying for every member of the bereft crew.

Together the friends contemplated Buckingham Palace through its enormously high black-and-gold wrought iron gates. Standing amid Londoners and foreign tourists, many in exotic uniforms, they gazed at the palace's iconic façade, which lent yet more gravity to the ancient monarchy. Wishing he knew more, Braden vowed to pursue learning for the rest of his life if he survived the war.

Continuing on, they saw grand buildings with sandbags piled by their entryways, some with improvised wooden roofs to deflect falling debris. Rubble-blocked side streets bore witness to entire blocks destroyed by bombing, and the tube stations along the way were all marked for double duty as bomb shelters.

Yet the Londoners carried on with remarkable spirit and aplomb despite the blackouts, rationing, and frequent air raid threats that all-out warfare with Adolf Hitler had brought. Everywhere they felt a sense of enduring community and indomitable determination.

The London Blitz had been front-page news before the Japanese attack on Pearl Harbor propelled the United States into the war. Furious that the RAF spoiled his planned invasion of 1940, Hitler abandoned daylight bombing against military targets to bomb indiscriminately day and night, switching to night-only bombing when the RAF proved too formidable. That eight-month onslaught cost forty thousand civilian lives, more than half in London alone.

*   *   *

Tiring of monuments and statues, the fliers stopped at Harrods and marveled at the sheer scale of the grand department store. After buying tea and comestibles for a bit of civilization at base, Braden let his map guide them eastward along the Brompton Road, which became Knightsbridge.

It was dusk when they arrived at Piccadilly Circus. Located at the heart of London, the thronged crossroads was a large square with a circular roundabout at its center. That artery bustled with cars, taxies, and red double-decker buses.

Above all, the square teemed with people. Braden saw the uniforms of the U.S. Eighth and Ninth Air Forces, U.S. Army ground forces, and U.S. Navy. He also saw those of the British Army and Royal Navy, including Canadian, Scottish, Anzac, and Sikh forces, this last group in the turbans they proudly wore instead of helmets even in combat.

There were WAAF, ATS, and WAC uniforms too. The British and American women wearing them all hurried through Piccadilly with harried looks on their faces indicating a strong desire to avoid unwanted male attention in the streets.

The headlights of the vehicles had slit covers that dimmed them for the blackout. Piccadilly's electric light displays were likewise dimmed although the huge advertisements for Bovril, Schweppes, Guiness, and other products still compelled one's attention.

Piccadilly was home to the clubs of many military services. This was the reason Jack and Frank finished their sightseeing there. Reaching the corner of Shaftesbury Avenue and Coventry Street, they spotted an angled entrance with the words *American Red Cross—Rainbow Corner*.

As they approached it, two "Piccadilly commandos" stepped out to block their way. They went around these prostitutes, ignoring their solicitations.

A pretty young American woman in a white AMC smock greeted them warmly at the club. Another served them a hearty dinner followed by after-dinner drinks. They lingered and talked.

U.S. servicemen packed the club. Many of them jitterbugged exuberantly to Artie Shaw hits with American servicewomen, English girls, and club hostesses. It was loud and frenetic. Although not seated right by the dance floor, Jack and Frank had trouble hearing each other.

"Why aren't you out chasing skirts with the rest of the guys?" Braden asked loudly.

"I've a girl back home," the copilot replied at equal volume. "You?"

"Something like that." Braden frowned. "Look, Frank, if hauling your ass into *Lola* scares you silly, why not tell the Central Medical Board? Plenty of guys with flying fatigue give all they've got and rotate home."

"You mean say I'm all through and let them ship me out? Doc Polling says he'll do that for me anytime—no court martial, no questions asked, not a blemish on my record." Frank raised his glass and contemplated it wistfully. "Just say the word and I'm home free…."

"So take him up on it. Hell, you've flown lots of missions."

"No, Jack," Frank Callard declared firmly. "Duty binds me to this particular circle of hell."

"How do you mean?"

"My old man flew with Rickenbacker in the last war, did you know that? It was the proudest time of his life and he lives and breathes Air Corps. So did my brother—"

Callard's voice broke. Braden looked at him. "Your brother?" he prompted.

His copilot nodded. "Todd was two years older than me," he said. "He died in a stateside training crash. Never made it overseas. I'm all my folks have left and it's up to me to uphold the Callard tradition. Just my crummy luck I ended up in B-26s."

"Hey, cut the Marauder some slack," Jack said. "She's great if you handle her right."

The alcohol was getting to them but Callard signaled for another round. "Let me tell you about my big brother," he said. "When

186

Todd was twelve, he climbed this huge tree all the way to the top, then spent hours figuring out how to get back down without breaking his neck. And me? I was too afraid even to watch."

The drinks came. Callard tossed his back. "I've been scared all my life," he confessed. "There's just one thing I'm even more afraid of than dying, and that's letting my family down."

Braden nodded. "I know what you mean. That's how I feel about the 328th bomb group."

Callard frowned. "Do you have nightmares?" he asked out of the blue. "I keep having the same two: Todd's training crash, and what happened over Le Havre...."

Braden saw his copilot had become maudlin. Time to get back to the hotel. He tossed money on the table, grabbed Frank by the arm, and steered him toward the exit. At that moment, air raid sirens blared their terrifying wail over the city. The music stopped and everyone streamed out into the night.

Piccadilly and London itself were now dark. Vehicles had stopped and been abandoned by people who walked off without fear. In the heart of Piccadilly Circus, Braden heard a London Bobby shouting, "This way to shelter, step lively!"

Hearing a deep, ominous chug-chug-chug sound, the two fliers stopped in puzzlement as the crowd broke around them. The noise grew louder until it echoed and reverberated off the buildings. Everybody looked up in dread.

Lit by searchlights, a winged torpedo shape appeared over the rooftops. Fiery streaks from its chugging engine punctuated the night with vivid pulses of flame. The noise gave way to terrifying silence as the weapon plunged steeply earthward beyond Trafalgar Square. The heavens lit up followed by a huge concussive boom, shouts, and the sirens of emergency vehicles.

"Must be that pilotless vengeance weapon they briefed us on," Braden said. "If Hitler thinks this will break civilian morale, he doesn't know a thing about the Brits."

"Kind of you to say, Dearie," said a matronly British woman who happened to be passing by. "You two best come along with us till the all-clear sounds."

They joined the line of people streaming down into one of the many entrances to Piccadilly's expansive tube station. It had been thoroughly transformed with folding chairs, cots, blankets, and pillows. Unflappable Britons calmly served tea as civilians of all ages mingled with servicemen and women, everyone gamely making the best of it.

Jack and Frank sat apart from the rest. "What happened over Le Havre?" Braden asked.

"What?"

"You said you have nightmares about something that happened over Le Havre."

Callard sighed and nodded. "It was my second mission. The ship ahead took a direct hit and its crew hit the silk." He swallowed. "One of the guys who jumped punched his quick-release and fell out of his chute. He meant to do this..."

Frank mimed pulling a parachute's ripcord.

"...but did this instead."

His hand slapped his breastbone and made a rotating motion.

"Oh Christ!" Braden said, realizing what he meant.

"Yeah," Frank replied, "we do that so often taking off our quick-release chutes back at base that it's second nature."

Jack now understood his copilot's insistence on the older clip-type harness "Could happen to anyone," he said.

"That ship was on my side. We nearly clipped the guy with our wing. He couldn't have been more than twenty years old. I saw the look of sick horror on his face as he realized what he'd done."

Frank's voice broke. "I can't get the guy out of my mind!"

They heard the wail of the all-clear and rose with the others to file out, Braden sobered by the needless death of a nameless young American who made one mistake in the heat of battle.

Chapter 34: Remembrance

"Gramps, Gramps!" Lisa shouted.

On the Vermont farmhouse's veranda, Dr. Wolcott hovered uncertainly over Judge Braden as he suffered what appeared to be a heart attack. Lisa looked up.

"Call nine-one-one!"

Quinn Wolcott pulled out her cell phone and hurriedly dialed.

*   *   *

Lisa and her husband Rob, their two children between them, sat tensely awaiting word in the hospital corridor. It was evening. The kids were tired and hungry.

On Lisa's other side, Quinn Wolcott sat blaming herself. "I'm so sorry, Lisa," she said vehemently. "It was too much—I should never have let the interviews go on so long."

Lisa smiled. "The way the words tumbled out of him over the past couple of days, I doubt you could have stopped him. He needs to tell this story, Quinn."

The historian nodded, grateful to be let off the hook.

"You're actually good medicine for him," Lisa added, dividing her attention between the conversation and a book she was reading to her daughter. "Honestly, it's the first time he's been his old self since grandmother passed away."

"Mrs. Braden? What was she like?"

"Very loving but proper," Lisa replied. "She was English, of course—"

"You mean," Dr. Wolcott interrupted, startled, "he married Georgiana?"

"You didn't know?"

Rob was also entertaining the children. "What was that bomb thing over London he described?" he asked in passing.

"The German V-1 revenge weapon, a primitive cruise missile. The British referred to it as the Doodlebug. We called it the Buzz Bomb. I think your granddad witnessed the very first V-1 attack a week after D-Day."

"Wow," said Lisa.

Quinn nodded. "Hitler began building launch facilities for it as far back as late 1943. Between them, the AAF and RAF destroyed as many of those sites as they could. Those were the NOBALL missions Judge Braden flew under the code name OPERATION CROSSBOW."

A doctor approached. Lisa and Rob stood up and joined hands, bracing for bad news. Quinn also stood. Taking Lisa's other hand, she gave it a supportive squeeze.

"Mr. and Mrs. Graham?" the doctor asked.

"Yes?" Lisa said hesitantly.

"Your grandfather suffered a mild coronary artery spasm."

They digested the news. "It wasn't a heart attack?" Rob asked.

"No. We've stabilized and are treating him. He can go home tomorrow."

"Thanks heavens!" exclaimed Lisa. "Can we see him?"

"Yes, but just for a few minutes."

The family entered the brightly lit hospital room where Braden sat propped up in bed. He gave them a lopsided smile. "Sorry for the scare."

He was instantly mobbed by his loving family. Lisa hugged him and kissed his cheek. "I called Mom and Dad," she said, babbling with relief. "They'll be here tomorrow. So will Uncle Tim and family unless I can reach them in time to say it's a false alarm."

Braden patted her hand reassuringly and looked around for Dr. Wolcott. Seeing her out in the hallway, he waved her in. "Come in, Quinn. Come."

"I shouldn't intrude...," she began hesitantly.

"Nonsense. You want to hear how *Lola* ended up in the drink, don't you?" He turned to the nurse. "Have more chairs brought in, please."

"It's not a good idea at your age," the doctor said.

"Doc, I've been living on borrowed time since nineteen-forty-four," Braden assured him. "A little more won't hurt now!"

Minutes later, the adults were seated around his bed listening with rapt attention while the children played on the floor with toys provided by the hospital. Quinn Wolcott pushed her digital voice recorder close to Judge Braden.

"With good weather," Braden began, "my crew and I quickly racked up the missions, sometimes flying two a day. Then came our group's devastating third night mission. I assume you know about that, Quinn?"

The historian nodded grimly. "Yes, the 328th Bomb Group lost nine Marauders that night—including *Lodestone Lola.*"

Braden sipped more water. "The British bombed by night and we by day," he said, "so it made zero sense to us. But the brass thought it would avoid some of the flak around our target."

"What was the target?" asked Rob.

"A key *Wehrmacht* headquarters nestled in the Ardenne foothills of Northern France. It oversaw the launching of pilotless V-1 flying bombs against England."

"The night of July 7th and 8th, 1944," Wolcott added.

Braden nodded. "They had us wear red lenses during the briefing to preserve our night vision before takeoff. We put up more than thirty ships that night and the Pathfinder Squadron contributed several more crammed with electronic navigation gear to lead the way. They dropped glowing pyrotechnic target indicators to show us where to lay our bombs."

"What was the weather like?" asked Lisa.

"Crystal clear with a full moon," Braden replied, "but nobody wanted to fly that one."

"Why not?" Wolcott asked, intrigued.

Braden shook his head. "I don't know, Quinn. Maybe we sensed trouble. Colonel Swan certainly did because he had chaplains and medical staff standing by in the briefing hut to calm our jitters."

Braden's eyes grew distant with memory as he spoke....

Chapter 35: The Night Mission

The fliers on the benches wore Polaroid B-8s over their eyes. These large black-rubber goggles, which resembled those worn by tank commanders, had dark red filters.

On the platform at front, Colonel Swan watched as Lt. Colonel Nielsen dismissed his men at 02:15 hours. The fliers rose and filed out of the 517th Squadron briefing hut. Elsewhere in the ops block, two other squadrons were finishing their briefings at the same time.

On the way out, some young men chose to stop and receive blessings from chaplains at one side of the hut's door. Others lined up at the other side where medics dispensed amphetamine tablets and paper water cups to wash them down with.

As flight crews spilled out into the night, Lieutenant Thomas Prestridge stopped and looked at the sky. *"Deep into the darkness peering,"* he quoted theatrically, *"long I stood there, wondering, fearing."*

His fellow fliers jostled, pummeled, and verbally abused him for this choice of quotes. A major intervened.

"Knock it off, you lugs. As for you, Prof, stow the poetry."

"Yes Sir," Prestridge said.

"Tonight's your sixty-fifth mission, isn't it?"

"Yes, Sir," he said again.

"This time your farewell celebration won't be canceled. Good luck to you and your crew!"

Prestridge winced, feeling the premature congratulations might jinx him. He joined the other grim-looking men climbing aboard the 4x4s, among whom were Jack and his crew. The fleet of Chevy

G506 trucks jounced off into the night to deliver the crews to their bombers.

Lodestone Lola shared a dispersal with *Tennessee Henhouse,* another veteran Marauder that had survived in defiance of the odds. The crews of both ships jumped off the truck and crossed to confer with their respective ground crews.

Lola had eight 500 GP bombs in her belly. After a preflight walkaround with Rotten, Braden climbed aboard. At the briefed time, a green signal flare arced brilliantly up into the night. Pratt & Whitney R-2800 radial engines spluttered to life around the field, their throbbing bellow echoing like thunder.

"The loo-tenant says it's one hour to the target and another back home," Wrotnowski shouted to Miguel and Butch. "They should be okay. I mean, what can happen in two hours, right?"

The others looked far from confident.

*   *   *

The noise awakened Georgiana, who in her dreams had been running from a raging storm. *It's American aero engines I hear,* she realized groggily.

On one elbow, she tried to make sense of Kingsholme Field roaring with the familiar pulse of daytime activity, then lay back with a sigh.

The war constantly intruded on the tranquility of her ancestral home before dawn, although never this loudly in the middle of the night. Sleep was impossible. She sat up, switched on her bed table light, and fluffed pillows behind herself.

Can the Yanks be flying a night mission?

The thought popped into her mind, and with it a stab of fear for Jack's safety mingled with renewed grief for dear Alistair, her childhood friend who died in the night sky. Tears welled.

"Be careful, Jack," she whispered softly. "Be careful and come home to me."

*   *   *

A moon one day past full accompanied the 328th Bomb Group's Marauders across the English Channel. Having turned off their running lights, they flew for safety in a loose gaggle at staggered altitudes varying from 6,500 to 9,000 feet.

The members of this force could not see one another. Exhaust suppressors sent to England for Northrop P-63 Black Widow night fighters had been borrowed and temporarily installed on the B-26s to eliminate the blue streaks of incandescent exhaust gases that would otherwise have betrayed their presence at night.

Only when moonlight momentarily glinted off the wings or fuselage of a Marauder did it briefly become visible. As *Lola's* tail gunner, Lew Jacobs had a perfect view of this phenomenon. It was magical, like whales breaching for an instant before disappearing again beneath the waves.

Ignoring the fact that he was yet again hurtling ass-backward into war, he pondered how he could ever describe this night to friends and family after the war. Or to the guys up front, since they couldn't see it from the cockpit.

*   *   *

Like everyone else, Jack Braden had cast aside his red goggles upon climbing into *Lola*. He found no solace tonight in the simple discipline of flying. From the time took off, he'd felt nervous, vulnerable, and exposed by this very bright moon. They would be penetrating airspace where survival depended on *not* being seen.

Moonlight revealed the folds of the land below. Black shadows marked hedgerows around fields and meadows and betrayed blacked-out towns. The ground itself was featureless except where rivers, lakes, or even railroad tracks reflected moonlight.

A bombers' moon, Braden thought.

That famous RAF phrase now had an ominous ring. The people below knew that a full moon on a clear night rendered them less safe, but Braden now saw that it worked both ways, endangering British bombers and now American ones as well.

He glanced to his right. Frank was staring fixedly through the windshield, probably fearing a collision with another B-26 in the dark. A shout of dire warning looked was ready on his lips.

Callard's battle with the demons of fear now bothered Braden a new way. For the first time, he himself felt vulnerable aloft. Back when he arrived at Kingsholme, Tom Prestridge had explained to him that young replacements show up with a sense of psychological invulnerability, but that it wanes over time.

Braden hadn't believed it then; he did now. His personal supply of invulnerability was all used up—he'd run too many risks, flown too many missions, seen too much happen....

Jack also remembered something that the college professor had quoted. *Act well your part; there all the honor lies.* He couldn't recall which long-dead poet had said it, but it sustained Braden too now. He resolved that, no matter what, he would not let down his crew, his buddies, Keith Nielsen, Mike Swan, or the entire 328th.

He loved Kingsholme Field and its pastoral surroundings. Different as Essex was from his childhood homes, the base meant the world to him, for it was here that he finally found both identity and community. It shocked him to realize that he felt this way about a place that wasn't even in the United States.

It's my home until my number comes up or this war ends, he thought.

The glow of falling red target indicators ahead snapped Braden out of his reverie. He thumbed the mic button. "Pilot to navigator, enemy coast markers observed."

"Navigator to pilot, Roger," came Captain Poole's reply. "Marking the time as thirty-eight minutes past midnight."

At the briefing, Colonel Swan had mentioned that his ship would carry six 500-lb bombs instead of the usual eight, freeing up space for two 250-lb target indicators on the bottom racks. The group

CO would release these TIs at landfall to give every ship in the group, which was not flying in formation, an exact jumping-off point for the course leg to the IP.

You can count on Mike Swan, Braden thought, proud to serve under someone who led courageously by example. It embarrassed him to recall how rebellious he'd felt that day they first met in his office.

By the time they overflew the pyrotechnic marker, it had landed and was burning brilliantly red on the ground below.

"Pilot to crew," Braden went on, "we made landfall over France. Thanks to Captain Poole's navigating, we hit the marker right on the button—no course correction required."

Derek Poole, a lead navigator in the 517th Squadron who taught math in civilian life, glanced at the cockpit. He saw Jack Braden twist in his seat and gave him a smiling thumbs-up. Poole grinned back and nodded before returning to his work.

His charts, straightedge, circular slide rule, calipers, notepad with pencils, watch, and the slaved repeater instruments mounted by his station were what allowed him to track their progress and estimate arrival times at milestones along their planned route.

He did this without visual reference to the ground. There was a high window beside him but he didn't bother with it; even in daylight, it provided a far better view of the wing and right engine nacelle than it did of the ground below.

"Navigator to pilot," Poole transmitted, "we'll pass exactly halfway between Lille and Arras in nine minutes. It's along this corridor that we're briefed to expect maximum enemy resistance."

"Roger," Braden said, purposely sounding relaxed to reassure his crew. "Keep your eyes open, boys."

*   *   *

Knowing they were over enemy territory, Sergeant Gonzalez grabbed a packet off of the pile near him. He tore it open, pulled out a fistful of 1"x10" aluminum-backed paper strips, held them out the open waist window, and released them.

Pausing before climbing into his top turret, Bidwell watched as the slipstream blew these strips apart and sent them spinning wildly off into the night.

Bidwell knew the Army called the radar-jamming strips *chaff* whereas the Marauder men usually referred to them as *window,* the British term. *Hey,* he thought, *the Brits invented radar so they can call it what they like.*

But then again, as he knew from his Pacific tour of duty, it was the U.S. Navy that came up with the term radar, an acronym for *radio detection and ranging.* So maybe he'd call it chaff after all.

"Does that stuff really work?" he called out.

Sitting on his scrounged red cushion, Gonzalez looked back and grinned. "We'll find out soon enough, *compadre!"*

*   *   *

Long-range Freya radar picked the Marauders up while still over Southeast England. Misidentified as an RAF raid, they were tracked across the English Channel. At landfall, parabolic Wurzburg-Riese radar antennas took over, following their progress.

Kammhuber Line personnel alerted all the flak and searchlight batteries within the sector through which this enemy force would pass. In the *Himmelbett* operations center, ground controllers calmly began vectoring the patrolling night fighters to intercept the threat. No other bomber streams then being aloft in the area, this one claimed their full attention.

Luftwaffe controllers saw when the inbound aircraft began dropping *Düppel.* They responded to this jamming by directing their fighters—including *Wilde Sau* single-seaters—to the leading edge of the cloaked mass now displayed by their radar screens.

The enemy hid within that cloak. While the *Luftwaffe* controllers could no longer vector fighters to specific targets, they could guide them to the general area at the correct altitude and let each individual *Nachtjäger* locate its own prey.

Even as the 328th's Marauders advanced, more fighters were being summoned from neighboring control sectors. *Nachtjagd* units at all *Luftwaffe* bases within striking distance stood by with freshly refueled and rearmed night fighters to take over for those currently hunting if they ran low of fuel or ammunition.

*　　*　　*

The countryside below began winking with muzzle flashes. It looked benign from cruise altitude until 88-mm flack began to explode with glaring brilliance.

In daylight operations, ground radar served to preposition optical sighting systems so that the flak battery personnel could take over and visually fine-tune where the cannons pointed. At night, these shells were fired by radar guidance alone, posing less danger of direct hits or shrapnel damage. The fact the bombers weren't clustered in tight formations also worked in their favor.

This changed as night missions wore on. *Luftwaffe* battery crews combined the Kammhuber Line radar input with acoustic tracking to close in on targets. And if any bombers caught fire or were illuminated by searchlights, optical rangefinders also came into play. All of this, combined with height calculations based on perceived formation angle versus radar-derived distance, further refined azimuth and elevation settings for the flak gunners.

The Marauders saw searchlights spring to life across a wide swath of enemy territory. Ever more of them lit up to perform a scything hunt. Their beams, brilliant when close and dusky orange at a distance, quickly numbered more than a hundred.

The searchlights rattled Frank Callard aboard *Lodestone Lola.* "Any ship caught by those lights will get clobbered!" he predicted.

Right on cue, one hunting beam swept across the belly of a silver B-26 half a mile away at ten o'clock. Having splashed it, the brilliant light quickly backtracked to lock onto it. Two more dazzling beams joined the first, thoroughly transfixing the Marauder.

"Flak will chew them to pieces!" the copilot exclaimed.

Braden shook his head. "We're not all flying at the same height, Frank, and the time fuzes in those shells need to be set to explode at the right altitude before the rounds are even loaded and fired. There's no way a flak gunner can do all that in time to catch us except by pure dumb luck."

Callard was unconvinced. "They've got proximity fuzes."

"No they don't," Braden replied, shaking his head. "We do but the intelligence boys tell me the Krauts haven't been able to solve that challenge. Their flak still relies on fuzes that explode at whatever altitude they enter manually."

The copilot nodded.

*   *   *

The coned Marauder was *Roxie* of the 516th Squadron. Her twenty-one-year-old pilot maneuvered hard but couldn't shake the searchlights. "Goddam it!" he swore furiously.

"Dive for the deck!" shouted his equally young copilot.

"Dive for it? I can't even see it!"

*   *   *

Tom Prestridge watched the transfixed bomber's plight. "Poor bastards are catching hell," he said. "I wonder whose ship that is?"

Buddy didn't reply. Tommy glanced at him and saw his pilot looking stunned. Returning his attention to the coned plane, he saw it rear up and fall into a diving spin. The pilot had pulled hard back on his wheel and kicked the rudder hard over in a desperate bid to free himself from the blinding lights.

My god, who would do that in a Marauder? Prestridge wondered with a sick feeling in the pit of his stomach.

There's a reason why bombers are strictly placarded against snap rolls. Seven thousand feet isn't a huge amount of altitude to recover from an upset event, not if you want to avoid overstressing the airframe on pullout so your ship didn't come apart in midair.

*   *   *

The number of searchlights passed 150 to now total 200 or more. At least a dozen B-26s were coned and striving to break free even as they forged ahead with the mission.

Those ships attracted constant antiaircraft fire. Each barrage produced brilliant yellow-orange blossoms as the shells exploded. Their glare transformed the moonlit night into a fiendish hellscape.

Dozens of bursts blossomed near one coned ship. Bursting into flames, the B-26 rolled over on its back and plunged earthward, dragging a fiery trail behind it until it exploded on impact with the unseen ground below.

Two parachutes drifted down in its wake. Fellow Americans mutely observed the fireball and chutes as they flew past, every flier wondering who's luck would run out next.

At the controls of *Spirit of '76,* Mike Swan didn't see the crash but he did witness the flak hit that caused it. He knew they were goners and felt no need to ask the tail gunner for confirmation.

A cold white glare pulled Swan's eyes upward. Through the overhead panel, the CO saw three white flares falling like shooting stars. In quick succession came three green flares and then three red ones.

"This damn war is getting on my nerves!" the CO exclaimed.

"Who launched those flares, Sir, and why?" asked his copilot.

"The *Luftwaffe.* The white ones are star shells to make us visible. I'm guessing the colored ones signal the flak gunners to lay off." Swan scowled uncertainly at the night. "Chester, I suspect there's a whole hungry pack of night fighters out there."

Chester looked down through his side window and saw the flashes of antiaircraft fire taper off. Within seconds, no more shells exploded around them. "Oh shit," he said.

"CO to gunners," Swan transmitted via interphone, "keep your eyes peeled for night fighters. Navigator, how long till the IP?"

"Navigator to pilot, thirteen minutes to initial point," came the reply.

If we make it that far, Swan thought grimly.

*   *   *

Serving as Jack Braden's copilot, Frank Callard had made significant strides in controlling his fears. This mission saw a major relapse. Jack could feel his copilot's stark terror even as he struggled to control his own growing unease.

Another white glow splashed the cockpit from above. He looked through the roof and saw more white flares. The Marauders raced past their stark glare, but not before it gave German night fighters the opportunity to pick out targets.

"Pilot to crew," Braden warned, "be on your toes."

"Look!" cried Callard, pointing.

Ahead in the fading glow of the flares, a sinister form had slipped behind a brightly coned Marauder a thousand yards away.

"Pilot to top turret," Braden transmitted, "Two o'clock level, Milt. Do you see it?"

"Yeah, Jack, it's a Focke-Wulf 190."

Braden was stunned. "Are you sure?"

"Yes," Bidwell replied.

Twin-engine, multi-seat night fighters were the norm, but single-seat day fighters? Was the *Luftwaffe* that desperate?

"Top turret to gunners," Bidwell transmitted, "short bursts only. The flash suppressors on your guns can only do so much, so shut one eye when firing to preserve night vision."

"The searchlights haven't found us," Callard added. "Don't forget that if you fire, you'll give away our position!"

Braden glared at his copilot. "Pilot to crew, no chatter on the interphone unless you have critical information to share."

The FW 190 savaged the B-26 with explosive 20-mm shells. The bomber's pilot reacted by yawing his ship side to side using rudder alone to throw off his attacker's aim. The Focke-Wulf's tracers went wide. Muzzle flashes from the bomber's tail and waist guns showed its crew was really dishing it out.

Get him! Bidwell mentally willed.

Bidwell wished the top brass hadn't done away with tracer ammo for U.S. bombers. Visible fire could deter an enemy at night and help the Marauders hit their swift targets.

"Pendejos, lots of them!" said Gonzalez. "Eight o'clock high!"

Glancing over his shoulder, Braden saw moonlight glint off the wings and canopies of enemy fighters as they banked to sweep down onto their prey.

"Pilot to crew," Braden ordered, "call it out if one of them tries to slip beneath us."

Braden couldn't forget the RAF Lancaster pilot's description of the Messerschmitt 110's upward-angled "gutting knife" cannons. B-26s would be especially vulnerable because, unlike Flying Forts or Libs, they were too small to have a belly turret.

The night sky, awash with muzzle flashes and tracer streams, erupted in blazing slaughter as night fighters opened up on coned B-26s. Those vulnerable ships valiantly returned fire while trying desperately to evade the clinging lights.

Lola's pilots watched as the first coned B-26's tail guns stopped firing, the turret knocked out of commission or the gunner injured or dead. Smoking from both engines, the bomber fell off to dive at a jaw-dropping rate of descent. The FW-190 stayed with it, firing relentlessly as the flashing barrels of the Marauder's top turret responded in kind.

Two parachutes blossomed as crew members hit the silk. Just before the B-26 disappeared beneath *Lola's* nose, Braden had the satisfaction of seeing flames erupt from the Focke-Wulf. He hoped the Marauder made it home because the chances of a successful belly landing in a dark field at night were vanishingly small.

More coned ships plunged to destruction. One exploded in midair, its *Luftwaffe* victor briefly glimpsed as it sliced through the searchlight's beam. In that instant, Braden recognized the bulbous-nosed silhouette of a Messerschmitt 410.

Descending parachutes showed many fliers had bailed out. Their white canopies picked up the reflected light of probing beams and explosions.

A strange ululation pulled Braden's attention back to *Lola's* cockpit. Frank wailed and rocked rhythmically back and forth in his seat, eyes squeezed shut, his hands slapping his knees.

This was butterfly-net behavior. Braden feared losing his friend to it. "Frank, snap out of it!" he said, gripping his arm.

Frank opened his eyes, realized where he was, and nodded. "At least we're not coned," he said glumly.

*   *   *

In *Baltimore Blitzkrieg,* a livid Buddy Hasbrook exploded in fury. "Those Kraut bastards—"

A sudden yawn interrupted this shout, after which Hasbrook couldn't seem to catch his breath. Tom Prestridge watched as his stressed pilot continue trying until he completed the yawn.

Chapter 36: Duel in the Dark

The lead pathfinder was the B-26 *Hobblin' Goblin*. Code named Makehome One, this Marauder flew ahead of the main attack force. Two more pathfinders, Makehome Two and Makehome Three, accompanied her in loose trail at staggered altitudes.

These three special ships belonged to a top-secret unit based at Great Saling Army Airfield in Essex. Designated the 1st Pathfinder Squadron (Provisional), this highly classified Ninth Air Force unit was an entity unto itself rather than part of any bomb group.

The First Provisional, as it was known, shepherded the Ninth's Marauders and Havocs when bad weather hindered or precluded visual bombing. The First Provisional's B-26s were equipped with advanced electronics that allowed them to navigate to and then drop bombs on targets without ever seeing the ground.

Each of the three squadron elements comprising a combat box formation would have a pathfinder to lead it. In daytime operations, the bombers following these specially equipped lead ships knew to release their bomb loads when the pathfinders did theirs.

Things worked differently this night mission. Copying the RAF, the pathfinders would use incandescent flares and target indicators to mark key junctures for the 328th's squadrons, which would cross the target at staggered heights and intervals.

*   *   *

Captain Danylko "Wilco" Levchenko sat tall and confident at the controls of *Hobblin' Goblin*. Nothing fazed this strapping young Ukrainian-American from Chicago, whose Form 5 showed much more instrument flight time in theater than the average American bomber pilot had. Levchenko's logbook also showed nearly two hundred hours of night flying, most of it logged getting to the bases of shepherded bomb groups ahead of early morning missions.

Wilco had sandy hair, gray eyes, Slavic cheekbones, and a wolfish grin. He'd been called Danny all his life until a flight instructor gave him this nickname. It stuck, providing a dashing wartime moniker the Marauder pilot loved.

In the succinct parlance of military radio communications, Wilco meant *message received, will cooperate.* For Levchenko, it was also his personal philosophy—whatever the mission, he'd fly it.

The navigator's compartment behind him was crammed with special electronic gear from two classified systems. The first was *Gee,* which enabled aerial navigation in darkness and bad weather. Two of the unfamiliar boxes in this compartment were for Gee.

The second and more complex system was Oboe Mk II, whose name was unrelated to the coincidental use of the word to signify the letter "O" in Allied radio communications. The Oboe aboard these pathfinders facilitated blind bombing.

Oboe was cumbersome and balky. Its receiver, filter, and control junction box were in the navigator's compartment but its guts occupied the aft bomb bay, reducing the amount of ammunition a pathfinder ship could carry to feed its rear-fuselage machine guns.

Gee and Oboe both relied on electronic beams transmitted from towers in England. When these systems worked perfectly, which was rarely, Allied bombers could accurately navigate to and bomb military targets at night or in bad weather.

Wilco's navigator completed his Gee plot and squeezed a push-to-talk switch clipped to his parachute harness. "Navigator to pilot, coming up on the initial point."

"Roger," said Wilco. "Pilot to bombardier, bomb doors open."

"Wilco, Wilco," came the reply of their bombardier, who had trained for pathfinder duty under the expert tutelage of RAF bomb aimers at Otmoor Bombing Range in Oxfordshire.

A buffet felt through the controls and the simultaneous drop in cockpit temperature confirmed for Wilco that the bomb-bay doors were open. He flew steadily, waiting patiently.

"Fire the green flare… now!" transmitted the navigator.

The copilot rose, stepped behind his seat, and fired a loaded flare pistol mounted to shoot through the cockpit roof. Its cartridge soared up, exploding into a green flare to alert the 322nd Bomb Group to watch for the IP markers to drop.

Wilco's navigator turned and looked back through the low door into the bomb bay. As he watched, the two 250-pound target indicators fall away into the night. The TIs burst immediately after release, sending brilliant green light flooding back up into the bomb bay as its doors closed.

The navigator turned back to his chart. "Come to a heading of zero-three-seven degrees," he transmitted.

Wilco Levchenko complied, banking onto the bomb run.

*　　*　　*

Mike Swan was heartsick. Another Marauder had gone down. More aborted with battle damage and were limping home, some presumably with wounded or even dead aboard. Swan knew many of them wouldn't make it and prayed none had to bail out over the English Channel at night.

Dozens of B-26s were transfixed by searchlights. Their light-gray underside camouflage, which worked to their benefit by day, made them easy prey for the probing lights. The shiny aluminum undersides of the newer ships were also a liability.

Having looked over the wrecked Lancaster as it was removed from his base, Swan knew that the RAF painted the undersides of its night bombers a rough, sooty, utterly non-reflective black. Hard experience lay behind Britain's development of that flat coating. The Americans were now learning the same lesson all over again the hard way. If he got home alive, Ninth Air Force HQ would get an earful from him!

Jinking to shake free of the searchlights, the coned Marauders nevertheless plowed doggedly on toward their target. This made them sitting ducks for, by Swan's estimate, forty or perhaps fifty *Luftwaffe* night fighters. The ruthless savagery of those nocturnal attackers reminded him of the blood lust displayed by piranhas in their Amazon River feeding frenzies.

At least the flak was temporarily gone. But Swan knew in his bones it would be back with a vengeance over the target. *If we make it that far,* he thought again….

His copilot called out the green flare. Twenty seconds later, the green IP markers burst open. Those incendiary munitions merged into a glittering ball that flooded the night. It slowly assumed the shape of a Christmas tree as it drifted down.

Swan's racing Marauder ate up the distance to that shining mass. "Pilot to bombardier," he ordered, "let me know when we're smack dab over those TIs."

"Roger, Skip," came the reply. "Hey, you should see them refracted in the nose down here—I'm ready to hang stockings!"

Mike Swan smiled despite himself. Looking at the shining guidance this moonlit night, he felt gratitude for the unknown pathfinder crew who was shepherding them through hell.

That same ship had previously dropped yellow TIs to mark the French coast. As planned, Swan's bombardier had sighted on them and laid his red TIs right on top of them to extend this centering coastal jump-off to the entire bomber stream. Now they had hit their mission's next waypoint.

"Bombardier to pilot, we're directly over the IP," came the call.

"Roger," Swan acknowledged.

He banked *Spirit of '76* north-northeast onto the bomb run heading. A third of the following B-26s individually did the same, turning left over that glowing marker toward their mission's goal.

The other two thirds flew on watching for different colors from their respective pathfinders, yellow TIs from Makehome Two and later blue ones from Makehome Three. Each time, the unseen shepherd led his portion of the flock in a turn toward the target.

This coordinated division of the 328th's strike force saw each element approach the drop zone from a slightly different angle. It also spaced them out to reduce the number of B-26s overflying it at any one time, minimizing the chance of collision.

*   *   *

The searchlight batteries were adept at handing off ensnared prey to other lights down the line as the mission progressed. More ships still were coned on the runup to the target. As Swan had anticipated, the night fighters broke off as heavy antiaircraft shelling commenced from the target's batteries.

Pathfinder bomb runs lasted at least nine minutes, twice as long as the average B-26 visual run. This agonizing one seemed endless to the group CO, who watched anxiously for the next milestone: red-on-green TIs marking the aiming point.

The enemy was known to drop decoy markers to trick night bombers into unloading in the wrong place. Therefore, only this color combination would be accepted as the true indicator.

Spirit of '76's bomb bay doors came open. Its bombardier, a captain, lowered his face to the eyepiece of his Norden bombsight. There was absolutely nothing to see yet, but he was ready. The same thing was happening aboard every other B-26 as they converged at varying heights on the runup to the *Wehrmacht* headquarters.

Squinted through the glare at their PDIs, the coned pilots flew as steadily as they knew how. Their bomb bays too came open. In their noses, bombardiers bent over bombsights whose magnifying optics fortunately worked despite searchlights.

Hit by shrapnel, one coned airplane began to trail smoke from its left engine nacelle. Moonlight and searchlights rendered this thickening plume visible. Some 500 feet and flying lower was *Baltimore Blitzkrieg,* whose pilots watched this ship framed in their windows.

"Guy's got guts staying on the bomb run," Prestridge said. "Anyone else would salvo and hightail it home."

Buddy Hasbrook didn't reply. Prestridge glanced at him. "I hope they make it, Buddy," he said feelingly.

Still no response. Tom Prestridge frowned, not knowing what to make of his pilot's peculiar silence.

Mike Swan squirmed in his seat in *Spirit of '76,* his frustration barely in check. "Come on, come on…!" he muttered.

Relief flooded through him as two of the pyrotechnic munitions blossomed in the distance, the first one green and the second red. A slight delay in their automatic release let the colors fall separately, one after the other.

"Pilot to bombardier, you have your aiming point!"

"On it already," came the clipped reply.

Refracted colors from the pyrotechnic munitions played in the nose of the B-26 as he worked. Flak burst repeatedly. Hunched over his bombsight, he ignored the jolts shaking him in his seat and worked his adjustment knobs.

"They're on the ground now, Sir," he transmitted, "Keep the PDI centered. Steady, steady…."

Their burdened ship bobbed upward from the release of two tons of weight. "Bombs away!" he said.

*   *   *

In the nose of *Lodestone Lola,* Chick Spottedbird straightened from his Norden with equal satisfaction. "Bombs gone!"

"Pilot to crew," Braden asked, "how did we do?"

"Tail gunner to pilot, bull's-eye!" Lew Jacobs enthused. "We placed our bombs right between the target indicators."

Paco Gonzalez paused while dispensing chaff to frown down at the scenery as it slipped by below. Burgeoning bomb flashes continuously illuminated the scene as one Marauder after another dropped on the burning pyrotechnics as they lay on the ground.

"Waist gunner to pilot," the Latino replied, sounding puzzled. "Looks to me like we flattened a whole lot of empty woods, Boss."

In the cockpit, Frank Callard's mouth fell open. "All this... for nothing?" he said incredulously.

Braden shook his head, his lips tight.

*   *   *

Having dropped, the 328th turned to sprint for home. There was no rally point because there was no formation to reassemble.

Still following the damaged Marauder, which like them had successfully dropped its load, Prestridge and Hasbrook watched as visible flames erupted from its engine. The unidentified B-26—its markings not visible from behind—flew steadily on despite the growing fire.

"They'd better break off and hit the silk," Hasbrook said, finding his voice.

Cold white light yet again flooded the cockpit. Prestridge's heart sank as he looked up and saw new star shells descending. The fighters were back!

A briefly silhouetted form darted past the moon. "What was that!" exclaimed Hasbrook, rattled.

Before Prestridge could speak, another *Luftwaffe* night fighter—this one at one o'clock level and startlingly close—revealed itself by firing its upward-angled cannons as it slipped beneath the crippled bomber. Like a shark drawn to blood, this Me 110 blasted away at the B-26 until it exploded with a horrific concussion.

Baltimore Blitzkrieg rocked violently as debris rained down on her. Bellowing with rage, Hasbrook rammed his throttles forward and wrenched his control wheel hard over to pursue the departing fighter.

Despite being strapped in, Prestridge was thrown to the side and bruised his shoulder against the metal window frame. With no warning to brace themselves, the top turret gunner tumbled out of his turret while the waist gunner hastily grabbed the mount of his machine gun with both hands.

The bomber's gyrations lifted him bodily off the deck plates and smacked him down again as he held on for dear life. He drew a shaky breath, knowing how close he'd come to being hurled out the window.

The waist gunner saw his friend and fellow crewmember sitting on the deck plates clutching the base of his turret. Their eyes locked. Neither man dared let go as the wild ride continued.

"Maybe we should clip on our chutes?" suggested the waist gunner.

His crewmate winced in pain. "Don't make me laugh—I busted some ribs!"

Up front, Prestridge was aghast. "Buddy, what the hell are you doing!"

"I'm gonna get that son-of-a-bitch!"

"Are you insane? We'll never find him in the dark."

"Shut up!"

"You'll get us all kill—"

Hasbrook sucker punched his copilot. Prestridge slumped back, stunned. Blinking in disbelief, he probed his bleeding mouth with his hand and glowered at his pilot.

Hasbrook threw *Baltimore Blitzkrieg* one way and the other, firing frequently and erratically. In the blisters low on the Marauder's sides, his four .50 caliber packet guns chattered, sending pounding vibrations through the fuselage.

But the Messerschmitt had vanished without a trace. They saw and hit nothing, yet Buddy kept on firing.

*   *   *

From the pilot's seat of *Spirit of '76,* Mike Swan watched the gun flashes that drew attention to this rogue Marauder's erratic flight. Switching his interphone jackbox to Command, he jabbed the transmit button on his control wheel.

"Unidentified B-26, this is Pickpocket leader," he transmitted urgently. "Cease fire. I repeat, cease fire—you're giving away your position to the enemy!"

Searchlights were already sweeping *Baltimore Blitzkrieg's* direction and moments later it too was transfixed.

"B-26 just coned, identify yourself!" Swan demanded.

"It's *Baltimore Blitzkrieg,* Sir," came the shaken reply. "Captain Hasbrook has gone berserk!"

*   *   *

Braden and Callard watched this play out from the cockpit of *Lodestone Lola,* which remained undiscovered. As copilot, Frank routinely monitored the command frequency in case radio silence was broken. Having heard the group CO's transmission, he called his pilot's attention to it.

Braden switched to command frequency just in time to hear the reply. "That's Tom Prestridge!" he exclaimed.

"Hasbrook's gone nuts," Callard said. "He's got them coned!"

Baltimore Blitzkrieg stopped its wild antics when Hasbrook could no longer see. The light-splashed Marauder instantly attracted unwanted attention. Braden and Callard watched an Me 110—visible in moonlight and the reflected glow of searchlights—slide stealthily in from below and behind that bomber.

214

"Their gunners don't see it!" cried Frank. "The searchlights must have blinded them."

Braden switched his jackbox back to Inter. "Pilot to crew," he transmitted, "grab hold and hang on tight!"

Callard barely had time to brace himself before his pilot rammed the throttles forward and banked steeply to come to the aid of his best friend. Bidwell braced himself in the top turret, but not before the maneuver inflicted painful bruises.

Hard maneuvering threw Jacobs against the side of his cramped tail turret and tumbled him out. Gonzalez grabbed a fuselage ring former with one hand and an ammo feed chute with his other. Seeing his remaining chaff packets tumbling out the window, he tried to grab one but immediately abandoned the effort because both hands were needed to keep himself from following them out.

Lola leveled out and raced at maximum speed toward *Baltimore Blitzkrieg,* approaching from its left rear quarter. It loomed large, brilliantly illuminated.

The twin-engine Messerschmitt opened fire with its angled guns. The fiendish armament chewed into the Marauder's belly.

*   *   *

Baltimore Blitzkrieg's gunners dove aside as the floor erupted in devastating havoc. Shells stitched a ragged pattern of debris-filled destruction up the deck plates from back to front. The men pressed tightly into the side walls as high-velocity shards and splinters flew. Finding themselves miraculously unhurt when it ended, they gaped in disbelief.

*   *   *

Milt Bidwell had his twin machine guns already trained on the attacking Messerschmitt. He fired, as did Chick Spottedbird using the handheld fifty in *Lola's* nose. With no deflection angle, neither man could miss.

Braden pressed his firing button and his packet guns added to the pounding. Using the control wheel and rudder pedals, he aimed *Lola* herself to send the .50-caliber slugs where he wanted them.

The heads of the Me 110 two occupants turned as it staggered under this withering broadside. Belatedly recognizing their peril, the German pilot broke off and fled at top speed, corkscrewing as he dived. *Lola* shot past *Baltimore Blitzkrieg's* tail guns in hot pursuit, Bidwell, Spottedbird, and Braden firing as they closed the gap using the momentum Braden had built up.

The *Luftwaffe* night fighter flew unsteadily. Devastated from the constant fire from behind, it faltered. Braden saw a wing fly off as he zoomed past.

"Pilot to tail gunner," he demanded, "what's the status of that night fighter?"

"It broke apart, Skipper," came Jake's voice.

Cheers rang out over the interphone. "We got 'em!" exclaimed Bidwell.

Frank Callard laughed out loud. "You got your wish, Jack!"

"How do you mean?" Braden asked, confused.

"You're a fighter pilot!"

Jack laughed heartily in this shared moment of tension release.

Chapter 37: Cat and Mouse

Baltimore Blitzkrieg fell off in a spiral. Assuming it was crashing as a result of the attack, the searchlights released it to hunt other prey.

Tom Prestridge had chopped the throttles and was purposely diving. With grim concentration, he advanced them slowly and began gently pulling out of the dive.

Buddy Hasbrook reached for the control wheel. Prestridge slapped his hand away and glared at him. The 517th Squadron's notorious bully meekly submitted.

The college professor leveled out low over the nighttime terrain. Guided by his navigator, he set course for England, undetected as searchlights hunted on. Via interphone, he and Hasbrook learned what had happened from their tail gunner, who recognized their rescuer's markings as it flashed by.

"*Lodestone Lola…,*" Hasbrook repeated, dumbfounded.

"Jack Braden!" Prestridge said happily.

*   *   *

Lola's luck ran out. A searchlight found the veteran Marauder and clung to her before she could climb back to cruise altitude. More joined in until she too was caught in a brilliant vice.

"I can't see!" exclaimed Braden.

"We're sitting ducks!" cried Callard, imagining Messerschmitt ME 110s racing up by the dozens to exact revenge. And Me 410s and Junkers Ju 88s too.

But it was flak's turn again. Ground batteries all around opened up on them. A cluster of near bursts rocked the bomber.

Braden touched the transmit button. "Pilot to crew, hang on!"

"Again?" wailed the copilot, bracing himself.

Less than seven thousand feet above sea level, Braden heeled over into a steep dive, corkscrewing to shake off the searchlights. He made it dramatic because he needed the flak crews to believe they had mortally wounded *Lola*.

In the navigator's compartment, Derek Poole hung on for dear life as his chart and tools went flying. He watched his straightedge, circular slide rules, pencils, and a chart float eerily around him, briefly defying gravity.

"Pull up before we crash!" Callard shouted in the cockpit.

"Not yet," Braden said.

He kept at it until the external illumination winked out. Only then did he begin hauling back on the control wheel, being careful not to overstress the airframe in the high-*g* pullout.

Lola bottomed out. Braden trimmed for level flight, not bringing the power back up until their excess diving speed had dribbled off. Moonlight revealed high dark walls of mountainous terrain to both sides. They had plunged into a steep-sided valley.

"Cutting it a wee bit close, aren't we, Skipper?" came Bidwell's voice on the interphone.

"Yeah," Braden replied dryly.

Frank Callard stared at him in admiration. "That's amazing, Jack! How did you know where the ground was?"

"I didn't," Braden admitted.

Callard looked like he was going to be sick. *Just how close did we come to rounding out below ground level?* he wondered.

In the compartment behind them, Derek Poole had gathered up his tools. Strapping back in, he tapped his repeater instruments, made calculations, and double-checked the work on his open chart.

"Navigator to pilot, we've crossed the Belgian border heading north," he transmitted. "Come left to three-zero-zero degrees."

Before Braden could reply, bright tracers streamed past. He shoved the throttles forward and began evasive action.

"Pilot to crew," he said, "we can't seem to catch a break. There's a night fighter sitting on our tail. Have at it, men."

Lola's gunners responded but were unsuccessful. They simply couldn't see their pursuer if he didn't fire. Holding their breath, nerves stretched to the limit, the gunners waited for more flashes to betray the position of this demon in the dark.

By the light of that initial burst, Jacobs recognized the angular form of another Messerschmitt 110, Hitler's ubiquitous nocturnal predator. From gunnery training, he knew the Me 110 mounted four forward-firing 20-mm autocannons and two light-caliber machine guns in its nose. This ugly foe's radar antennas had also been visible in that brief instant of flashing cannons.

Jacobs reported all this to the Skipper via interphone. "Good work, Jake," Braden replied. "Stay alert."

In the cockpit, the pilot's mind raced. The moon was at a low angle and its light didn't penetrate to the valley floor. So how had this enemy found them? Jacobs had just provided the answer.

It could only be radar. Jack didn't have to see the angular array jutting from their pursuer's nose for confirmation. Still, it came as a surprise because he'd been told radar works well up high but is defeated by ground clutter at low levels.

This Me 110 likely had those upward-angled 30-mm cannons installed. *The gutting knife,* he thought with a shiver, having just seen it used on Baltimore Blitzkrieg. *I can't let this guy get beneath us!*

If this Messerschmitt was tailing them now using radar, why hadn't its pilot opened fire again? Could his opponent be short of ammunition and waiting until he could be certain of success? This was all that made sense.

"Could he have followed us down?" Frank asked out of the blue.

Before Jack could consider the question, a second burst of fire streamed past.

*   *   *

The foe revealed himself! In the tail turret, Jacobs instantly fired back at the spot from which the tracers had come. A devastating return volley violently hammered his turret, tumbling him back off his padded stool. When he sat down again, he saw that the thick armored glass he sighted through had been turned opaque.

"Holy shit!" he exclaimed, still shaken by the ferocity of the attack. Cold as it was, he felt drenched in sweat.

The turret didn't move when he tried to rotate it and elevate the guns. It being totally dead and blind, Jacobs abandoned it to join Paco Gonzales at his waist guns.

The Marauder's tapering rear fuselage was too narrow for both of them to man a machine gun, so Jacobs knelt forward of his friend where he could see rearward out whichever waist window Gonzalez wasn't manning at the time. He'd call out warnings and firing opportunities as he saw them.

Survival depended on seeing the *Luftwaffe* night fighter first, but there was little hope of that. The moon was now so low that the rugged terrain and high ridges cloaked them in profound darkness.

*   *   *

Braden saw that he'd climbed a bit and pushed the nose back down. Callard glanced at him in alarm. "What are you doing?" he asked via interphone.

There seemed little point to shouting with his copilot when their crew needed to know real-time how things stood. Braden joined Callard in dispensing with interphone protocol.

"I'm staying low so he can't get beneath us," he transmitted.

Callard looked like he wanted to shout *Are you crazy?* "How did he find us in the first place?" he asked instead.

"My guess is the bastard was upstairs with us. He followed us down to make sure we crashed," Braden replied. "When we didn't, he began hunting for us at low level."

"Makes sense," Frank admitted.

"The terrain would make using radar difficult," Jack went on. "His operator is either very good or very lucky."

Milt Bidwell's voice came in their ears. "They were probably the nearest fighter when we were coned," he speculated. "I'll bet he was setting up an attack on us when you ducked out on him."

"Could be, Milt," Braden said. "Too bad our death throes didn't fool him."

"You may have deprived him of an easy kill, Skipper," came Chick Spottedbird's grateful voice. "Looks to me like he got mad and is determined to bag his prey."

Nobody answered but it all made sense. Grimly, it painted the picture of an experienced and implacable foe.

More tracers flashed past. Braden jumped, his nerves stretched to the limit as he strained to follow the folds of a long valley with invisible walls. With the moon low, only the absence of stars now revealed where those ridges were.

The tracers had again gone wide. This Kraut couldn't see them any better than *Lola's* gunners could see him. Once again, Braden changed heading slightly and stayed low, knowing that moonlight could still betray them if the terrain granted it access.

"Poole, where the hell are we?" Braden demanded.

"Over the Ardenne Forest," came the reply, "but we're headed the wrong way. England's the other direction."

"Can't do anything about that now," the pilot replied. "Paco, you can resume dispensing chaff."

"Sorry, Boss, all out," came Gonzalez' voice. "Jake's here with me—the *pendejo* knocked out his tail turret."

"Oh great!" exclaimed Callard.

"Don't worry, we'll nail him," came the Latino's confident reply. "Just give me or Bidwell one clean shot!"

Enemy fire ripped through the rear compartment, punching holes in *Lola's* aluminum skin. The crewmates flattened to the deck at the waist windows. In the cockpit, Braden and Callard felt *Lola* ship take hits.

There was a sudden sloppiness to the controls. *That bastard chewed up our tail feathers!* Braden thought.

He changed course five degrees again in case the German pilot had seen where they were and planned to fire again, but once again he did not. Probing the controls gingerly, he assessed the damage to *Lola's* rudder and elevators. Their responsiveness was reduced but they still worked.

"You guys okay?" Braden called as he adjusted the heading again to follow a half-seen turn in the valley.

"Yeah, we're okay!" came Jacobs' voice.

"That pen-day-hoe's hiding behind my cam cutouts, damn it!" muttered Bidwell, unable to fire to the rear because of his top turret's protections against shooting off their own tail.

Braden stayed low, banking from one valley into another as the opportunity presented itself. He avoided the ridges by keeping the star field centered as seen through the plexiglass roof panels. It was like driving on a highway in the dark without headlights. The fear of running into unseen terrain was nearly overwhelming.

At the time, he was acutely aware that he was leading a mortal foe whose radar wasn't precise enough for firing but sufficed for staying glued inexorably to their tail.

In the aft fuselage, Jacobs and Gonzalez watched vigilantly through opposite-side gun windows.

"He's still back there," Jacobs said, overwhelmed with peril.

"Yes, Jake, he's still there," Gonzalez agreed.

"What's he waiting for?"

The Latino gestured out the window. "Take a look."

Jacobs did and saw the first faint hints of gray above the valley wall. "Oh crap!"

This was what their pursuer was counting on! Soon enough, he'd have enough light to ensure a kill. Before they could react, he'd rise up and dive down over *Lola,* riddling her with focused fire at her most vulnerable points.

Up front, Braden used these hints of a new day to force *Lola's* belly closer to the ground. He racked his brains furiously but could come up with nothing to prevent them from being shot down.

"Am I right that he's low on ammo?

He pondered the question. From Air Technical Intelligence briefings, Braden knew that *Luftwaffe* warplanes were notoriously short ranged by U.S. standards. The reason was Hitler's formative experience as a corporal in World War I.

Shaped by that conflict, the dictator thought only in terms of the battlefield. Why order planes to be built with extended range that permitted strategic use, when their purpose was tactical support of troops on the frontlines? This was one reason the RAF prevailed in the Battle of Britain despite being outnumbered more than two to one the *Luftwaffe.*

If *Lola* was low on fuel—and by now she was—their pursuer must be running on fumes. Moreover, the ammunition supply for his upward-angled cannons could not be diverted in flight to feed the nose guns. So all that really mattered was how many explosive 20-mm shells remained in the Messerschmitt's nose cannisters.

He's saving what's left for the first light of day! This realization struck Braden a physical blow.

That night fighter had been on patrol, he reflected, so its pilot had probably already expended some fuel and ammunition before encountering them. So why hunt them so doggedly now?

He's risking everything for this! Braden breathed, recognizing an obsession that could lead his pursuer to make a mistake.

It grew lighter. *Lola's* pilots could now just discern a bottleneck ahead. The valley through which they snaked appeared to narrow into a deep ravine ahead. A hill protruding from the right further constricting their path.

Thank heavens we didn't run into that in full darkness! Callard thought. There would have been no avoiding a horrific disaster.

Braden's mind continued to race. *Know your enemy* was a maxim the Army had drilled into him during his training. He reviewed what he and his crew surmised about the *Luftwaffe* pilot clinging to their tail. Braden could almost feel him plotting his attack.

A desperate plan occurred to Jack. Thumbing his transmit button, he shared it with the crew.

*   *   *

With a bit of light to sight by, the Messerschmitt swung out, first to one side and then the other, taking potshots at *Lola's* engines. These bursts were very short—a few rounds each. As the tracers streaked past, Braden used the rudder to slew *Lola* away from them.

Callard jumped as one quick burst found its mark, exploding the cowling off the engine beyond his right window.

"We're hit!" he shouted, gaping out his side window.

Shredded aluminum was all that remained of the top portion of the engine's cowling. The Pratt &Whitney R-2800's magnetos, cylinders, and valve covers were exposed to sight.

Braden scanned his panel. "Number two shows normal oil pressure and it's maintaining RPMs," he said with guarded optimism. "Keep an eye on it, Frank."

Meantime, the gunners focused their attention entirely on the Messerschmitt, oblivious to what was happening up front. Cued by Jacobs, Gonzalez quickly switched sides from one gun to the other, firing each time the Me 110 showed itself.

The floor-level windows gave his swivel-mounted Brownings a wide field of fire everywhere but upward and to the rear, which was where he needed to fire. *Lola's* upward-canted horizontal stabilizers were in the way. The Latino could only sight below them, hoping to catch the enemy as he swung out to the side but before he rose up to fire.

But the twin-engine Messerschmitt popped up too quickly each time. Unable to catch it, Gonzalez swore rapidly in Spanish.

*   *   *

Wary of those muzzle flashes, *Oberleutnant* Hansjörg Schröder of NJG 5 abandoned the pop-up attacks. Cruising level 300 meters behind the now discernable form of the bomber, the night-fighter ace concluded that his attempts to shoot out its engines had failed. He'd done nothing but waste precious ammunition.

Schröder closed the gap between himself and the bomber further until it loomed very large. Having knocked out its tail guns, he was where that rearward-firing side armament couldn't reach him. Allowing himself to relax, he reflected upon the surprise still spreading through him.

Dark as it still was, that white star insignia he'd seen atop the airplane's left wing was unmistakable. *Amerikaner!* What were the *Amis* doing flying at night?

He prided himself on Germany having the most lethal weapons of any nation on earth. But those American's 12.7-mm machine guns were to be respected. They combined a withering punch with a far higher rate of fire than his 20-mm autocannons. This was the weapon that decimated the ranks of the *Luftwaffe's* day fighter force.

The events of the previous night still rankled the *Oberleutnant*. He'd been mere seconds away from downing this enemy when its pilot threw it into a sudden dive. Determined not to be denied his kill, he'd followed it all the way down to the deck and lost it.

Determined not to be foiled, he'd flown around until his back-seater picked it up again on his radar scope. Pure luck.

Since then, the enemy had continued to frustrate him by flying too low for him to employ the *schräge Musik*. Those cannons had plenty of ammo but the American pilot rendered them useless.

All he had left were the two 7.92-mm machine guns and four 20-mm cannons in the nose of his Me 110. He'd used up much of their latter's ammunition on the previous night's patrol and was nearly out of cannon shells.

Guided by his radar operator, he risked short bursts in the dark trying to down this speedy foe. If any of them hit their mark, they had no effect—this tough bird kept on flying!

He cursed his light machine guns, which were just as useless as the equivalent .30 caliber popguns used by RAF bombers. Guided by his back-seater's radar, Schröder fired them in full darkness into the American, but they failed to send it crashing down.

The four MG 151 autocannons in his plane's nose had at most a dozen precious rounds each. He wouldn't waste them on the backside of a bomber; that might kill crew members but it wouldn't deal a mortal blow.

No, thought the *Luftwaffe* ace, *you shoot down airplanes by disabling their engines, setting their wings ablaze, or killing their pilots.* He smiled grimly. *Better still, all three at once!*

This was how he'd earned his *Ritterkreuz des Eisernen Kreuzes,* the Knight's Cross to his Iron Cross.

"Herr Oberleutnant, unser Mangel an Sprit ist ja dringend!" protested his *unteroffizier* radar operator yet again over the intercom.

Schröder checked the fuel gauges with irritation. His back-seater was right; they were critically low on fuel. But this American was a unique battle prize he could not forsake. It would be his 35th aerial victory and there could be no more delay in claiming it.

* * *

"Now!" Braden said via interphone, putting his plan into effect.

He retarded *Lola's* throttles and pulled the wheel back to keep her at the same height as they decelerated to a slow cruise.

* * *

It being light enough now to see, Schröder steeled himself to deliver his coup de grâce. The attack could not fail because the enemy would have no time to react. He would rise high over his enemy and dive back down on it, hosing his remaining explosive rounds from side to side into the cockpit, engines, and wings.

After that, he would fly to the nearest airfield or, if they ran out of fuel, bail out. But nothing would deny him his kill.

Schröder rammed throttles to the stops, only to suddenly realize that the bomber ahead was slowing down! This alarming fact caught him at the worst possible instant. Swearing, the *Luftwaffe* ace broke hard to the side to avoid colliding with the bomber's tail.

* * *

"You guessed it, Skip, he broke right!" transmitted Bidwell.

The pilot drew a breath. *So far so good,* he thought.

Jack's gamble was based on a flight instructor's observation that fighter pilots nearly always break right when startled. It didn't matter whether they were right- or left-handed. Everyone holds the stick in their right hand because the throttle is at left in trainers and fighters. And when you have to react instantly, it's more natural to yank the control stick hard right than push it left across your body.

Braden had timed his slowing so that it occurred just as they reached the valley's chokepoint. This was to force the fighter out from behind them and make him rise up to clear the terrain, which he hoped would place this foe within Bidwell's field of fire.

With Schröder's accelerated approach, the plan worked better than Braden could have hoped. Finding a jutting hillside in his way, the *Luftwaffe* ace pulled hard back on his stick at full power and barely avoided scraping the hill's tree-clad flanks.

Bidwell saw the Messerschmitt balloon into sight high over his turret. To regain flying speed and avoid stalling out, it's pilot now had no choice but to dive back down into the valley.

Glancing over his shoulder, Schröder was jolted to see a power turret forward of the bomber's tail. Realizing too late the trick that had been played on him, he banked hard as he angled down, cutting into *Lola's* path in a desperate bid to race away to safety.

It was a terrible situation for the night-fighter ace, who could not bring his nose guns to bear on his intended victim. With sick horror, he and his back-seater watched helplessly as the barrels of that twin-gun turret tracked them.

Aboard *Lola,* Tech Sergeant Milton Bidwell focused the shining reticle of his reflecting gunsight over the Messerschmitt and squeezed his handgrip controllers. A withering hail of bullets from the .50 caliber Brownings struck a devastating sledgehammer blow with a combined rate of fire of 1,500 rounds per minute. The *Luftwaffe* warplane exploded instantly and violently, raining debris down on the valley floor.

This happened directly in front of Braden and Callard. The latter swallowed. "It's like being in the front-row seat of a movie theater," he said.

Braden turned to reply and froze, staring past his copilot.

Frank looked out his window and blanched. Flames engulfed their damaged engine.

Chapter 38: The Choice

Braden chopped the burning engine's throttle, hit its fuel cutoff, and "pulled the bottle" to actuate the fire extinguisher within the nacelle. It didn't work—the fire continued unabated.

Adding power to the good engine, Jack pulled up for altitude while using the propeller feather switch. To his dismay, the engine's wide blades remained broadside to the slipstream instead of rotating edge on into it to reduce aerodynamic drag.

Combined with the disrupted airflow of a missing cowling, the unfeathered prop created enormous drag. That and an uncontrolled fire meant there was nowhere to go but down.

"Pilot to crew, prepare to abandon ship," Braden transmitted tersely. "I'm climbing for whatever altitude I can give you. Bomb-bay doors are coming open."

Lola shook badly as Bidwell slipped out of his turret. He clipped his chest-pack parachute onto his harness and stepped over to join his fellow gunners. Jacobs and Gonzales had donned their chutes already. The tail gunner looked very worried. The Latino smiled but it looked forced and he chewed his gum too quickly.

"Wait for one long and three short rings of the bell," Bidwell reminded them. "Don't pull a Canfield or we'll land too far apart."

The flight engineer turned and went forward. The countryside below slid by beneath the open bomb bay as he crossed the catwalk, his chute making it a challenge to squeeze through the bomb racks.

At the catwalk's other end was Poole, the navigator. He stood cinching his parachute harness tight. Seeing Bidwell, he ducked back into the navigator's compartment to let him pass.

Chick Spottedbird emerged from the nose compartment just as Bidwell arrived. He let the bombardier/navigator slip by before stepping up into the cockpit and stationing himself behind the pilots.

He saw Braden muscling the controls hard. The pilot looked haggard as he strove to *Lodestone Lola* climbing and strove to prevent her from falling off to the right. It took all his strength and focus as she shuddered on the ragged edge of a stall.

"Better drop the gear," he told his copilot. "Don't know how much higher we can climb."

"Gear won't extend," Callard replied. "Jack, we can't use the nosewheel hatch!"

"You'll have to jump from the bomb bay," Braden replied, only then noticing Bidwell. "Damn fine shooting, Milt. How are the boys doing back there?"

"Safe and ready to jump," he replied. "Feels like the ship's trying to flip on us."

Braden nodded, breathing hard.

"Propeller won't feather?"

The pilot shook his head. "That fighter made a mess of the prop, engine, and our tail surfaces."

Bidwell looked past him at the instrument panel. The altimeter needle showed their anemic climb had topped out at a paltry 2,200 feet above sea level. How high that was above the rugged terrain below, the flight engineer couldn't guess.

"Can we continue climbing?" Callard asked.

Jack shook his head. "It's been milking a mouse just to get this high. *Lola's* done her best for us but she's had it."

"You talk like she's a living thing," Frank said.

Braden's throat constricted. "She is—she's one of the crew."

Callard nodded, belatedly realizing he loved their ship too.

"Hit the bell, Frank," Braden ordered.

The strident clangor of the bail-out bell filled *Lodestone Lola:* one long ring followed by three short ones.

Braden glanced back over his shoulder. "See you downstairs, Milt."

Bidwell knew what his pilot faced and didn't budge.

"Get out of here," Braden said. "That's an order."

Bidwell clapped his captain on the shoulder. "It's been an honor, Sir," he said and departed the cockpit.

When he heard the bell, Paco Gonzalez dove headlong out one of the waist gun windows. Lew Jacobs tumbled out the other a second later. Farther forward, Derek Poole and Chick Spottedbird stepped off the catwalk, one after the other, as Bidwell waited his turn in the navigator's compartment. Stepping through, he positioned himself on the narrow beam. Taking a last look around, he patted the cold metal structure around him fondly.

"Goodbye, old girl," he said, "you've been swell!"

He stepped off, fell away, and pulled his ripcord as soon as he was clear. Five parachutes drifted down in the wake of the stricken bomber.

*　　*　　*

"Hit the silk, Frank," Jack Braden said.

"I can't."

"Jump! That's an order."

"I can't, I can't!"

Braden wrestled with the controls. "I don't give a damn about your nightmares—get the hell out of here!"

"You go, Jack. I'll hold her steady for you."

Without waiting for a reply, Frank slid his seat forward, folded down the rudder pedals, and gamely took over.

"Damn it!" Braden shouted furiously. "Haul your butt out of that seat right now or there won't be enough altitude left for either of us to hit the silk."

"You go! You said so yourself—when things go wrong, it's every man for himself."

"All right, I will!"

Braden unbuckled hastily and stood in a crouch, glaring at his insubordinate copilot. *Lola* rocked alarmingly as Frank labored to avoid a fatal plunge.

The conversations they'd had in London played in Braden's mind. Frank had confessed to his recurring parachute nightmare, and Braden had shared his own about holding the ship level for others to escape, leaving no one to return the favor for him.

You're welcome to my nightmare if yours scares you! he thought angrily.

But he didn't leave the cockpit. Precious seconds ticked by, *Lola* descending, as he grappled with violently conflicting emotions. His face betrayed this raging inner battle.

It's every man for himself. Those callous words of his—uttered in anger what seemed a lifetime ago—now pierced his heart.

So much had happened since then. It was a philosophy to which he no longer ascribed....

*   *   *

Bidwell watched *Lola* dwindle as the first golden rays of sunlight touched his parachute. The bomber was dropping fast and was now nearly too low for a survivable jump.

"Bail out, you guys!" he shouted, dangling helplessly.

*   *   *

Jack Braden's rage vanished. Having reached a decision, he sat back down, buckled in, and calmly reassumed control. "Bomb-bay doors coming closed," he said, flicking the overhead switch.

Callard stared at him in astonishment, a question on his lips.

Braden smiled. "We'll ride her down together."

"Why didn't you bail out?" the copilot asked incredulously.

"Call me old-fashioned, Frank, but a captain doesn't abandon a member of his crew."

Braden assessed the situation. *Lodestone Lola* could *only* go down. Releasing some of the backpressure on the controls helped him keep her wings level, but it also hastened the inevitable. He scanned the terrain ahead with a grim frown.

"So what's the plan?" Frank asked nervously.

"The plan?" Braden shrugged. "Hope for a stretch of open ground free of boulders. Barring that, put her into the trees at a hundred-and-sixty plus—any slower and she'll flip inverted."

They descended inexorably, now just five hundred feet or so above the ground. As the terrain flattened out before them, the trees grew taller with no hint of a clearing as far as the eye could see. Just more forest, washboard terrain, and a stream with sandy banks too small for anything larger than a Piper Cub.

Wooded ridges slid by on both sides of the valley. As Callard watched, the high terrain off their left wing ended, revealing a pristine mountain lake shining in full sunshine.

"Look!" he exclaimed, pointing.

Braden turned, saw the water out his side window, and instantly banked toward it. He was grateful to be turning away from the dead engine, not into it—that would have been fatal.

"Half flaps!"

"Half flaps," Callard repeated, moving the handle with alacrity.

Sky, hills, and deep blue lake now filled their windows. With his free hand, Braden fumbled at his collar. His fingers found the charm Georgiana had given him. He squeezed it for luck.

"Master switch off," he commanded. "Brace!"

They braced themselves against the brow of the instrument panel, he with one hand on the control wheel. *Lola* touched and skimmed the water, her tail throwing up a wake. The waist windows and engines dug in, slamming her nose down with a huge splash that stopped them almost instantly. Both pilots were thrown hard forward against their seatbelts as a truly thunderous waterfall broke over their plexiglass roof.

They unbuckled, threw open the escape panels, and clambered up out of the bobbing airplane. Spluttering and laughing, they sat atop *Lola's* fuselage, their feet dangling in her cockpit as they stripped off their flight gear.

"We're alive!" Frank shouted with joyous incredulity.

"I'll break out the life raft and—"

Jack broke off and looked around in dismay. "It's gone!"

"What's gone?"

"My good luck charm!" he replied, fumbling frantically as he checked his clothes. Giving up, he stared bleakly down into the cockpit of the bomber as she filled up with water.

Chapter 39: Happy Landings

"That was the last time I was ever at the controls of an airplane," Judge Braden concluded, his voice husky.

The night was dark beyond the hospital room windows. Lisa lifted a metal water glass and placed its straw in her grandfather's mouth. He swallowed and settled back on the propped-up pillows.

"Frank was a good man, Quinn," Braden told her. "You say my crew's gone. He as well?"

Dr. Wolcott nodded sadly. "Granddad died last year."

Murmurs of surprise filled the room.

"Frank... was your grandfather?" Braden asked.

She smiled. "Yes, I would have told you sooner but I didn't want to interrupt our sessions." The historian paused, choosing her words. "My grandfather felt he owed you everything, Judge Braden. He said you didn't just save his life; you changed it."

A youthful grin played briefly on the judge's face as he accepted this gift. Then it was back to business. "Where were we?"

Dr. Wolcott picked up her voice recorder. "You were saying that your last mission was a failure—"

"War itself is the failure, young lady," Braden interrupted. "But yes, the pathfinder boys got it wrong and we missed our target."

Wolcott started to reply when Braden suddenly stiffened in pain. Monitoring equipment sounded an alert and hospital personnel again raced in.

The doctor checked his patient. "I need you all to leave."

*   *   *

Lisa and Quinn sat glumly together in the hospital corridor. Rob and their children were gone; he'd taken them home.

"He'll be all right," Quinn insisted gently.

Throat clenched, tears on her cheeks, Lisa shook her head. The doctor approached just then.

"You may see you grandfather now, Mrs. Graham," he said.

Lisa rose fearfully.

"Wait," Quinn said, "give him this!"

Quinn fumbled in her briefcase and handed her something. It was the small box with the handwritten note *"Ask!"* on it that she'd wondered about that first day of the interview.

"My restoration team found it," she added.

*   *   *

Judge Braden wore a cannula tube delivering oxygen to his nostrils. He raised a weak hand as his granddaughter entered.

"Sweetie," he whispered.

She took his hand tenderly, tears forming in her eyes. "Hi, Gramps," she said with a twisted smile.

"Don't be sad." His voice failed. He swallowed and continued. "I need you to say my farewells."

"Don't talk like that—you'll be fine!"

Jack Braden smiled wryly and shook his head. "My number's finally come up." He noticed the box in her hand. "What's that?"

"Quinn asked me to give it to you," she said, reminded of it.

Lisa opened it to reveal a velvet-covered jewelry box suitable for something the size of a ring. She opened that and lifted out a thin gold chain with a dangling flak fragment. A jeweler had repaired the broken chain and left every part of the necklace gleaming brightly.

Braden stared in wonder. He lifted his hand to touch it.

Lisa cleared her throat. "Grandma's not around anymore," she said, "so I guess it's up to me...."

She removed his cannula, slipped the chain around his neck, replaced the oxygen, and took his hand in both hers. Slowly and lovingly, she repeated words she'd learned during the interview.

"This is good luck," she said. "Wear it and it will keep you safe."

Tears of gratitude in his eyes, Jack Braden wordlessly lifted his free hand and shakily gave the charm a familiar squeeze for luck. His eyes lost focus.

"Love you, M'Lady," he whispered, drifting away.

"Love you, Yank Flier," she replied, a huge lump in her throat.

His eyes closed and he died peacefully. She collapsed sobbing, not aware that the monitoring equipment had sounded or that the doctor, his staff, and Quinn Wolcott had all respectfully entered.

Chapter 40: Lest We Forget

Situated at the base of Normandy's Cotentin Peninsula, Utah Beach was alive with surf, sun, and seagulls. Lisa, her husband, and their two children toured the invasion beach. Snatches of laughter were audible as the vacationing family strode the sand, played, and read D-Day historical markers.

On the bluffs above, they entered a covered display to gaze in wonder at an actual Martin B-26 Marauder named *Dinah Might*. Crouching by their children, the parents talked earnestly to them, pointing things out about the bomber. The youngsters gazed up at it, eyes large, mouths open in wonder.

*   *   *

At the Historic Aircraft Recovery Trust Museum's restoration hangar in Washington State, Dr. Quinn Wolcott and her team of restorers were busily at work on *Lodestone Lola* as loud alt-rock music blared. Their jovial banter and painstaking ministrations showed this to be a true labor of love.

Wearing T-shirts decorated with the HART logo, a huge version of which adorned the white hangar wall, they tapped, drilled, and fitted parts by hand. What had required massive factory tooling and skilled master machinists to create when *Lola* was built in April 1943 could now be repaired or replicated through automated CNC machining, additive manufacture of castings and forgings using industrial 3D printing, and laser cutting and welding technologies.

Lola's fuselage, wings, engine nacelles, and horizontal and vertical tail components already looked better. Disassembled and mounted on wheeled stands, they could be pushed around the shop floor and rotated to whatever angle the work required. The fuselage itself was in two sections. Nearby sat two freshly overhauled radial engines and propellers wrapped in protective plastic sheeting.

Elsewhere, the shop was dotted with seats, turrets, radios, and other components as *Lodestone Lola* was painstakingly returned to functional wartime condition. She would be capable of flight but would never fly again, being far too valuable for that.

Even as repairs were made, her flak patches and other battle scars were carefully preserved to document the plane's operational history. The tail turret had new armored glass and was again functional, and a new right engine cowling had been manufactured. A company specializing in historical fabric reproductions worked from original Army specifications to recreate new wall insulation, and so on. The end goal was to roll *Lola* out on her own wheels looking ready to take off again for another mission.

This was technically a preservation, not a restoration. *Lola* had effectively been in a time capsule in the unoxygenated depths of that freshwater mountain lake in Belgium. She was thus more original than almost any other surviving World War II bomber with an operational history. Judicious fill-in paint was applied by hand to address postwar damage or loss, and modern coatings now ensured that her skin and internal components were protected from corrosion and other hazards far into the future.

Dr. Wolcott sat working at her desk in the central work area. It was an island of tables, computers, flat files for manufacturing plans, books, and assorted other reference materials. Taking a break from her research, she stretched and yawned.

The framed photo on her desk caught her eye. It was a wartime shot of Lieutenants Braden and Callard standing together in their flight gear before *Lodestone Lola*. The two friends were smiling.

Quinn Wolcott picked up the frame and studied the photo in it with fond gratitude. The warmth of her expression showed she was much the richer for having known both men.

Flak-Bait's Preservation

My real-life inspiration for *Lodestone Lola* is Martin B-26B Marauder *Flak-Bait* (serial number 41-31773, fuselage code PN-0). A crown jewel in the collection of the National Air and Space Museum, Smithsonian Institution, *Flak-Bait*—which flew with the 322nd Bomb Group's 449th Squadron—completed more missions over Europe in World War II than any other U.S. bomber.

Logging 202 combat missions from late July 1943 through to the end of the war in Europe, *Flak-Bait* survived everything that *Luftwaffe* fighters and flak batteries could throw at her. Jim Farrell, her first assigned pilot who also named her, loved his plane and fondly called her a "flak magnet," a reputation that she more than lived up to with countless visible battle scars to prove it.

General Henry "Hap" Arnold, head of the U.S. Army Air Forces in WWII, decreed that examples of the warring parties' military aircraft be preserved. Thanks to his foresight, *Flak-Bait* avoided the fate that befell all the rest of the USAAF Marauders in Europe. Considered too unforgiving for postwar use, these valiant warbirds were scrapped in Germany even though the B-26 finished the war with by far the lowest loss rate of any U.S. bomber flown over Europe.

Flak-Bait remained disassembled and untouched in dead storage, first at the hands of the U.S. Air Force and then in the care of the National Air Museum, predecessor to today's NASM. *Flak-Bait* thus remained totally stock and is fully authentic, unlike most surviving bombers that were stripped of their military gear for civilian use in the postwar era. In this sense, she is emerging from a time capsule.

As of this writing, *Flak-Bait* is undergoing painstaking preservation at the Steven F. Udvar-Hazy Center in Chantilly, Virginia, NASM's large aircraft and spacecraft facility on the runways of Washington Dulles International Airport. When finished, this amazing historical artifact will roll out looking once again ready to fly.

Jay Spenser

For More Information...

Anyone interested in learning more is encouraged to visit the B-26 Marauder Historical Society (https://B-26MHS.org). This volunteer-driven organization works to preserve the memory of the 300,000 men and women who were involved with the Martin B-26 Marauder. It ensures that the contributions of these valiant air crews and their hardworking ground-crew mechanics are not forgotten.

The United States and other armed services flew Marauders in many theaters of World War II. For anyone wishing to perform historical research about these operations or learn more about family members or the B-26 units in which they served, the Historical Society is a gold mine of information.

This donor-supported online community is the largest organization dedicated to preserving the memory of the B-26 Martin Marauder. It publishes newsletters and historical materials, maintains a museum with artifacts, photographs, and memorabilia related to the B-26; and performs educational outreach to promote awareness of this aircraft type's amazing role in history.

Author's Bio

Jay Spenser is a Seattle author who's written more than a dozen books and many hundreds of articles. He's won professional writing awards at the national and international level. His first two children's chapter mysteries took back-to-back 1st Place Blue Ribbons in category from the Gertrude Warner Book Awards for Middle Grade Fiction, part of the annual Chanticleer International Book Awards competition.

Jay served as an assistant curator of aviation at the National Air and Space Museum, Smithsonian Institution, in Washington, DC, USA. He was subsequently the curator of the Museum of Flight in Seattle. Switching careers, he spent more than two decades with The Boeing Company as a communications professional. Now embarked on his third career, Jay pursues his passion for fiction by creating original screenplays and novels.

Lodestone Lola is a labor of love. Although fictionalized, this work is based on the author's decades of exhaustive primary and secondary research. Astonishing as it may seem, almost everything depicted in the novel actually occurred among the eight U.S Martin Marauder bomb groups in the European Theater of Operations.

Acknowledgements

My thanks go first and foremost to my new friend Sylvia Muri Saadati, an astonishingly fine editor who helped me through multiple drafts of this novel.

Sylvia knows a great deal about the Martin B-26 Marauder in her own right. Her father, James Muri, helped introduce the then-new B-26 to the public during the Battle of Midway in the early days of WWII. On June 4th, 1942, he piloted a torpedo-launching Marauder and brought his crew back safely in the face of withering Japanese defenses. Famously, he did so by buzzing the entire length of the aircraft carrier *Akagi's* flight deck in a never-to-be forgotten escape.

Sylvia joined the B-26 Marauder Historical Society in 2017 and began editing their publications the next year. In her own life and through the MHS, she has known countless "Marauder men." Like me, she wishes their contributions to be remembered.

I'm greatly indebted to my friend Tom Farrell, a superb interpreter of the B-26 and his father Jim Farrell's career as *Flak-Bait's* first and longest pilot. In my mid-teens, I contacted Jim to learn more about his wartime experiences. He and his family made me feel welcome. Tom and I remain in touch all these years later and he keeps me up on *Flak-Bait's* preservation by the National Air and Space Museum.

Heartfelt thanks go to Ron Bolesta, another new friend whose father was a bombardier/navigator in Jim Farrell's squadron. One of his father's missions, flown on rotation, was in *Flak-Bait*. The depth and quality of Marauder research that Ron has independently performed over many decades has been of material help to me in this novel.

Among experts on all aspects of the B-26, few if any can rank higher than MHS historian Brian Gibbons, who also kindly assisted me.

Finally, I thank my brother Jon, son Brian, and wife Deborah for their great help with this book. They made it possible for me realize my goal of showing what wartime life was like for the Marauder men.

www.ingramcontent.com/pod-product-compliance
Lightning Source LLC
Chambersburg PA
CBHW022003170626
46808CB00001B/268